4/23

BOOKENDS

SHORT STORIES FROM A LONG LIFE

ELLIS M. GOODMAN

RED
PENGUIN
Books

Bookends – Short Stories from a Long Life

Copyright © 2021 by Ellis M. Goodman

All rights reserved

Published by Red Penguin Books

Bellerose Village, New York

Library of Congress Control Number: 2021911415

ISBN

Print 978-1-63777-074-0

Digital 978-1-63777-075-7

AUTHOR REVIEWS

"This collection explores a wild variety of subjects, including fraud, romance, greed and even murder. The stories range over 60 years and multiple continents, and are highly entertaining, full of vivid incidents and surprises. Goodman writes with wit, great understanding of human nature, and keen observation of cultural nuances. His knowledge of European culture is vast. His finely drawn characters sparkle. Highly recommended."

   - Jian Ping, Author of *Mulberry Child: A Memoir of China*

"The author has assembled an intriguing format for a collection of stories that focus on key inflection points over a sixty-year timespan, loosely connected to an established English family of landed gentry. The vignettes, some with a whiff of Dickens, others with a strong dose of John LeCarre, focus on the fragility of life and the tenuousness of the line between fulfillment and disaster. How a delightfully ordinary day, holiday or business trip spent savoring stunning scenery, exciting work, wonderful cuisine, or good company can erupt, without warning, into loss, danger and violence. Goodman takes us across international locations through stories of romance, greed, murder, and kidnapping. He refines the devastating impact of a life-altering plot twist."

   - Rita Dragonette, Author of *The Fourteenth of September*

ACKNOWLEDGMENTS

I believe most works of fiction are based on fact. This collection of short stories is based upon my own experiences and loosely on some of the events, circumstances and characters I have met in my long life.

I could not have completed this book without the dedication of my executive assistant, Lana Quinn, and the diligent work to help finish the final manuscript by Pamela Gingold.

I would also like to thank my wife Gillian and my family for their continued encouragement, advice and support.

I also received outstanding creative advice and support from my friend Jennifer Hou Kwong, and my meticulous and talented editor Emanuel Bergmann.

Finally, I would like to thank Stephanie Larkin, JK Larkin and the team at Red Penguin for their enthusiasm and professionalism.

CONTENTS

For Diddles, as always.

1 THE AUDIT - 1956

"Well, young man, do you think you can handle it?" asked Mr. Bamford, with a stern glance at Harry Bishop.

"Yes, Sir," Bishop responded, albeit with more confidence than conviction. He was a stocky, young man of nineteen, with a shock of reddish-brown hair, green eyes, and freckles that seemed to shine in the summer. Whenever he smiled, which was often, two dimples appeared on his cheeks. He was an articled clerk at the small accounting firm of Haslam, West and King. His supervisor, Mr. Bamford, was a rotund man in his fifties, with streaks of greyish-brown hair combed across his bald pate. He usually wore a formal, black jacket and pinstriped trousers, displaying a fob watch and gold chain. But he always seemed to have a smile and a twinkle in his eye behind his rimless glasses. He had risen through the ranks to become a partner. He had always been kind and considerate to Harry, perhaps because he knew they both came from humble backgrounds.

He was giving Harry his opportunity of handling a client audit on his own. The person who would normally handle this, Peter McFarland, the senior articled clerk in the firm, was ill. He allegedly had the flu, although Harry suspected he might be taking an extra week off before his final examinations. Harry didn't like McFarland very much, a pale-faced and rather arrogant young man. He was always trying to copy the partners in every way, walking around with what Harry and some of the clerks called a "smell under his nose."

Harry was sitting opposite Mr. Bamford in his small office overlooking Chancery Lane and a large bomb site. London still bore the scars of the Blitz. Ten years after the end of the second world war, with Britain nearly bankrupt, there were hundreds of similar sites. Large holes in the ground, now filled with rainwater and weeds, surrounded by temporary brick walls, awaiting the redevelopment of the city. The Haslam offices were pockmarked with shrapnel damage,and the building had not seen a lick of paint since the mid 1930s. The office furniture was old, worn, even Victorian.

On Harry's lap was a notepad, ready for instructions.

"Well then, Bishop," Bamford said. "You could spend tomorrow morning going through the audit file, but I thought I should give you some background to Summers & Co."

"Yes, sir."

"They're among our most loyal clients. An extremely old, established firm of solicitors. They are located in Bedford Row. They've been in the same building for over a hundred years. I believe they were originally established in Lincoln's Inn around 1785."

"That long ago?" Harry said.

Bamford smiled and wrinkled his nose. "Indeed." He leaned forward and spoke in a conspiratorial tone of voice. "It is rumored that they represented Marie Antoinette and that for many years they housed her jewelry in their basement vaults."

"Really?" said Harry, suitably wide-eyed.

"Well, I don't know whether it's true. She certainly doesn't appear as a client these days." Bamford gave a loud guffaw, then he continued. "The firm today consists of three partners. Mr. Arthur Sharpe is the senior partner. He must be in his mid-sixties now, a rather crusty individual, somewhat difficult to deal with. Hopefully you won't have to see him. You should steer clear if you can. He has two junior partners, Mr. Greville Thornton and Mr. Robert Beasley. There were two junior partners before the war, but one of them died in action in France, and the other one apparently did not want to return to Summers."

Bamford paused to allow Harry to catch up with his notes. "The partnership does not do very well financially. The junior partners, in particular, are not well remunerated. Summers & Co. has been struggling. Most of their clients are dead, you see." Bamford gave a little chortle. "By that, I mean that most of their clients are trusts. The firm has always represented a large number of landowning trusts. You know, English and Scottish aristocracy, some going back hundreds of years, that sort of thing. In fact, Greville Thornton, I believe, is a direct descendant of *the* Sir Greville Thornton."

"Who?"

"Well, dear boy, he fought with the Duke of Marlborough at the Battle of Blenheim."

Harry paused with his notes and gave him a blank stare. Bamford went on. "You see, he was rewarded by a grateful nation with four thousand acres of land, mostly farms and villages just north of Plymouth. He was subsequently ennobled as the first Lord Marsden, and the family estates still exist today. They have spread into Cornwall and other parts of Devon and Dorset." He paused, as Harry was scribbling furiously. "You will report to the cashier, which is just an old-fashioned name for today's accountant. His name is Mr. Barker. You will find him on the second floor. I should tell you that the building is in need of considerable maintenance. To my knowledge, it hasn't had a lick of paint since before the war. Mr. Barker has been with the firm for over thirty years and has always been very helpful and cooperative. If you have any questions or run into any problems, you can call me on the telephone. You should be able to complete the audit within two weeks, and you can requisition your supplies from Mrs. Webster this afternoon or tomorrow morning." He paused. "Any questions?"

"No, sir," replied Harry, thinking he would probably have some questions as soon as he walked out the door.

It was Friday afternoon, at the end of March 1956. The firm of Haslam, West and King worked a half-day each Saturday. That's when the staff was allowed to come to the office wearing sports jackets and a soft collared shirt, as opposed to the more formal suits, waistcoats, and stiff collars that Harry had to endure during the week. Mr. Bamford handed him the audit file and he retreated to the general office. He found Mrs. Webster and told her that he would be doing the audit of Summers & Co. He signed a chit requisition for a bottle of green ink and two nibs for the dip pen that he would be using.

On Saturday morning he spent his time going over the audit file. This contained the income and expenditure accounts for the previous financial year, together with work papers, audit certificate, and notes from Peter McFarland, which, Harry had to admit, were very thorough. There really didn't seem to be any problems and he was beginning to feel a little more confident that he could do the job.

On Monday morning, Harry came out of the underground station at Chancery Lane with thousands of other workers heading for their offices. Harry was dressed, like many of his co-workers, in the "uniform" of the day. He wore a beige gabardine trench coat over a three-piece blue suit, tie, and, of course, the stiff collar that always pressed into his throat when he was feeling under pressure, as he was now.

Unlike many of his co-workers, he was not wearing a hat. He had been told by Mr. Haslam that he would be expected to buy a trilby hat or a bowler hat for work and client visits. He was directed to Dunn & Co. They had a very catchy slogan: "If you want to get ahead, get a hat." But Harry felt the trilby didn't suit him, and he looked ridiculous in a bowler. So far, he had managed to avoid wearing either of them. The group was interspersed with some young women, usually with scarves wrapped around their heads against the cold wind. March had come in like a lamb and was certainly leaving like a lion.

After a brisk walk, he arrived at the Bedford Row offices of Summers & Co., a three-story brick terrace building in the Georgian style with a white front door in need of some paint. The company name was embossed on a brass plate on the right-hand side of the door, but it had been polished so often over the years that the letters had nearly disappeared into the brass. Harry pushed open the door. It led to an entrance hall of black-and-white marble squares in a diamond shape. There was no receptionist or reception area. The lighting was very poor. He could hear typewriters clacking in the distance as he passed double mahogany doors with a small sign on the wall with the words "Conference Room." He made his way up a poorly-lit, uncarpeted, sweeping staircase, with portraits on the walls, possibly of past partners, and passed more mahogany double doors and a small hand-painted sign to the right which read: "Mr. Sharpe."

He followed the stairs up to the second floor which had two offices with names attached to the wall, "Mr. Thornton" and "Mr. Beasley." Another door must have led into some sort of typing pool because he could hear typewriters clacking away furiously. He also found the door with the word "Cashier" on it, knocked quietly, and entered.

"Mr. Barker?"

In front of him sat a rather rumpled figure in a complete fog of pungent smoke. It was coming out of a pipe clasped between his teeth. "I'm Harry Bishop from Haslam, West and King."

"Ah, yes, of course, come in Mr. Bishop," Mr. Barker said with a welcoming gesture. "We are ready for you. You can make yourself comfortable over there, at that high desk. I have got the general ledger ready for you. You can hang your hat and coat on this hat stand. Oh, you don't have a hat."

"No, not today, Mr. Barker."

Harry made his way over to a Victorian style, sloping desk near the window. The rest of the office consisted of bookcases, which were full of ledgers and receipt files, and a small kitchen area in one corner with a sink and a gas ring. Harry unpacked his audit file, together with his bottle of green ink and pen. The bottle did not quite fit the inkwell on this old Victorian desk, so he had to balance it on the narrow ledge on the top of the desk. The desk had a sloping front, but there was a ridge at the bottom on which books could be balanced. His seat consisted of a tall stool of cracked leather.

Harry took in the contents of the room. Mr. Barker's desk was on a small square of a worn Persian carpet. He had a hat stand behind his desk, on which, unsurprisingly, was his bowler hat, gabardine raincoat, and a jacket on a hanger. The jacket seemed to belong to the suit that Mr. Barker was wearing. However, Harry noticed that he had three or four jackets, one on top of each other, on the back of his office chair. It appeared that he had taken one off to wear for the day while today's suit jacket was placed on the hanger. Harry had seen a similar practice in many offices. The idea was to avoid developing shiny arms because of perpetual rubbing on the desk.

The fog of smoke from Mr. Barker's pipe was giving off such a pungent smell that it seemed to have invaded the walls of the office. Next to Mr. Barker was an old-fashioned voice tube. When one of the partners wanted to speak to him, they would blow into the tube, which gave off a whistle. He would then withdraw a plug from the tube and shout down to the partner who was communicating with him and they would exchange messages in this fashion. *Oh my God*, thought Harry. *I have stepped back into Victorian times.*

Mr. Barker's smoking had taken its toll over the years. Not only did the room smell of his herbal mixture, but the walls, particularly around his desk, had a brown sheen. Like the rest of the building, this office was sorely in need of a paint job and a major spring clean. Dust was everywhere, the windows were grimy, and the frames had cracked, white paint around them. Harry doubted that they could even be opened. Finally, he noted that Mr. Barker had a hearing aid connected by wire to a square metal receiver poking out of one of his waistcoat pockets.

"Well, Mr. Bishop," said Mr. Barker in a warm, gravelly voice, "where shall we start?"

Harry had already looked at his audit notes and, following the audit guide, asked for the general ledger. Mr. Barker handed over a thick, rust-colored, leather-bound general ledger. It was medium-sized, but easily and comfortably sat on the ledge of the sloping Victorian desk. Harry got right down to work and started checking the numbers and ticking away with his green ink.

After about an hour and a half, there was a slight commotion at the door. It opened to reveal five members of the Summers & Co. staff. This, apparently, was tea break time. Mr. Barker was very gracious—he explained who Harry was and made the introductions: Mr. Humphries was a short, well-dressed man in his mid-forties, with slicked-back, gray hair and a pipe in his mouth. He was described as the senior clients account manager who maintained all the client accounts trusts books. Ms. Whipple was a delicate-looking, older lady, probably in her early sixties, with gray, streaked hair pulled back in a bun on her head. She wore rimless glasses and no makeup. Her cotton dress and black cardigan hung off her thin frame. Harry subsequently found out from Mr. Barker that she had lost her fiancé in the First World War, had never married, and had been Mr. Sharpe's personal secretary for over thirty years. Next was Mrs. Handley, who was Mr. Thornton's secretary. She was a stout lady, probably in her forties, with dyed blonde hair, lots of makeup, and very red lipstick. Then there was Mr. Davies, a tall, slightly stooped man with curly gray hair, glasses, and a disinterested expression on his face. He was described as the senior legal clerk and assistant to Mr. Sharpe. And finally, there was Miss Higgins. She was a young woman, probably in her early twenties, the switchboard operator and file clerk for the partners. She had short, black hair, blue eyes with thick mascara, large circular earrings, and heavy white makeup with a slash of red lipstick. She was dressed in an all-black, pencil-tight skirt nearly down to her ankles with flat shoes in the rebellious Teddy girl style.

"Would you like to join us in a cup of tea?" asked Mr. Humphries. Harry accepted and was presented with a cup of hot tea, which had too much milk for his liking and not enough sugar. Amazingly, Mr. Humphries then asked him for tuppence. "We do require everybody to contribute to the cost of tea breaks in the morning and afternoon," he said pompously. "I'm sure you understand." Harry handed over his tuppence, but decided that even though the tea was hot and wet it was not worth the investment.

Ms. Higgins was all eyes, clearly interested to see somebody of the younger generation in the building. "Where do you come from then?" She said it in a broad cockney accent. Harry replied, "South London" not wanting to elaborate. The Teddy girl look really didn't appeal to him. Harry then got on with his work, but Mr. Humphries launched into a loud discourse on the number of "negroes" that were "flooding" into London. He said they were changing the culture of the city, bringing "disgusting, dirty habits" with them, and taking jobs from the British working class. Before he finished his diatribe, he had also given his opinion of the

Irish, the Pope, Catholics in general, and the Jews who "control everything in the city." It was clear that Mr. Humphries had some serious social problems. The rest of the staff generally ignored him and didn't take up the argument, particularly Mr. Davies, who took his cup of tea and sat down to do the Times crossword. The tea break lasted about fifteen to twenty minutes and would repeat during the afternoon. The members of the staff who did not participate apparently either had flasks of tea or coffee that they brought with them or took a quick dash around the corner to Theobald's Road for a cup of tea and a biscuit, which is what Harry decided to do.

As he was leaving for his afternoon tea break, he bumped into Ms. Higgins. She asked if she could join him, pleased to have some company. She took him to Dino's, a small café on Theobald's Road, and they both ordered a cup of tea and a penguin chocolate biscuit. Underneath her Teddy-style clothing and make-up, Harry could see she was quite an attractive girl. She was tall and slim, with a pretty smile and beautiful blue eyes. Her name was Sally. She was just twenty years old.

"I am taking an evening course at Pitman's College to learn shorthand and become a secretary," she said in her cheeky, Cockney accent. "I should be finished by the beginning of June, and then I'm getting out of here."

"What are you going to do?"

"I shall be looking for a much better job. Summers & Co. is too old-fashioned. Some of the staff are really weird, like Mr. Humphries. 'Sharparse' is a pain in the whatsit, and very mean, even at Christmas." Harry laughed. "The junior partners are really miserable," she went on. "Mr. Thornton seems to have a perpetual drip under his nose, and Mr. Beasley is hardly ever in the office. I think I can do a lot better. What about you?"

"I come from Southwark. I'm halfway through my studies to become a Chartered accountant."

She said she was from Whitechapel Road in the East End. They had a few laughs together. Harry liked her. She seemed smart and ambitious. The next day, when they met up for their tea breaks, she was dressed in a blue wool dress with long sleeves, a much shorter skirt, and high heels. She wore less make-up. Her pale lipstick set off her blue eyes. Harry said nothing, but he realised that she was doing this for him. He thought she looked much more attractive.

The audit proceeded quite well. Harry had no difficulty in keeping to the program. He finally met the elusive Mr. Thornton, who came in to complain to Mr. Barker about some client payments. Harry heard numerous shouting exchanges through the voice tube, suffered through the fog of Mr. Barker's herbal mixture in his pipe, and navigated the ground floor of the building whenever he needed to use the toilet. When Harry inquired about that facility, Mr. Barker said the partners didn't allow any of the staff to use the toilet on the first or second floors, so Harry was directed to a toilet in the rear garden. The small structure contained only a toilet and a washbasin. Generally, it was in good working order, except the room itself was freezing, and there was only cold water in the basin. Harry decided that he would try to avoid further visits at all costs.

Harry enjoyed his tea breaks with Sally Higgins. He found her personable and interesting. He would have liked to ask her out on a date, but that was against office regulations. He would have to wait until the end of the audit. They liked the same sort of movies, they both enjoyed jazz at Ronnie Scott's, and he was interested to learn that she loved to read.

By Friday morning, he was ready to review the client ledgers. Mr. Barker had them brought up to his office. They were two large, thick, red leather ledgers inscribed with the words "Summers & Co." in gold. They were extremely heavy, maybe twenty pounds each. Inside were the client accounts, recording receipts, and disbursements, some going back many years. They were beautifully written in copperplate script by Mr. Humphries. Some of these client accounts were more active than others. They were recording the affairs of large and ancient family trust accounts of the English and Scottish aristocracy. Harry picked up one of the ledgers from Mr. Barker's desk. It was really heavy.

"Can you manage?" asked Mr. Barker.

"Yes, I think so," responded Harry. But he had difficulties getting the ledger up on the sloping desk. Once that task was completed, he had to make sure the book was steady and secured, resting on the rim at the bottom of the desk. However, when he opened the ledger, it started to slide off the desk. As he tried to stop it from falling, the top of the ledger hit the bottle of green ink. The bottle, seemingly, jumped up into the air and then flooded the book in bright green. The ledger crashed to the floor with an enormous thump, sending a large puff of dust particles into the air. Harry was rooted to the floor. It was a disaster. Even Mr. Barker had a look of horror on his face as he surveyed the green ink flowing over the open pages. Immediately, there was a whistle on the voice tube and Harry could hear Mr. Sharpe loudly, demanding to know what happened.

Mr. Barker explained in fairly gentle terms that there had been an accident and that the clients' ledger had dropped on the floor and a bottle of ink had splattered onto the clients' accounts pages. This generated more screaming up the tube. Harry knew he was in trouble. He was anxiously grabbing Mr. Barker's blotting paper, trying to soak up the green ink on the pages. This was difficult. The ink had leaked onto the top of each of the pages, so no one single spot could claim his attention. Mr. Barker joined Harry in this task, but there was no hiding the mess. The ink had run amok. Some of the entries were just a blur.

Within a couple of minutes, Mr. Sharpe arrived in the office. He was a short man, wearing rimless glasses. His grey hair was parted down the middle. He was dressed in a black, chalk-striped, three-piece suit with an old-fashioned winged collared shirt and a silver-grey tie. The suit was splattered with white streaks and there were pieces of white plaster on his shoulders and in his hair.

"Are you the auditor?" he asked aggressively.

"Yes, sir. I am Mr. Bishop, and I'm halfway through the audit." Harry spoke in a subdued, trembling voice. "I'm very sorry, sir, about this accident. The ledger just slid off the desk... I couldn't control it."

"That's ridiculous! Nobody else has had that problem before you. What happened to that other young auditor, Mac something or other?"

"McFarland is ill at the moment. He's not in the office."

"Well, young man, it's your responsibility," Sharpe responded with a cold steely-eyed glare. You better clean up this mess now and make good!" With that, he left the office, shouting at Barker to get Bamford on the phone. Harry knew what that meant.

Harry and Mr. Barker tried as best they could to mop up the green ink. Within another couple of minutes, the door burst open and Mr. Humphries arrived. When he saw the scale of the disaster and the mess on his beloved ledgers, he turned to Harry and shouted "Are you some sort of juvenile delinquent? Or just a total idiot?"

Mr. Barker intervened. "It was an accident, Mr. Humphries. It is difficult to balance these ledgers on those old Victorian desks, you know." His plea fell on deaf ears.

"I shall send Ms. Higgins up with a damp cloth and some dry towels," Humphries said. Then he turned on his heel and left the office, slamming the door behind him.

Within a few minutes, Ms. Higgins arrived, but there was not much she could do. "This is a right old bloody mess," she said with a grin. "It's about time Summers & Co. got rid of those old high desks and joined the 20th century. They should provide us with better working conditions." She continued as if she was a local shop steward of the clerks union and supporting a member.

About five minutes later, the telephone rang. Mr. Barker picked it up. He looked over at Harry, who was working with Sally Higgins, trying to remove green ink stains all over the room. "It's for you." Harry's stomach sank. He knew what was coming. It was Mr. Bamford on the other end. "I hear there's been a calamity, with one of the client's account ledgers," he said in a cold tone. He paused. Harry said nothing. "Mr. Sharpe has asked for your immediate removal," Mr. Bamford continued. "You better pack up your things and come back to the office." Harry had no answer. He would have a chance at an explanation later on, but he knew it would do no good.

"I'm sorry," said Mr. Barker. "It's not really your fault."

Ms. Higgins was clearly disappointed that Harry would be leaving. She hastily scribbled her phone number on a piece of paper and gave it to him.

"Please call me," she said, blushing.

He was too flummoxed to focus. As he went downstairs, he was surprised to see various members of the staff on the landing, many of them smiling and giving him the thumbs up. A couple of them even slapped him on the back and said "good job."

Within twenty minutes, he was back in Chancery Lane. Mr. Bamford was waiting for him. "You better give me a good explanation, Bishop." Harry apologized and did his best to explain. Mr. Bamford listened patiently. "Well, McFarland has done this audit for two years, he doesn't seem to have had the same problem." Then he paused and said: "In addition to the damage that you have done to their ledger, Mr. Sharpe is particularly annoyed because dropping the ledger apparently caused a large lump of plaster to fall off the ceiling right onto his desk. He is covered in white."

"I know, sir. I saw Mr. Sharpe. I am so sorry," Harry said.

Mr. Bamford scoffed. "You'd better go now and we will find you some new work on Monday morning. I shall have to do damage control as best I can with Mr. Sharpe."

Harry apologized again and, as he turned to leave the office, Mr. Bamford, looking pensive, said, "Humph."

Harry knew it had been a disaster. He had failed on his first independent audit. But it wasn't all bad. After all, he had met the lovely Sally Higgins. He was off the audit. He felt around in his jacket pocket for the crumpled piece of paper.

2 AMORE – 1961

I t was an overcast afternoon, which was unusual for the time of year. The old man replaced the faded red rose at the base of the gravestone with a fresh one. He then took out a damp cloth from a plastic bucket he had brought with him and wiped down the gravestone. The man was tall, slightly stooped, with disheveled white hair. He was very thin, and his clothes were hanging off of him. His cheeks were sunken. His eyes were full of sadness. He stood by the gravestone at the little cemetery on Via Del Paradiso in the Tuscan village of Forte Dei Marmi. He said his prayers, then he realised it was nearly fifty-five years to the day that he had first set eyes on her.

A lifetime, he said to himself, a *full and wonderful lifetime.*

* * *

Charlie couldn't take his eyes off of her. She was a black-haired girl in a bright, green bikini showing off her dark tan. Her hair was held back by a green band, to match the bikini. She was lounging with three others on the beach in Alassio, an

Italian seaside town about fifty miles from the French border. Charlie couldn't see her eyes because they were covered by big, round sunglasses. She was animatedly talking to her girlfriend, a blonde in a white one-piece bathing suit, wearing similar sunglasses. Two young men were with them, both appeared to be around Charlie's age. One of them – probably her boyfriend, Charlie thought – was tall, slim, and athletic looking.

"Greg!" Charlie said. "Look at that girl over there." He nodded towards the dark-haired beauty.

"Yeah. Very tasty," Greg responded. Greg Westbury was Charlie's best friend. They were on vacation together with two other friends, Steve Bloom and Patrick Fisher. It was an exciting time. The four of them had just graduated from Bristol University and had been planning their trip to Europe for many months. Charlie Thornton was a tall, young man with a gregarious personality, fair hair, blue eyes, and a strong physique from years as a varsity rower. At the end of summer, Charlie would be joining NM Rothschild, the London merchant bankers. He'd been accepted after an introduction from his father, Roger Thornton, who was the bank manager at Barclays, Mayfair. This vacation was to be his last hurrah, at least for a while.

They had crossed the Channel on the P&O car ferry to Boulogne, the first stop of their journey. They drove through France in two convertibles—a Sunbeam Alpine, which Charlie had bought second-hand just a few weeks previously, and a Triumph Herald, which was owned by Patrick's mother. On the French Riviera, in Juan-les-Pins, they had met four Swedish girls and spent some time with them on the beaches, or dancing the night away at an open-air nightclub called Le Vieux Colombier. After a few days, they had driven across the Italian border to Alassio, a seaside resort with white, sandy beaches and a vibrant nightlife. The recommendation had come from a classmate of Charlie's. He'd also suggested a place to stay, Pensione Alberto on Via Boselli, less than ten minutes from the beach. The rooms were sparse, but they were bright and clean. They had arrived late the previous night.

And now, Charlie and his friends were looking forward to a few more weeks of sun and fun... and girls! In particular, Charlie thought, *this* girl. He was captivated.

"You've got a whole beach of Italian beauties like that to choose from," Greg said. "Most of them won't have their boyfriends with them."

"I know, I know," Charlie replied, sounding rather despondent. "But she's the most beautiful girl I've ever seen."

"Come on," Greg said with a laugh. "We've only been here half an hour!"

Steve and Pat returned from their walk along the beach. "These Italian girls are beautiful," Pat said, "but for the most part they seem to be with their families or boyfriends or brothers or whatever."

"Some of them are walking up and down the beach on their own, so maybe we should try our luck," said Steve.

"We'll probably have a better chance at the bars tonight," Greg said. "But there's no harm in trying."

They all went down to the water's edge, grinning at the girls, saying *buon giorno*, and receiving some smiles and giggles. None of them seemed very interested in striking up a conversation. The beach was rather full by now, mostly with English, French, and German tourists. Charlie and his friends spent some time running in and out of the warm Mediterranean Sea and splashing around to cool off. After a while, the midday heat started to burn. As people began leaving the beach for lunch, Charlie and the others put on their shorts and T-shirts over their swimsuits and wandered up to the edge of the town. They bought some crêpes and Coca-

Colas for lunch. By the time they went back to the beach, Charlie's beautiful Italian girl and her friends were gone. They had apparently retreated from the heat of the day.

That evening, Charlie and his friends found a little café in the old part of town where they had an excellent fixed-price dinner., within their limited budget. Just after nine-thirty, they found Mario's Bar, near the beach, and got a table by the dance floor. A five-piece band started up, playing a combination of Italian, American, and English tunes, many of which were slow and romantic. The bar quickly filled up with young tourists and Italian families. There was a cover charge, and the boys had to buy a drink, so they bought a bottle of Asti Spumante between them that came with a plate of crisps, nuts, and olives. Steve, deeply suntanned after one day on the beach, approached a pretty, dark-haired Italian girl, sitting with her family. He asked her to dance: "Permesso, Signorina?"

The others, too, found plenty of girls to dance with: English, French, German, and Dutch. They had a great evening dancing under the stars, but there was no sign of Charlie's Italian beauty.

The days passed blissfully. During the day, they lounged on the beach. When the sun went down, they danced the night away, either at Mario's or another club, Tino's, two hundred yards up the beach. They quickly made friends. Steve's Italian girlfriend, Laura, invited him to meet her family, and he seemed to get on with them very well. Her brother Armando suggested a soccer game on the beach. From then on, they regularly met for a match every morning at the water's edge. The Italian boys had tremendous mastery of quick flicks and numerous tricks. They were impressed with Steve's speed and Pat's considerable dexterity. However, they were better than the Brits, and they beat them every day. But they all had a lot of fun, and after the game, everyone would rush into the Mediterranean to cool off.

Charlie's Italian girl, her boyfriend, and their friends were sitting in a row behind him every morning. He couldn't help but stare at her. He took in her every movement. On the fourth day, she took off her sunglasses and smiled at him.

"Hey Greg," said Charlie. "She just smiled at me. She obviously knows that I've been looking at her day in and day out."

"Of course," Greg replied. "How could she not see you staring at her like an openmouthed goldfish?"

"Do you think it means anything? That she smiled at me? Do you think there is some way I could approach her if her boyfriend isn't around?"

"Look, Charlie," said Greg. "She's with someone. You can't just walk up to her and start talking. That would be bad form. How would you like it if that happened to you? You have got a pretty German girl, Anke. the one you met at Mario's? She seems nice. Why embarrass yourself?"

"I know, I know... but I just can't take my eyes off her."

Later that day, Steve and Laura came to visit with the boys under their umbrella. Laura asked if they had been to La Luna nightclub, at Capo Mele, on the road out of Alassio. She said it was more sophisticated and expensive than Mario's or the other clubs on the beach. She also said the music was fantastic and the view was amazing.

That night, they decided to try La Luna. By the time they got there, just after ten o'clock, it was already crowded. Parking the car was difficult, and they had to pay an entrance fee before getting into the club, after waiting in a long line. Inside, however, it was beautiful. The palm trees were lit up in white and green, and there was a marble dance floor with sofas and lounge chairs around it. From the terrace, they could look out at the sea, all the way to Alassio. The music was great, and the band was in full swing. They had a table for three. Steve wasn't with them. He had decided to stay at Mario's with Laura for the evening. They ordered the usual bottle of Asti Spumante and settled down. And then Charlie's heart jumped. There she was. His beautiful Italian girl. She was wearing a white dress, with a scooped-out neckline, her black hair held back by an orange and white chiffon scarf, which matched a similar scarf around her waist. Her high-heeled shoes were bright orange, and she wore sparkling bracelets on her right wrist. She certainly stood out in the crowd. This time, there were no sunglasses. She saw Charlie and her face lit up with a smile. He made up his mind that he was going to speak to her and try and dance with her.

After about twenty minutes or so, her boyfriend got up and walked away, perhaps to the bar or the men's room. Charlie decided this was his chance. Under normal circumstances, he wouldn't dream of approaching a girl who was with her boyfriend, but he had a deep feeling that if he didn't speak to her now, he would regret it for the rest of his life. Greg was already dancing with a Danish girl, so before he could interfere or stop him, Charlie bounded over to her. "Permesso, Signorina," he said politely, asking her to dance.

"Grazie," she replied. She gave him a warm smile.

"Do you speak English?" Charlie asked.

"Yes, but not very, very good," she said with a thick accent.

"I've been looking at you on the beach for days, you know."

"I know, but you never come to speak."

"Well, every day, you have been with your boyfriend and your other friends."

"My boyfriend!" She stopped dancing as she laughed. "No, that's Flavio, my brother, not my boyfriend. And my friends are Fabiana and her brother, Paolo."

Charlie was dumbfounded. It took a moment or two, with his heart pounding, to start talking to her again. The music turned to a romantic Italian song. He held her closer and could smell her intoxicating perfume. She was smaller than he had thought, looking at her on the beach. She was perhaps five foot four, but, with her high heels, her head and hair nestled gently into his shoulder. She seemed quite content to be dancing so close to him.

"What is your name?" Charlie finally said, croakily.

"Anna Maria Sanguinetti, and what is yours?"

"Charlie Thornton."

"Sharlee," she said in her Italian accent. "I like that name." She smiled.

"Now that I have finally met you, I want to see as much of you as possible, as long as you are in Alassio," Charlie blurted out, without even thinking what response he might receive.

"That would be nice, but I am sorry, it would be impossible."

Charlie's stomach took a nosedive. "Impossible? Why?" His voice was almost pleading.

"Because we leave tomorrow morning."

"Oh no," said Charlie. "Can't you stay a few more days?"

She gave a short laugh. "No. I have to go with my brother, home to Milano. This was a short holiday from my school in Geneva," she said.

"I don't understand," said Charlie.

"I have just finished year-end examinations at my school. Now I go home to my family."

Charlie was feeling desperate. How could he lose this beautiful girl after having only just found her?

"What time are you leaving tomorrow. Which hotel are you staying at?" He was desperate to spend at least a few final minutes with her.

"We are at the Hotel Victoria. But we leave at eight in the morning."

"I shall come to see you," said Charlie. "I would like your address and phone number, and if you don't mind, I would like to keep in touch."

Amazingly, there was a definite chemistry between them. She seemed to be as interested in Charlie as he was in her. "Okay, Sharlee Tornton, come to the hotel early in the morning, and I will give you all my information." She paused, then she said quietly, "I would like you to write to me." It was too dark to see her in the dim light of the dance floor, but somehow, he felt she was blushing.

They danced every dance together, and Anna Maria introduced Charlie to her brother Flavio and their friends. They all had a good laugh when they heard that Charlie had thought Flavio was Anna Maria's boyfriend.

"Nice girls in Italy do not go out alone," Flavio said. "They have a chaperone. It might be an elder brother or another member of the family, or a close friend. That's the way it is in Italy," he concluded with a laugh. At last, Charlie understood why the girls here seemed never to be alone.

Anna Maria told Charlie a little of her background. She came from Milan and was studying art and design in Geneva. She was nearly twenty years old, and she would graduate at the end of the next school year. Charlie told her a little of his background.

Charlie loved La Luna, and the romantic music under the stars. He had never had a vacation like this before. Charlie held Anna Maria tightly. They danced cheek-to-cheek during nearly every dance until the club closed at one-thirty a.m.

"I don't know how, but I am determined to see you again. I shall never forget tonight."

Anna Maria laughed." I would like that also, Sharlee. I think I will also remember tonight."

At the end of the evening, he gave her a little kiss on the lips, and he received a sweet response. He felt he was drowning in her perfume and her beauty. He had never felt like this before. Something in this girl shook his core.

The next morning, he bounced out of bed early, got

dressed, and made himself look respectable in order to say farewell to Anna Maria. They had met less than twelve hours ago, but he knew that he would see her many times again in the future. He ran over to the Hotel Victoria. It was easy to find, since it had a large sign that could be seen from Pensione Alberto. It was a small hotel, but it looked more upmarket than Alberto's. Anna Maria's group was just packing up their cars when Charlie arrived. He got a big smile from Anna Maria and a friendly nod from her brother Flavio and their friends.

"I write down my address and phone number in Geneva for you," said Anna Maria with a smile that made Charlie melt.

"As I said, I will write regularly," responded Charlie and looked at the piece of paper. It had her address and phone number written in red ink. He folded it and put it in his pocket.

"Have a safe journey, and enjoy the rest of your summer." They didn't really have any time for anything else. The cars were packed and ready to go. He stood in the hotel driveway waving goodbye to his newfound love, and, within a minute or two, Anna Maria was gone. He walked slowly back to the hotel, in time to meet up with the boys for breakfast.

"I hope you're not going to mope around because of your lost love," said Greg. "I know she is lovely, but it is not going to be easy to keep a relationship going between London and Geneva."

Steve and Pat nodded in agreement. "And anyway, we've got a couple of weeks left in this vacation, so I hope you make the most of it. There are other fish in the sea, you know."

Charlie nodded his agreement. He would have a good time.

They enjoyed the rest of their stay in Alassio, making new friends on the beach and at Mario's. Charlie joined in the fun, but he kept thinking about Anna Maria. At the end of the week, they said goodbye to Alberto, the owner of the pensione, packed up their cars, and drove on to Florence. They took in all the major sights, the Cathedral, David, the Ponte Vecchio, and Uffizi Gallery. They met students from the University, ate some lovely food, and had a lot of fun. At last, it was time for the journey back home to London. They decided not to follow each other. Charlie and Greg would choose one route to Paris, and Stephen and Pat another. They agreed to meet up at the Arc de Triomphe at eleven a.m., four days after leaving Florence.

Charlie and Greg took a route that took them to Monte Carlo and then around the edges of the French Alps to Grenoble. From there they were going to move on to Dijon and Paris. They were making good time on the second day when the skies suddenly darkened. They could see a gathering storm approaching.

"I think we should get off the road and put the hood up," said Greg.

"I will, but at the moment there is no layby that I can pull into," Charlie replied.

They were driving right into the rainstorm. Large blobs of rain were starting to hit the windscreen. And then the heavens opened up. Massive sheets of rain poured down on top of them. The windscreen wipers were working furiously. Charlie had to slow down to a crawl until he eventually was able to pull into a panoramic viewing area. They jumped out of the car, which was filling up with water. They eventually got the hood up, a major engineering achievement. There were about six inches of water in the car. They tried to bail it out with their bare hands and hats. They were soaked through, but the water was warm, and the rainstorm was beginning to pass. Within a few minutes, the rain stopped and the sun came out. Soaked to the skin, they continued on their journey.

Eventually, they reached a small village. It appeared to be

totally deserted like so many French villages. At the end of the main road, they found a café that was open. They pulled up, got out of the car, and again struggled with the hood. This time they were taking it down so the sun could dry the contents of the car. They took out Greg's holdall and Charlie's backpack, which was soaked through. Then they opened the boot and took out some dry clothes from their suitcases. They took turns going into the foul-smelling WC to change and then sat outside in the sunshine and ordered a couple of coffees.

They decided to unpack the holdall and backpack so they could dry out the contents. When Charlie opened his luggage, he was gripped by panic. He realised that he had put Anna Maria's name and address in one of the small pockets on the outside of his backpack. He opened it up and there it was, folded neatly, but totally soaked through. He unfolded the piece of paper and could make out neither her name nor her address. All that was left was a wet, runny red smudge. The words had completely disappeared.

He felt sick. "Oh God," he said to Greg. "Look what happened! I've lost Anna Maria's information. I don't have her address, phone number, or anything. What am I going to do?" There was desperation in his voice.

"Come on, Charlie," said Greg. "You must be able to remember something! The name of the school, or where she is living in Geneva, or something about Milan? You know her name. You should be able to find a phone number or her family's phone number."

"I only knew her for a few hours. Her name is Anna Maria Sangretti or Sanditti or something like that. I don't even know how to spell it because I didn't concentrate that much."

"Well," said Greg, "we will have to work out a plan."

As they drove through the French countryside, they discussed the problem and tried to find a solution. But they were stumped. After focusing on the issue for hours, Greg finally said, "I'm sorry mate, but I think you're screwed. Perhaps the only way you will find her again is to go off to Geneva and wander around the schools."

"Oh God," Charlie cried despondently. "You may be right, but even then... I wouldn't know where to begin. And, of course, I'm starting work in a few weeks, so I won't have another vacation until next summer."

They eventually made their way to Paris where they stayed in a modest hotel on the left bank. They all met up under the Arc de Triomphe at eleven a.m., four days after having left Florence. Steve opened a bottle of Champagne. They drank to each other's health and the great vacation that they had just enjoyed. Charlie told the other boys about losing Anna Maria's information.

Patrick came up with a feasible idea. "Why don't you write to the Hotel Victoria in Alassio? You could ask for her address or her brother's address and you could then write and explain what happened."

Charlie's heart jumped. "Yeah, Pat, that might work. I shall definitely give it a go."

Charlie didn't even think about making a phone call from the UK to Italy because it was quite an undertaking. It wasn't just expensive, it was also difficult, and the connections were notoriously finicky, especially if you were trying to connect to a small hotel in Alassio. Writing a letter was the only practical form of communication. After another day and night in Paris, they headed off to Boulogne and caught the ferry across the Channel to England.

After returning home, they went their separate ways. Charlie spent a month working on his grandfather's farm in Dorchester, Dorset, which he had done every summer for years. Then, on September 4th, he started work at Rothschild's in London. He had already written to the Victoria Hotel and was anxiously awaiting a response. Two weeks later, a letter arrived. His heart was pounding as he opened it. The English was not particularly clear, but he understood the gist of it, which was that the hotel would not give out information relating to any of its guests. They were apologetic, but Charlie's heart sank. Despondent, he threw himself into his new job. He did well. But despite having other girlfriends, and meeting up with his pals Greg, Steve, and Patrick, his thoughts were always on Anna Maria.

When spring came around, he asked his office manager whether he could take a week's holiday in June. He was granted permission and made arrangements, booking a ferry passage across the Channel and a youth hostel in Geneva. The idea was to spend a few days visiting every art school he could find. On June 16th, he left England. By Monday afternoon, he was in Geneva checking into the Geneva Youth Hostel on Rue Rothschild, a few blocks from the lake.

He had compiled a list of four art and design schools. After a comfortable night and an adequate breakfast at the well-appointed hostel, he set out on his search. His first call was at the L'Ecole des Fines Arts, a small building located on Rue Patrice in the center of the old town. He was directed to the Office of Admissions. The people were not very helpful. They were unsympathetic to his story, and, in the end, they merely confirmed that no one had registered under the name Anna Maria Sangritti or Sanditti. He moved onto the next school on his list, L'Ecole Bruno Boucher, located not far from the first school. He was kept waiting for over half an hour. At last, someone from the administration office came out to see him. They informed him that they were not allowed to confirm or deny the name or whereabouts of any of the students. This was understandable, but not helpful. However, since it appeared that the classes were ending for the day, he sat outside across the street in a café and waited and watched. After about twenty minutes, a slow trickle of students started to exit the building. He anxiously looked for Anna Maria. He stayed for over an hour, but there was no sign of her. Finally, a janitor came out and locked the front doors to the building.

Charlie realised this was going to be more difficult than he had anticipated. He wandered around the old town during the evening, looking for the Café La Clemence, which Anna Maria had told him about when they had been dancing under the stars. She said it was a hangout for the local students. He hoped she might show up. He arrived there at five in the afternoon and stayed until about nine-thirty. No sign of Anna Maria. He went back to the youth hostel feeling despondent. He was kicking himself that he didn't even know her true surname.

The following morning, under a bright blue sky, he headed out again, walking briskly past the shimmering lake. This time, he went to the Haute École d'Arts Appliqués. It was in a grand building on James Fazy Boulevard. He walked through an inner courtyard towards the administration office. Once again, he explained his situation. The lady in the office was rather dubious when he didn't know Anna Maria's real name. She said they could only give out student's names and addresses in a case of emergency, and this didn't really qualify. She did, however, seem to have some sympathy for his situation. She suggested that he wait at the exit by the courtyard. Perhaps, she suggested, he would see Anna Maria when the students left for lunch. But she also gave Charlie the nod that she didn't recognize the name. Still, he stood by the gate and watched the students flood through at lunchtime. They certainly looked like art students, with a variety of colored outfits and hairdos. There was no sign of Anna Maria. He kept waiting and watched the students come back into the school, just in case he had failed to see her. But there was still no sign of her. He was beginning to wonder whether she was even in Geneva. Maybe she had graduated early? He sat in a café across the street and had a *Sandwich Jambon* and a cup of coffee. He wondered if he was on a wild goose chase.

After lunch, he headed to the last school from his list. This was the Ecole supérieure des Beaux-Arts, part of Geneva University, in a large, imposing building. Again, he asked to meet with the administration office and was told to wait. He sat on a hardwood bench in the large gallery of the old stone building, trying to think of any alternatives. After about forty minutes, a middle-aged lady approached him. She introduced herself as Madame Simone and asked him what he was looking for. He explained his situation. She said it was not their practice to release information about their students, not unless it was an emergency. Charlie put on the charm and said he understood. Then she asked Charlie whether he thought this was an emergency. He said absolutely. He had been looking for her in three other schools to no avail, and if he failed, he didn't know what he would do. It was imperative that he find Anna Maria in Geneva somewhere. She asked for the girl's name and he said she wasn't sure whether it was Sangritti or Sanditti or something similar. She laughed and said that was not very helpful. She then told him to wait on the bench. He sat there with his heart pounding, praying that perhaps there was a glimmer of hope.

After about twenty minutes, the door at the end of the corridor opened. There she was. Anna Maria. She was escorted by Madame Simone.

"This may be the young lady you are looking for," said Madame Simone as she approached Charlie with a smile on her face, "Mademoiselle Anna Maria Sanguinetti."

Anna Maria was dressed in a black apron splashed with paint. She smiled brightly at him. "Sharlee, you are here in Geneva," she said, "why didn't you let me know you were coming?"

Charlie gave her a big hug. "It's a long story," he said with a big grin on his face. "But I found you, and I will explain everything."

"I'm in the middle of a class," she said, "but I will be finished in about forty minutes. Can you wait here?"

"Absolutely, I will wait as long as it takes."

Charlie grabbed Mme. Simone's hand and said: "Thank you so much. This is wonderful. You have saved my life."

She laughed. "You are very welcome, Monsieur."

After about forty minutes, Anna Maria reappeared, all smiles. She grabbed Charlie's arm and said, "I will take you to my apartment, and then we can go to the old town, and La Clemence Café. I have arranged to meet some friends there this evening, and I would like to introduce you."

"La Clemence," responded Charlie. "I remember you told me about that place, and I was there last night, but you didn't show up."

"Well, yesterday evening, I met up with some other friends at the Lido Beach. We stayed the whole evening. It is lovely. I'm looking forward to showing you Geneva and having you meet all my friends." She sounded excited.

They had been walking for about twenty minutes and were now in a residential area with stately apartment buildings. Anna Maria led him through a doorway and up to the fourth floor of an old building, then they entered one of the apartments. It was expensively furnished. A small, grey-haired lady came out to greet her.

"Oh, Anna Maria, you are home early this evening."

"Yes, Madame, I have an English friend visiting Geneva. He came to my school to find me. I'm just going to change and we are going out for the evening." She introduced Charlie to Madame Bonnet. Then, from one of the rooms along the corridor, a couple of young women came out, laughing. Anna Maria introduced Charlie to her two roommates. "This is my friend Sharlee, from London," she said in her accented English. "Sharlee, this is Eleanora from Rome, and Francine from Paris." Charlie shook hands formally. The girls giggled at him.

"We weren't sure if you existed," said Francine in near-fluent English.

"Even if you did exist, we were not sure that you would show up in Geneva," Eleanora added, laughing.

"Well, here he is," said Anna Maria, "as handsome as ever."

Charlie was quite taken aback by this reception. He had been thinking about Anna Maria every single day. It had frustrated him that he had been unable to contact her or find her for a whole year. It now appeared that she had been thinking of him as well.

"Come on, Sharlee," said Anna Maria. "We are off to La Clemence, and then we have a party to go to."

"Don't be late, Anna Maria," said Mme. Bonnet. "You know you are in the middle of your final examinations, so make sure you are back here by eleven. Without fail!" Her voice was stern.

"Don't worry, Madame, we will definitely come back before eleven," she replied, kissing the two girls and Madame on both cheeks.

She linked her arm in Charlie's and guided him out of the apartment. It took them about fifteen minutes to walk to the famed café bar in the Place du Bourg-de-Four in the middle of the old town. It was packed with students, even on the large terrace outside. A couple of them were playing guitar, and there was excitement in the air. Anna Maria seemed to know a lot of people. She introduced Charlie to them all. He definitely felt she was treating him as her boyfriend, and not just a casual acquaintance from the beach in Alassio. He felt the same way about her. After spending about an hour at La Clemence, they moved on to a small apartment in a tiny building, around the corner in Rue Chausse-Coq, where one of her friends was having a party. There were bowls of food, including fondue, as well as plenty of wine. Loud music was coming from a record player in the corner. Once again, Anna

Maria knew everybody. She was greeted with hugs and kisses by practically everyone she spoke to. When the music was slow, he held her close, and she responded. From time to time he kissed her, starting on her cheek and moving to a soft kiss on her lips.

"I was really upset when I didn't hear from you," she said, "but, somehow, I knew that I would see you again in Geneva or somewhere else."

Charlie had already told her about how he had lost her address during a heavy storm. "I was desperately unhappy, but I was determined to find you. I didn't have much to go on, and I wasn't even sure of your last name. But here we are, and I can tell you, as far as I'm concerned, I'll never let you go again." She held him tightly. He saw a tear rolling down her cheek.

They were back at her apartment ten minutes before eleven. He held her face and gave her a long goodnight kiss. They arranged to meet the following day, as her final examinations were to resume in the morning. She would be free by one o'clock. She invited him to meet her outside the school and then to go to the Lido Beach club on the shores of Lake Geneva. She said it would be great fun. A bunch of her friends would be there as well. He asked if she needed to study for her next examination, but she told him that the finals were about creative design and ideas. Either she had the talent to pass or not. She seemed rather confident.

The following morning, a beautiful sunny day, Charlie left the hostel before nine and took a ferry ride down to Evian. He admired the scenery, the sparkling lake, and the hulking Mont Blanc in the distance. He was back in time to meet up with Anna Maria as she came out of school. She was wearing a white miniskirt and pale blue blouse. Her luxurious black hair was kept in place by a headband. She told him her examination had gone well. She had been working on designs for scarves, and she had submitted three of her designs to the panel of judges. They would be added to her other work and she would receive the results in about six weeks. She had a large backpack, stuffed with colored paper, brushes, pallets, and tubes of paint.

"Sharlee," she said, throwing her arms around his neck and giving him a soft kiss on the lips. Just the feel of her and her light perfume made his heart pound against his rib cage.

"I'm going to take you to my volunteer job," she said with a twinkle in her eye. "It's only an hour and a half, but I just feel you will fall in love with my students, just the way I have." She led him down the street to a building that appeared to be attached to a local hospital. They went in, and he quickly realised it was a Children's Hospital. It was catering to handicapped and autistic children, as well as those going through severe medical treatments. There was a small ward where some of the kids were sitting up in bed, and the rest were gathered at one end of the floor, sitting at miniature tables and chairs.

"*Bonjour, mes petites,*" said Anna Maria with a big smile.

"*Bonjour,* Anna Maria," Came the reply.

"This is my friend Sharlee, who has come all the way from London to see us." Every child was excited to see her. She handed out papers and pots of watercolors, as well as crayons and brushes. She explained the art project she had in mind, and everyone was very excited. There were squeals of delight as they all went to work. Anna Maria continually moved among the children, helping them, advising them, and sometimes painting a little bit to help them on their way. The time flew by. She collected the results from each child, putting a name on each piece. She then handed the paintings over to the ward nurse who promised that they would be put on the wall. She went around, kissing every child goodbye. Charlie was deeply moved. He knew that he loved her, but now he realised what a wonderful human being she was.

He felt that she made him whole. It was a miracle that she

had entered his life, and, even though their relationship might be complicated, his world would never be the same. It would only be more beautiful. As they left the ward, he saw that she had tears trickling down her cheeks. She vainly tried to smile at him. He took her in his arms and held her very close, feeling his own tears welling up. At last, she ended the embrace. "Come on," she said. "Let's go to the beach and have some fun."

As they made their way down to the beach club, she told Charlie about her family. Her grandfather had started a business in the late 1890s, making handcrafted ladies' shoes. At the end of the Second World War, her father had taken it over, gradually expanding the Sanguinetti brand. It now included three shops in Milan, Florence, and Rome. Anna Maria had two older brothers. Charlie had already met one of them, Flavio. He was two years older than her, and her second brother, Andrea, was six years older. He had joined the family business with an eye towards developing exports. Flavio was also in the business, and he had the responsibility of developing sales through other outlets and department stores in Italy. Andrea had opened accounts in major premium stores in London, Paris, and, most recently, New York. She said Andrea was very smart and ambitious and that he wanted to grow the Sanguinetti product range. The manufacturing plant in Florence had already been expanded, and they were planning to introduce a line of ladies' handbags. They were also developing other accessories, such as wallets, belts, and purses. She said that she would be joining the company and that her job would be to design a range of silk scarves that complemented the Sanguinetti brand. She couldn't wait to get to work.

Charlie told her some of his own background and about his current job with the Rothschild's Mergers and Acquisitions department. He even said that he had been thinking of applying for a position in the Milan office. When he said this, she gave him a big hug. He told her about his father's job as a London banker, and his grandfather's farm and estate in Dorset, where he and his brother and sister had spent much of their youth. Even now, he liked to work on the farm during his vacations. He told her that his family's connections to the land went back three centuries. Anna Maria was impressed, and she remarked how wonderful it was to have that kind of family history.

The Lido Beach Club had a clubhouse café and a large, grassy meadow leading to a narrow beach on the shores of the lake. Once again, Anna Maria met up with a bunch of friends and Charlie could see how popular she was. They had a good time talking, laughing, and running in and out of the water, or getting ice cream sodas and sandwiches from the café.

They spent the rest of the day talking, swimming, laughing, and holding hands, interspersed with little kisses and hugs. He found out that she had a few boyfriends, and that her mother was always pushing her to date the son of one of her closest friends. But none of her relationships were serious, particularly since she had met Charlie.

The two of them had a quiet dinner in a bistro in the old town. Charlie brought Anna Maria back to her apartment before eleven. She had no examinations the following day, so they drove down the lake to Lausanne. They had a wonderful time exploring the old town. They had lunch in a restaurant overlooking the lake. The Swiss countryside was spectacularly beautiful. Anna Maria was affectionate and cheerful, and they spent a lot of time kissing. Charlie's head was spinning. He was having the best time of his life. He knew he was madly in love with her. Moreover, he knew that he wanted to marry her. When the thought entered his head, he initially tried to push it away. *Don't be silly*, he told himself. *You barely know her.* And yet, deep down, he knew it was true. Anna Maria Sanguinetti was the love of his life.

They enjoyed every minute of each other's company. They

were both very sad when he had to say his goodbyes. He had to get back to London and go to work the following Monday. He left in the middle of Saturday afternoon and drove at a good pace until it was dark. He found a small pension near Paris, where he spent the night. He was up early, and, after a quick breakfast at a nearby café, he headed for Boulogne and the ferry back to Dover, and eventually to London.

When he arrived late in the afternoon, his parents were at home. His mother gave him a hug and a warm welcome. He excitedly told her the news. "I found Anna Maria. Amazing, considering I didn't even have her right name. She is the most wonderful girl I've ever known... and I'm going to marry her."

His mother stood very still. Finally, she cleared her throat. "Don't be ridiculous," she said. "You are far too young. This is just an infatuation. You should be focusing on other things, like your work at Rothschild's." As she spoke, her face reddened and her voice hardened. "Anyway, we don't know anything about this Italian girl. There are lots of wonderful English girls. I don't know what your father will say about this, but I think you should get your head straight."

Charlie's father had been in his study, on the phone. As he came into the living room, Charlie made the same speech. His mother jumped in. "I told him that it is a ridiculous suggestion. He is far too young and needs to get himself established in the city. He needs to focus on other things before considering marriage... to anyone. And certainly not some girl he met on the beach in Italy last year!"

His father seemed to agree. "Your mother is right, Charlie," he said calmly. "I think you should get this out of your mind, get back to work tomorrow, and continue to learn the ropes at Rothschild's. That doesn't mean you can't have a good time. There are many beautiful, young, English girls, Charlie. I don't want to hear any more about this." As he finished, his voice sounded more irritated.

Charlie knew when to shut up. He didn't raise the matter again with his parents. When he next met up with Greg, Stephen, and Pat, he told them all about his trip to Geneva. They were wide-eyed when he said that he was in love with Anna Maria and that he intended to marry her. "Good on you mate," said Greg. "But take your time."

Stephen nodded in agreement. "She seemed lovely when we met in Alassio, but holiday romances don't always get too serious, you know."

Pat, however, was all smiles, "Love at first sight. How incredible. You know what you're doing, Charlie, and you're always very determined, so I hope it all works out. What are your plans?"

"Well," said Charlie, "we are going to keep in touch. Either I will go to Italy to meet her family in the next few months, or she will come here, maybe for Christmas. We shall have to see how things develop. I am going to learn Italian and start agitating at Rothschild's. I want to see if I can get transferred to their Milan office."

Charlie and Anna Maria did keep in touch via mail, but it was not easy to arrange their next encounter. Neither sets of parents were keen to extend invitations. Both parties were perhaps waiting to see if this romance survived and was indeed serious. However, the following summer, Anna Maria invited Charlie to come and spend a week in August at her family's villa in Forte Dei Marmi, on the Liguria-Tuscany coast. Charlie was over the moon when he received this invitation. He really wanted to meet Anna Maria's family... and also try out his Italian. The letters got more frantic and passionate as the days counted down.

Eventually he boarded an Alitalia flight from Gatwick to Pisa, where Anna Maria had agreed to meet him at the airport. But she was not there. 10 minutes passed, and then 20. He was getting frantic; he did not know how to communicate with Anna Maria. All sorts of thoughts were going through his head. Had her parents not given their permission? Had she gotten cold feet about meeting him at all? The small airport slowly emptied, and eventually he was the only one standing forlornly outside.

At last, in the distance, he saw a small grey Fiat coming into the airport. It was almost the only vehicle in sight. It had been over an hour since his flight had landed. But suddenly she was there, flinging open the door of the car, running round to greet him, and throwing her arms around his neck.

"Oh, Sharlee," she said, "I am so sorry. There was an accident, right ahead of me. That road is treacherous. It is an old road, winding through little villages and over railway crossings, and there is always heavy truck traffic. There are always accidents. They're building an autostrada, which will be ready soon and will go right past Forte dei Marmi. It will be faster and safer." She was gushing out her explanation. Charlie didn't care. He had her in his arms. All would be well.They loaded up the small car with his luggage. It took less than forty-five minutes for them to get to the family villa, which was located on a quiet tree-lined street leading down to the beach.

The villa had been built around the turn of the century, and it was set in a mature garden with shade trees, flowers, and palms. There was even a pool with plenty of loungers and umbrellas. The house itself was cool, with marble floors and a square turret, which funneled the breeze down into the house. There was a large outdoor terrace at the rear of the house, with a vine-covered trellis providing shade over a long, wooden dining table. This was where the family took most of their meals. Anna Maria's mother and father were welcoming, smiling and casual, and Charlie immediately took to her elder brother, Andrea. He already knew Flavio from their vacation two years previously. There was also a cook and a housemaid to look after them all, and Charlie was made very comfortable.

Charlie and Anna Maria had a wonderful week together. She took him on some sightseeing visits to Pisa, Lucca, and Pietrasanta, a small artists' village where Carrara marble came from. They swam a lot, in the sea or the pool, and even went water skiing behind Mr. Sanguinetti's speedboat, which he kept moored in the small harbor.

On their last evening together, Charlie booked a table for two in a quiet corner of one of the upscale restaurants on the beach. He had butterflies in his stomach because tonight was the night! He had used all his savings to buy a diamond engagement ring from Boucheron in Bond Street. It was now in his jacket pocket. He knew they loved each other, but he didn't know whether she was ready for marriage, or whether her love for him was deep enough to spend the rest of her life with him. He also had no idea whether her parents saw him as just a nice boyfriend or something more serious.

They ordered their food and a bottle of wine. Anna Maria was bubbly, as usual, and chatting away. Charlie was subdued. He was tormented by his thoughts. *What if she turns me down?* He decided to propose between the entrée and dessert, but the waiter kept coming over and checking in on them.

"I hope everything is all right, sir?"

"Yes," Charlie responded for the third or fourth time during the meal. When the waiter left, Charlie saw his chance. With his stomach churning, he reached out for her hand. "Anna Maria," he said. "I want to ask you something. It's very serious..." His voice suddenly failed him. He realised how stilted and formal he sounded. He tried to smile.

"What is it, Sharlee?" said Anna Maria. An anxious frown was creasing her forehead.

With a shaking hand, he bought out the tiny ring box from his pocket and placed it on the table. He wanted to say something, but found himself unable to speak.

She looked at him, wide-eyed. "Sharlee," she said in almost a whisper. Then she fell silent.

"Anna Maria," Charlie suddenly blurted out nervously. "I love you with all my heart. I will never let you go, and I want us to spend the rest of our lives together." He cleared his throat. "Will you marry me?"

She looked at him. She was perfectly still. She didn't speak. His heart was pounding. She stood up. He followed suit. Suddenly her face lit up. Tears filled her eyes, and she gave him a big, wonderful smile. "Sharlee, I also love you with all my heart. Yes, I want to marry you! I want to spend the rest of my days with you!" She flung her arms around his neck and they kissed passionately in front of all the diners. Applause broke out.

Anna Maria was bubbling with excitement. The words were coming at a rapid pace. When could they get married? Would he agree to marry in Italy? Who would be his best man? Where would they live? Did he want children? Did he like dogs? He answered all those questions and more. The waiter brought them two glasses of champagne and a small chocolate cake in the shape of a heart – compliments of the house. They finished their dinner and walked slowly back to the villa, holding each other tightly under the stars. The moon was shining on the Mediterranean.

The next morning, he asked Mr. and Mrs. Sanguinetti whether they would agree, which led to rapid outbursts of Italian. When the dust settled, Mrs. Sanguinetti started crying, and everybody started hugging and kissing one other. The brothers came in, smiling broadly. The deed was done. Anna Maria had clearly thought this out carefully. After talking to her parents, she asked Charlie whether he would agree to get married at the Villa the following summer. He said yes. The scene was set.

It was Christmas before Charlie was able to introduce Anna Maria to his family. She came over to England for the holiday, which the Thorntons always spent at Charlie's grandfather's estate in Dorset. Anna Maria was warm, confident, beautiful, and outgoing. Everyone in Charlie's family was completely charmed by her. Both his mother and father told him that he had made a wonderful choice. Their previous arguments were all but forgotten.

The wedding took place the following June in Forte dei Marmi. The ceremony was held at the small, picturesque Sant' Ermete Church on the Via Trento. This was followed by the reception, dinner, and dancing at the Sanguinetti villa, where two long tables were laid out in the garden, under the trees, with large candelabras and lights strung across the trees. It was an ideal setting. The champagne flowed, the food was magnificent, the music soft, and everybody had a wonderful time. Steve and Patrick had been ushers in the church. Greg made a speech to the newlywed couple. It was more of a roast than a toast, witty and sharp, greatly appreciated by the English guests and their family, but perhaps it caused some confusion among the Italians. But, at the end of his speech, he said, "If any of you have doubts about love at first sight, I can assure you that it does happen. I was there when Charlie first laid eyes on the beautiful Anna Maria on the beach in Alassio. So here we are, and I'm sure this is a marriage that is made in heaven. This wonderful couple will live happily ever after."

Reminiscing about Greg's speech brought a little smile to his face and helped him think of all the wonderful times, and years they had together. Greg was right. They had lived happily ever after. They had three children and eight grandchildren. Forte dei Marmi had become their full-time home after his retirement as a senior executive of Banco Popolare di Milano. He looked at the gravestone and said, "We were truly blessed, weren't we, my love?" He sighed. The despair and misery again gnawed at his insides, as it had for the past two years. Apart from the vast emptiness in his life, he also had a sense of guilt. For the thousandth time he told himself that he should have never let Anna Maria take their daughter, Sylvia, from the villa to the airport. He remembered every word of their last conversation.

"Darling, let me drive Sylvia," he had said. "The weather is looking a bit rough. I'm sure it's going to rain. I don't want you driving through thunderstorms. You hate driving in the rain!"

"Oh, I'll be fine. Sylvia and I can talk on the way. We may not see her again for some weeks, maybe even months."

He didn't really put up a fight, and she gave him a peck on the cheek. Sylvia gave him a hug. As they left the villa, Anna Maria turned, smiled, and waved, as she had done a thousand times. And that was it. The last time he would ever see the love of his life.

Sylvia was returning to London after having spent a few days with them. There had been a rainstorm. The roads were slick, and as Anna Maria was driving back home from the airport, she had slowed down for an accident. However, a large semi-trailer truck on the inner lane had been going too fast on the slick wet road surface. The rear part of the truck jackknifed across the two lanes and smashed into the back of her Fiat. The police and ambulances were on the scene quickly. It took three hours to cut her out of the wreckage. By that time, she was long dead. Charlie collapsed when he got the news. She had been an energetic, healthy, outgoing woman in her seventies, beloved by all who knew her.

A deep depression settled over Charlie, and, even though their children and grandchildren made regular visits to keep him company, he could not break away from the despair that he felt. He wanted to die and join her as soon as possible, but life doesn't happen according to one's plans.

They had many friends in Forte dei Marmi, Milano, and London, and most of them had kept in touch with him, but he wasn't good company. Gradually, one by one, the communications and get-togethers had become a rarity. He did not want company.

The tears rolled down his cheeks as they did at the end of every visit. "I shall be back to see you again next week, my darling. Remember, I'll never let you go." The old man turned and shuffled away into the gloomy afternoon.

3 THE BLACK ROSE – 1968

Billy Rose and Eddie Gardner had known each other nearly all of their lives, having grown up next door from each other in South London. Billy was the youngest of four children, and Eddie was the youngest of three. They were both from working-class, Catholic families. Billy's father worked in Smithfield Market and his mother on the buses. Eddie's father worked at Battersea Power Station, and his mother was an assistant nurse at St. Thomas's Hospital.

They were bright children, energetic and good-looking, and they both grew into strong young men. Billy had thick, reddish hair and large green eyes, just like the rest of his Irish family. Eddie was taller and darker and more athletic. They both won grammar school scholarships and chose careers in accounting, qualifying as chartered accountants at different small practices in the City of London. After three years, they decided to strike out on their own and set up offices in Albemarle Street under the name of Rose, Gardner, Chartered Accountants. They were both ambitious, outgoing, and quite successful in building their practice. By 1968, they had a staff of nine, including two articled clerks, two secretaries, and a receptionist.

One day in June, a man walked through the door and presented himself at the reception, asking to speak to either Mr. Rose or Mr. Gardner. He introduced himself as John Jakes. The receptionist called Eddie on the intercom. "Mr. Gardner," she said, "there is a gentleman here named Mr. Jakes. He said he would like to meet with you if you have time right now."

Eddie was reviewing a client's tax return. He had no idea who Mr. Jakes was. "Of course, Samantha," he said to the throaty receptionist. "Show him in."

Almost immediately, Samantha opened the door for Mr. Jakes. He was a slim, slightly disheveled, middle-aged man. His thin hair was prematurely gray. He had watery, blue eyes and a rather sallow complexion. He was dressed in a somewhat grubby raincoat with a tweed jacket underneath, a pale green shirt, and a woven tie. He held out his hand to Eddie. "Good afternoon, Mr. Gardner. I am John Jakes." His lopsided grin revealed yellowed teeth.

"Please, sit down, Mr. Jakes," said Eddie. "What can I do for you?"

Mr. Jakes paused. When he next spoke, Eddie noticed a country accent. "Mr. Gardner, I am John Jakes, the creator of the black rose."

"The what?"

"Oh, Mr. Gardner, have you never seen a black rose?" said Jakes, laughing.

"No, sir, I can't say that I have."

"Well, you see, I am a horticulturist, and I created something that has eluded men like me for decades, maybe even centuries."

Eddie chuckled. "You mean to say that you created a new rose?"

Jakes nodded. "Not just any rose. Perfectly shaped blooms. But its petals are dark as night."

"Congratulations, Mr. Jakes," said Eddie haltingly. He had no idea where this was going.

Jakes now looked serious. "Mr. Gardener, I have been living in Switzerland for the last twelve years, for tax reasons. But now my wife has insisted that we move back to England. I have been accumulating royalties from around the world for many years, and I have now received advice from Barclays' head office and the Bank of England on how to remit twelve million Swiss Francs back to the U.K."

"Did you say twelve million?" responded Eddie. His heart was pounding. He wasn't sure if he had misheard.

"Yes, Mr. Gardner. My kind of horticulture can be very lucrative. The black rose has certainly been good to me. It is one-of-a-kind, you understand?"

"I take it, Mr. Jakes, that you are no longer living in Switzerland?" Eddie was warming to the conversation.

"No, I recently moved to Kew, where I have rented a flat."

"I see. I assume you're planning to become a resident of the United Kingdom?"

"Yes, that is my intention. I will be investing in various businesses and philanthropy efforts. I have been consulting with a firm of local Putney solicitors, Hunter, Banks & Fielder, to help establish my legal status and advise me on the necessary legal structures. I don't have an accountant, but I was visiting my bank, National Westminster, up the road."

"Oh, you mean National Westminster Bank at Stratford place?"

"Indeed. And then I walked past your building with the brass plate on the door, Rose, Gardner. I thought that was a good omen, and so here I am. Perhaps you would be interested in representing me as I set up my various business entities."

Eddie nearly fell off his chair. He had made a quick calculation. Twelve million Swiss Francs was equivalent to approximately three million Pounds, a vast sum of money. If

Rose, Gardner were to represent Mr. Jakes, the man might quickly become one of the practice's largest clients.

"Well, Mr. Jakes," Eddie responded. He was trying to be professional and cool. "We would be delighted to represent you and help establish your various investments, and whatever else you have in mind."

Mr. Jakes responded with a toothy grin. "That would be wonderful, Mr. Gardner. My solicitor is already handling the purchase of Thornton's Camping and Caravan Park near Plymouth, in Devon. I have also been discussing the possible purchase of commercial and residential properties in Islington through Knight, Frank & Rutley."

"We know them well. We have done a lot of business with them. Very good estate agents," said Eddie.

"I've also agreed to make a donation of £100,000 to the Great Ormond Street Hospital for Children. They're going to name a wing for the John Jakes Family Foundation," he said with some amusement.

"That is very generous of you, Mr. Jakes, supporting such a worthy cause. I'm sure it will be greatly appreciated."

"Perhaps, to get the ball rolling, I could leave you a copy of the advice that I received from Barclays Bank head office, based on discussions with the Bank of England. I could also put you in touch with the Great Ormand Street Hospital." Mr. Jakes handed Eddie a copy of the Barclays bank letter and a business card from Sir Niles Davis, Chairman of the Board of Trustees of the Great Ormond Street Hospital for Children. "You can call Sir Niles and discuss the creation of the Jakes Family Foundation. I hope to proceed with the donation as quickly as possible. You can also call my solicitors in Putney. Ask for Mr. Hunter; his telephone number is Putney 7897." He paused for a moment. "Oh," said Mr. Jakes, as another thought came into his head, "it will take a few weeks before we can transfer the twelve million Swiss Francs to London. But I've opened a bank account at the National

Westminster Bank, and deposited a check for £125,000, drawn on my bank account in Geneva."

"£125,000," repeated Eddie slowly, barely able to register the large amounts of money. "Do you happen to have a deposit slip, Mr. Jakes?" Eddie realised he had to do his due diligence.

"Yes, of course, Mr. Gardner." He rummaged around in his jacket "Ah! Here it is, would you like to take a copy?"

"Yes, Mr. Jakes, that might prove to be helpful as we move forward. I'll just get that done." He called Samantha on the intercom and asked her to make a copy. Within a minute or so, she returned with the document. He handed the original back to Mr. Jakes.

Eddie had quickly taken in all these pieces of information and was already planning a series of calls to get the business relationship moving. "Well, Mr. Jakes. I think we have enough to start our work. Thank you for giving me the necessary contacts. We will move forward quickly. Perhaps we could have a further meeting next week, by which time I hope that I shall be able to lay out an action plan to meet your needs."

"That would be wonderful, Mr. Gardner. Let's meet again at this time next week. Please give me your business card, in case I need to contact you. Here is a business card with my Putney address. I'm looking forward to working with you. I think my feeling was right, I'm sure that Rose, Gardner will look after my affairs very well."

"I can assure you, Mr. Jakes, we will be at your service at all times."

The meeting was over. Eddie stood up and shook hands with Mr. Jakes. It was a rough hand, as if used to fieldwork. Eddie could hardly contain his excitement.

As soon as Jakes had left, he rushed to Billy's office next door. "You won't believe what just happened, Billy," he said. "A scruffy-looking character walks in off the street, and he says he wants us to represent him. He grows flowers for a living, can you believe it? He told me he developed a black rose, and that it made him a fortune... twelve million Swiss francs."

"Are you serious?"

"Yes! This could be the biggest thing that has happened to our practice. He wants us to do everything. He chose Rose, Gardner because he felt it was a good omen. By the way, he deposited a check for £125,000 to keep him going until the transfer permissions come through from Barclays. Isn't that amazing? I just can't believe it." Eddie was as excited as a young child who just received the best present ever from Father Christmas.

Billy looked up at Eddie from his desk. "Twelve million Swiss Francs from royalties? From roses? Amazing! Well, if this is all on the up-and-up, somebody out there loves us, Eddie." Billy was laughing as he crossed himself. "I agree, this could be an incredible new client. It does seem too good to be true, so we better check out all his contacts."

"Of course," responded Eddie, "I intend to do that immediately, starting with Sir Niles Davis at the Great Ormond Street Hospital. Very posh. I will put on my best British accent when I speak to him."

"You also better get on to his solicitors in Putney," said Billy, "if they are moving forward with this purchase of the caravan park. See how long they have been his solicitors, and what they think of him."

"Absolutely. That will be my next call," Eddie replied. "But if it all checks out, we're going to be very busy for the next few weeks."

With a big grin on his face, Eddie went back next door to his office and immediately phoned Sir Niles Davis at the Great Ormond Street Hospital.

"Good afternoon, Sir Niles," said Eddie in a posh accent. "My name is Edward Gardner, and I'm a partner at Rose, Gardner, chartered accountants. We represent Mr. John Jakes in respect to his business and philanthropic commitments. I understand that Mr. Jakes made a donation commitment to the Great Ormond Street Hospital for Children." He paused, waiting for a response from Sir Niles.

"Yes, Mr. Gardner. This was like manna from heaven. Out of the blue, Jakes marched into the hospital. He came to my office and then made this most generous commitment. Apparently, Jakes has made millions of pounds. He said he created a 'black rose.'" Eddie was pleased with what he heard.

"Well, Sir Niles," said Eddie, "we will start working, creating the foundation in the next couple of weeks. I will keep you up-to-date on progress, but in the meantime, if you need to contact me, please don't hesitate. My number is Mayfair 9400."

"Thank you very much, Mr. Gardner. We are truly excited about this generous offer. We appreciate your keeping us appraised of progress over the next few weeks." They said their goodbyes.

"Well, the financial commitment to the hospital seems to be genuine," said Eddie to himself. He then phoned Mr. Hunter, Jakes' solicitor.

"Good afternoon, Mr. Hunter," said Eddie. "I understand you represent a new client of ours, John Jakes. He recently moved from Switzerland. I also understand he has issued instructions to you concerning a business investment, Thornton's Camping and Caravan Park, near Plymouth in Devon, as well a large donation to the Great Ormond Street Hospital for Children."

"Yes, Mr. Gardner. Mr. Jakes just telephoned and informed us that you will be acting as his accountants."

"May I ask you how Mr. Jakes became a client of yours?"

"Well, he was introduced by Mrs. Alice Buckley. She and her late husband have been old clients of ours. She lives in the same apartment building as Mr. Jakes. In fact, she is going to invest £20,000 in his purchase of the caravan park.

They have become quite close friends apparently," said Mr. Hunter.

"Thank you, Mr. Hunter. That is very helpful."

A few days later, Eddie spoke to Gordon Austin at Knight, Frank and Rutley. Austin thought that Mr. Jakes' recent offer to purchase a block of shops with flats above in Islington was likely to be accepted, subject, of course, to due diligence. He also volunteered that he thought Mr. Jakes was quite knowledgeable about North London properties, and he felt this could prove to be a shrewd investment. He agreed to keep Eddie informed, but indicated it was unlikely that contracts be exchanged within the next two or three months.

The following day, Eddie received a standard printed note from Midland Bank in Richmond, Surrey:

Dear Sir,

We have been asked to open an account for Mr. John Jakes of 12 Northgate Gardens, Kew Gardens, Richmond, Surrey, and your name has been given as a reference.

Would you kindly inform us whether in your opinion he may be considered trustworthy and likely to prove a satisfactory customer of the bank? We thank you in anticipation of your kind assistance and assure you that your reply will be treated in the strictest confidence.

A stamped, addressed envelope is enclosed.

Yours faithfully,
  H. Wilcox, Manager

Eddie was beginning to feel uncomfortable. After all, Mr. Jakes was a new client about which he knew very little. He had no knowledge of his background. On the other hand, he had seen a copy of the deposit slip at National Westminster Bank.

He decided that he would ask Mr. Jakes for an advance, to cover the costs of setting up the various companies and the Jakes Family Foundation. In the meantime, he did not respond directly to Midland Bank, but waited for the further meeting with John Jakes. When he arrived at the office for the next appointment, Eddie gradually led the conversation towards receiving an advance and questioned him about the Midland Bank letter.

"Yes, Mr. Gardner, I've opened a bank account with Midland Bank in Richmond. I thought this would be sensible, just for my domestic expenses. I will make a transfer from my deposit at National Westminster Bank in the next week or so when they have collected the funds from my Swiss bank account."

"That does seem sensible," Eddie responded. "However, we are in the process of forming the company for your caravan park purchase, not to mention the Jakes Foundation, and we need to be put in the necessary funds. Perhaps you could advance us £2,000 towards fees to be incurred?"

"Of course. That seems reasonable. The only problem is that my deposit at National Westminster Bank needs to clear before I can use that money. Consequently... well, this is a bit embarrassing." He paused with a slight smile on his face. "I have to meet other expenses, such as rent at my flat, and I'm out of funds. In fact, I was thinking of asking you if you would be kind enough to advance me £2,500 just for a couple of weeks until the National Westminster Bank confirms clearance of my Swiss bank cheque."

The tingle on Eddie's neck was now going at full force. This did not smell right. He was certainly not going to lay out any money on behalf of John Jakes or give him any advance until he was satisfied that the deposit at National Westminster Bank had been cleared and that the funds were available. Of course, he felt he had to be diplomatic.

"I have to say, Mr. Jakes, that would be very unusual. We

are not in the habit of advancing monies to our clients. In fact, we usually request them to put us in funds in order to proceed. Of course, presumably, National Westminster Bank will advise you very shortly that your deposit cheque has been cleared and that will resolve all of these issues."

Jakes suddenly looked rather nervous and uncomfortable. "I understand, Mr. Gardner," said Jakes. "I realise this is a rather unusual request, and I don't want to put you in a difficult position. I will check with the National Westminster Bank today. Of course, once I have got those funds, I will be able to proceed with the Thornton camping purchase and deal with my domestic expenses. Hopefully, that will only be a few days. I was just seeking some help, in case of a delay."

Eddie then proceeded to discuss matters relating to the companies being formed, his discussions with Knight, Frank and Rutley, and Great Ormond Street Hospital. However, He thought he detected a certain amount of nervousness in Mr. Jakes' responses. The personal relationship seemed to be cooling somewhat. He thought he would have to do more research before spending any more time on this potentially large client. They agreed to meet the following week, by which time National Westminster Bank should have responded to Mr. Jakes.

When Jakes left the office, Eddie went in to see Billy to discuss the latest developments.

"You know, I have been skeptical about this guy," Billy said. "Too good to be true. But, since we bank with National Westminster Bank at Stratford Place, why don't we just go visit them and find out what's happening with the Jakes account? If there are any problems, I'm sure they would let us know."

"You're right," Eddie responded. "That's a good suggestion. Of course, it would be unusual for a bank to give us an indication of their business dealings with their clients, even if they happen to be a client of ours, but in the circumstances, perhaps they will make an exception. I will give Mr. Simpson a call and set up an appointment."

Robert Simpson was the assistant manager at the branch, and he agreed to see Billy and Eddie the following afternoon at 4 p.m. They had told him that they wished to discuss their own accounts and talk about clients' deposits. A lame excuse for a meeting, but nevertheless, Mr. Simpson seemed happy to give them the time of day.

They arrived at the bank on time and were ushered into Mr. Simpson's office. After chitchatting about the Rose, Gardener partnership accounts and general business matters, Eddie addressed the issue at hand. "We have a new client, and we understand he is one of your customers. We've been given substantial instructions to handle a variety of matters on his behalf."

"Really, Mr. Gardner," replied Simpson, "that's excellent news. Who is your new client?"

"Mr. John Jakes, a horticulturist and the inventor of the black rose. He is moving back to the UK from Switzerland. I understand he has made a deposit of £125,000 into a new account at this branch."

Simpson suddenly went red in the face. "Jakes! John Jakes, where is he? We've been chasing him for two weeks now. The home address he gave us doesn't exist!"

"What?" said Eddie, "It doesn't exist?"

"No," said Mr. Simpson, his cheeks still flushed. "And the check he deposited looked genuine, but it is drawn on a Swiss bank that also does not exist."

"Good Lord," said Eddie, exchanging a stunned look with Billy.

"Mr. Jakes is clearly engaged in some fraudulent enterprise. We turned down his request for a bridging loan until the money came in from Switzerland. I would urge you to be extremely cautious. We do not believe there is any truth to his story. We don't even know if he was living in

Switzerland or if he did really create this black rose." Mr. Simpson was clearly very upset.

"Well, Mr. Simpson," said Eddie, "that is very disturbing news."

"He may have shown you a bank deposit slip, but, as I said, it was drawn on a bank that does not exist. If and when we do hear from Mr. Jakes, we intend to terminate our arrangements and not represent him as a client of this bank. You may choose to follow our lead," Simpson said, clearly trying to guide Eddie in the right direction.

Eddie's heart sank. John Jakes was not going to be the bonanza client he had hoped for.

"Thank you, Mr. Simpson," said Eddie. "To be honest, we did have our concerns and reservations. But now you have given us a fuller picture, we shall act accordingly."

Eddie and Billy did not speak a word to each other until they left the bank. "Well," said Billy, "It was too good to be true after all. We don't have a big client, but we may have a legal mess. What do you think he was trying to do?"

"Yeah," responded Eddie. "I think the little bastard is trying to give us the run-around, trying to borrow money, open bank accounts, and probably start depositing checks into each account."

"And I bet he will try to draw cash, and maybe make some payments for expenses," said Billy. "I think we caught him at the right time. Maybe there's more to it than that. But we do have a problem. So far, apart from giving us a big story, he really hasn't done anything fraudulent. Lying doesn't count. We must be careful of accusing him of anything. What would you suggest we do?"

They were talking as they walked back down Bond Street to their office. The sunny afternoon seemed out of keeping with their black mood.

"Well, obviously we shall inform Mr. John Jakes, or whoever he really is, that we will no longer act for him. After we next meet with him, I think we should also inform the Great Ormand Street Hospital and his Putney solicitors, not to mention the Midland Bank enquiry we received. But then what? I'm not sure how much further we can go without risking possible legal action by him against us."

Eddie didn't respond straight away, but he was thinking. They were very near their office when it suddenly hit him. "Hey, Billy, you remember Johnny Wilkinson from school? The last I heard he was working in the fraud squad at New Scotland Yard. How about giving him a call, telling him the story, and getting some advice?"

"Yeah," said Billy. "That's a good idea."

Within ten minutes, they were back in Albemarle Street. Eddie got on the phone to New Scotland Yard and asked for the fraud squad. When he got through, he found that Johnny Wilkinson was not available that day. He left a message and asked him to call back as soon as possible.

He and Billy were feeling glum. Eddie did not sleep well that night. He was tossing and turning, all the while getting a lot angrier at John Jakes and the game he was trying to play.

The following day, he was only in the office for fifteen minutes when the phone rang. It was Johnny Wilkinson. They exchanged pleasantries, had a few laughs about the past, and then Eddie told him about John Jakes. Johnny asked for a description. Then he gave a chuckle. "That's Jimmy Jackson. He only got out of Norwich prison four weeks ago. He's a regular. A not very successful petty con man. He served three years for fraud. It looks like he is starting the same old games again. He usually talks about vast sums of money coming from abroad and working with legitimate professional bankers. It creates a believable story, and then he starts passing bad checks, borrowing money, converting as much as possible into cash, and then he disappears."

"Yeah, that seems to be the pattern this time as well," said Eddie. "What do you think we should do?"

"I suggest you keep all the papers that he has given you as evidence, then throw him out of the office. Tell him that you're on to his game and you've been in touch with the fraud squad at New Scotland Yard. At this stage, we've got nothing to arrest him for, but I can guarantee you won't hear from him again. And you might slow him down." He paused. "Let me know if you have any problems."

"Thanks, Johnny, that's great advice. Perhaps we could get together for a drink with Billy and some of the old gang?"

"Yeah. That would be fun."

After Eddie hung up, he went into Billy's office and described the advice that Johnny had given him.

"Well, that sounds good. That should get rid of a menace and get us off the hook. I'm sorry, Eddie, but it looks like we will have to go back to the grind." He spoke with a laugh.

"I'm not going to let the little shit off the hook so easily," responded Eddie. "I intend to put the fear of death into him. Maybe he will think twice about playing this game in the future."

Two days later, Jakes was back in Eddie's office. "Good afternoon, Mr. Gardner. It's good to see you again. We seem to be making progress on my investments."

"Indeed, Mr. Jakes," Eddie responded. He was playing a game, just waiting to put the knife in.

Jakes continued talking. "Yes, you see, one of my oldest and dearest friends, Mrs. Buckley, has kindly offered to invest £20,000. She has become a partner in my purchase of Thornton's Camping and Caravan Park. She is also going to instruct Mr. Hunter to release £2,000 to me, so as I can pay expenses until my check is cleared from my Swiss bank account. Unfortunately, National Westminster Bank has informed me that there's been some delay because of an error that my Swiss bank made. It seems I needed to sign an additional form. It's been taken care of. Hopefully they will move quickly now."

Eddie listened with a benign smile on his face. "So, everything is going according to plan, Mr. Jakes?"

"Oh yes, Mr. Gardner," Jakes responded confidently. "And now I am eager to hear how you are getting on with the company formations and the establishment of the Jakes Family Foundation."

"Well, I have been very busy. I've had help from my partner, Mr. Rose. In fact, I would like you to meet him."

"That would be very nice," said Jakes, clearly in a buoyant mood.

Eddie picked up the phone and asked Billy to join them. A few seconds later, Billy entered. He shook hands with Mr. Jakes, introducing himself.

"Well, Mr. Jakes," said Eddie. "Let me tell you what Rose, Gardner has been doing for the past week." He paused.

Jakes recognized the change in tone. He suddenly seemed nervous. Eddie continued talking. "We had an interesting meeting with Mr. Simpson at National Westminster Bank." He paused again as he watched the color drain from Jakes's face. "In addition, Mr. Jakes...or should I say Mr. Jackson? Well, in addition, I have been in touch with the fraud squad at New Scotland Yard."

Jakes started to shake. Eddie went on. "If I pick up the telephone right now, they will be in this office within a few minutes to arrest you." Eddie raised his voice now. "If you think you can fuck around with us, and play your disgusting con games, you've got a big surprise coming! The fraud squad has requested all the details of your little shenanigans. As soon as I press charges, your game will be up. You'll be back in Norwich jail quicker than you can say 'Black rose!'"

Jakes crumbled before their eyes. His shoulders sagged, and his head went down as tears started rolling down his cheeks.

"Oh, Mr. Gardner, please! I can't go back to jail again. Please don't call the fraud squad. I have spent nearly half of my life in jail." He paused for a moment, unable to speak. "I'm sixty-three. I have no wife, no family, no money, no prospects. The only thing I've ever known is... this." He made a helpless gesture with his arms. "You may think it's fraud, and I suppose it is if you want to get technical about it, but I prefer to think of it as stories. Is that so wrong? It's the only thing I'm any good at. I've never gone to school, you see, and I'm not in the best of health. I can't go back to jail. I would rather be dead." His voice trailed off and he started sobbing, his head buried in his hands.

Eddie looked at Billy, who nodded and gave a shrug. "All right, Mr. Jakes," Eddie said. "This is your lucky day, I suppose. We are going to keep all these papers. I'm going to get on the telephone to Great Ormond Hospital, also, Mr. Hunter, to make sure that any money received from Mrs. Buckley is returned to her immediately." Eddie took out some crisp notes from his wallet. "Here's a hundred quid. Now get out of here. Do not come back. And I strongly advise you not to try the same old con games again. You're right, you're too old to go back to jail. Try an honest living for a change."

Jakes looked up in disbelief. "Oh, Mr. Gardner! Mr. Rose! Thank you so much. I promise you will not see me again. I will take your advice and do my best to go straight." With that said, he stood up and shook hands with both Eddie and Billy, vigorously. After several more "thank yous," he left the office.

When he was gone, Billy turned to Eddie and chuckled. "Well, I guess he pulled another fast one. He took us for a hundred quid!"

Eddie laughed. "Well, the experience was worth it."

When Eddie went home to his wife that evening, he brought her a dozen white roses. The florist did not have any black ones.

4 LUV A DUCK – 1973

For four years, Henry Mason and his wife Deborah had owned a yeoman's cottage on the Sussex-Kent border. It was a wonderful country escape from their busy lives in London. Henry was a senior executive at J Walter Thompson, the advertising agency, and Deborah was a packaging designer for Marks & Spencer and other branded retailers. They lived in Hampstead, close to the schools their three children attended. Twelve-year-old Sarah and ten-year-old Claire were both at St. Margaret's, and six-year-old Philip had recently started at Lyndhurst. They were a handsome, young family. Henry was tall and fair-haired; he had some gray at his temples and long sideburns, which was fashionable at the time. He was energetic and athletic. Deborah was auburn-haired, olive-skinned, dark-eyed, and petite.

The cottage had been built in 1603, of wattle and oak beams and with a giant inglenook fireplace. It was surprisingly warm in the winter and cool in the summer. They enjoyed their weekends, breathing in the healthy fresh air, driving down to Hastings to buy fresh fish from fishing boats on the beach, and going to local food markets for cheese, eggs, or fresh vegetables. They also had their own vegetable garden, including a fruit cage, which produced raspberries, blackberries, and many other types of fruit. There were over two hundred apple trees on the 23-acre property, as well as a rather old swimming pool and tennis court.

During the school holidays, the family stayed for longer periods, but they tried to come every weekend. Deborah drove down on Friday morning. It could take over two hours in traffic to cover the 47 miles from Hampstead. Henry's company had assigned him a driver, who picked up the children from school every Friday afternoon and then collected Henry in time to catch the 5:30 p.m. train from Charing Cross to Etchingham, in Sussex, just a few miles from the house. In the winter, Deborah warmed up the house before they arrived, and, each Friday evening, they all ate dinner together. They had plenty to do over the weekends— golf and tennis for Henry and Deborah and horseback riding lessons for the children.

Henry always tried to find somewhere interesting for lunch on Sundays, and gradually got to know the best restaurants, pubs, and country hotels in the area. One sunny Sunday, at the end of May 1973, they decided to make a reservation for lunch at a new hotel south of Tunbridge Wells, a converted Priory, recently purchased by a retired London solicitor, Giles Thornton. The building, dating back to the 14th Century, had twelve rooms. The restaurant had received good reviews. They all packed into their Triumph Estate car, including their chocolate Labrador, Flash, who snuggled down on the floor of the front passenger seat, where he would stay while the family had lunch. It took them only about twenty-five minutes to reach The Priory Hotel, set in a thousand acres of beautiful parkland and forests. The day was warm and sunny, and the grounds could not have been more spectacular. Henry parked in the grassy car park next to a tranquil but slime-covered pond.

The Priory architecture was very interesting. There were

lots of peaks and turrets and ancient slit windows. On the ground floor, large lead glass windows looked out over a delightful stone terrace covered with large flowerpots of pansies, geraniums, and marigolds. Inside the hotel, there was an attractive bar and a large brick fireplace. The furniture consisted of comfortable brown leather chairs and small cocktail tables. Opposite was the reception area, next to a wooden staircase leading upstairs to the bedrooms. The restaurant was located through double glass doors near the reception, situated around an attractive courtyard with cloisters and alcoves. The courtyard was glassed-in but with sliding doors, with an open section on a flagstone surface beneath a spectacular tapestry, set between slit windows on what had probably been the altar of the Priory.

The restaurant was nearly full, and the Masons were shown an alcove with a horseshoe seating area around a polished oak table. The children, excitedly and somewhat noisily, settled into their seats after arguments as to who should sit where. The rest of the diners spoke in hushed voices, as the English often do in restaurants.

Henry explained a little of the history of the building to the children. When he had finished, Philip was the first to ask questions:

"Why are we having lunch in a castle?"

"It's not really a castle, Philip."

"But it looks like one!"

"Well, it's really an ancient church."

"Why are we having lunch in a church?"

"Well, Philip," responded Henry patiently, "it's no longer a church. Now it is a hotel and restaurant".

"Why did the church become a hotel and restaurant?"

"It used to be occupied by an order of ancient monks, who were vowed to silence, which means they didn't speak to anybody but God during their prayers," Henry said dramatically.

"Why didn't the monks talk to anybody?" asked Philip.

"Because, when they became monks, they agreed to only tend their garden, grow their vegetables, and pray to God every day."

"Where are the monks now?"

"There are no monks here anymore, and there haven't been for centuries."

"Why not?"

The waiter arrived with the menus and saved Henry from any more questions from his six-year-old.

The children were given orange squash, and Henry and Deborah ordered a chilled Bordeaux white wine. The menu had an interesting selection of both meat and fish, but in the end, Henry chose the Chef Special Duck à l'orange. The others chose the Sunday special, with small portions for the children: roast beef off the trolley, with Yorkshire pudding, roast potatoes, and green vegetables, and, as appetizers, potted shrimps for the adults and tomato soup for the children. The dining room was well-lit and pleasantly cool. The service was good, and the food was delicious.

After the main course, the children chose apple pie and ice cream for dessert, while Henry and Deborah preferred fresh fruit salad. The waiter informed them that coffee could be served on the terrace. So, they told the children that they could go to the car and take Flash for a walk around the grounds while they had their coffee. The scene was tranquil. Even on the terrace, the guests were talking in very low tones, even in whispers. It was mainly an elderly crowd, well-dressed and groomed, enjoying a Sunday lunch in the country.

The large terrace had a number of umbrellas and loungers on one side, and numerous small round iron tables. A set of very wide steps was flanked by white rosebushes, leading straight onto the parkland meadow. All was quiet and peaceful as Deborah and Henry chose a table. In due course, a pot of coffee with two demitasse cups, sugar, and cream was served, along with some Petit Fours. They sat there peacefully, their eyes half-closed, enjoying the ambiance.

After about ten minutes, they opened their eyes as they heard the children shouting and laughing in the distance. The noise got louder as they made their way back to the terrace, but they were preceded by the sudden arrival of Flash, charging at full speed, with a duck in his mouth, covered in water and green slime. He seemed very happy with himself. The dog stopped in the middle of the terrace near Deborah and Henry and dropped the duck. It looked like it had been shaken to death. Flash then proceeded to shake himself, and a spray of green slime and water came off his coat and splattered onto many of the diners. Some of them jumped up in shock, knocking over their coffees and drinks. Chaos ensued as Henry desperately tried to grab Flash. The dog ran around in circles, enjoying the game immensely. To Henry, it seemed like a slow-motion volcanic eruption. A total disaster was unfolding right before his eyes. Covered in water and slime, he eventually managed to grab Flash by the collar. The children arrived and made the scene appear even worse. They were laughing and Philip was screaming.

More spraying of wet slime ensued, until Sarah, seeing the disaster unfolding, handed the dog's lead to Henry, and he was able to attach it to the collar and hand the responsibility over to Deborah. She was also covered in a green, slimy mess. "I'm sorry, Dad," said Sarah, realizing the seriousness of the situation. "We just opened the rear door of the car, and Flash jumped out before we could grab him. He jumped into the pond and started chasing the ducks around. Before we could do anything, he had one in his mouth and was off to bring it to you."

Henry did not have time to respond because he was desperately trying to wipe the slime off his own clothing with his handkerchief and the little coffee napkins. The disturbance had brought Mrs. Thornton out onto the terrace. She looked in horror at the chaos.

"I'm so sorry, Mrs. Thornton," he said. "Apparently, the dog jumped out of the car when the children went to take him for a walk, and then he ran into the pond. He caught this duck, which, I'm afraid, appears to be dead."

"This is outrageous, Mr. Mason. You have the responsibility of looking after your children and animals. You should be considerate of the other guests. This hotel is not a playground for children. Our guests wish to enjoy the peace and quiet of the countryside. In addition, I regret to inform you that my husband is very fond of our local ducks, and he will be very distressed when I tell him what has transpired," said Mrs. Thornton with all the charm of a hospital matron imparting some dire medical news.

Henry felt he was being truly scolded, but he did not have much of a defense.

"I can only say, Mrs. Thornton, that I'm deeply sorry that this has occurred. Of course, I will compensate you for the loss of the duck."

"I must attend to the needs of our other customers, if you will excuse me," said Mrs. Thornton curtly, turning to speak solicitously to each of those customers who had green splashes on their clothing. A couple of waiters came rushing out with buckets of water, soda bottles, and fresh cloths to help the diners clean themselves up.

Mrs. Thornton then turned back to Henry. "I think it would be best if you and your family left the establishment immediately, Mr. Mason. I shall prepare your bill." She sounded as if he was being expelled from school.

"Of course, Mrs. Thornton," said Henry. He was relieved at the thought of being able to make a quick escape. Deborah and the children sat quietly watching the whole proceedings holding onto Flash's leash, although he was now laid out on the grass, drying in the sun. Henry made sure everything was secure and that Flash was unlikely to take off again. Then he went into the hotel to settle his account.

Mrs. Thornton prepared the bill quickly and added on £4 for the duck and £25 for "cleaning" allowances for the diners.

Henry did not argue. He was only too happy to pay the bill and get out of there.

He gathered up Deborah and the children, and the damp and smelly Flash, and they made it back to the car park and pushed the dog into the back of the Triumph Estate, as he tried to make a further lunge toward the slime covered pond. They drove off in silence. Henry felt that the children should realise that what had just transpired was very serious.

It was only when they had covered a few miles away from The Priory that Philip plucked up the courage to ask what he thought was a very important question.

"Dad, do you think they will cook the duck tonight in orange or serve duck soup? Flash told me he didn't mean to murder the duck," he said with a tear running down his cheek. Henry looked to Deborah for help.

"It was a very sad day for the owners. Mr. and Mrs. Thornton lost one of their favorite ducks because of Flash," she said in a very serious voice. "But probably they will just bury the duck close to home. I am pretty sure he will not appear on the menu. The lesson is that you all have to take responsibility for keeping a close watch on Flash when we go out and about."

Deborah tried not to laugh, but could not keep a straight face. Henry joined in, and the children, who were not quite sure whether they were going to be punished or not, were only too happy to laugh with them.

5 PLYMOUTH ROCK ...'N ROLL – 1976

Geoffrey Thornton, the tenth Lord Marsden, was worried. Very worried, in fact. The bank had been chasing him for months now. He had ignored yesterday's phone message requesting that he come in for a meeting with the manager, Mr. Bridges. He knew that there was a loan of a hundred thousand pounds due now, and he had no idea where he was going to find the money.

The Marsden estate, which had been in the family for over three hundred years, consisted of six thousand acres of land, farms, forests, and two small villages north of Plymouth. The ninth Earl Marsden had died in 1966, at the age of ninety-two. Geoffrey inherited the estate and all its problems. His older brother Henry, a Major in a tank regiment, had been killed in France five days after the D-Day landings in 1944. His younger brother Douglas had taken an inheritance from his grandfather and bought a substantial farming estate in Dorset, which he had successfully developed.

Geoffrey was sixty years old. He had three children. His oldest, Peter, was the vicar of a local parish not far from the Marsden estate. His middle son, Gregory, was addicted to drugs and alcohol. He lived in some squalor with his boyfriend in Shoreditch in London. Geoffrey had not seen him for seven years. His youngest was Amanda, who had graduated from Exeter University and had moved to London. She had a job with a public relations firm. As far as Geoffrey knew, she was doing well. His wife Sheila was an alcoholic. Despite numerous treatments and visits to rehab centers, she had relapsed many times.

Geoffrey Thornton had a vague and irritating inkling that he was, perhaps, not a very bright man. His acquaintances occasionally remarked, usually behind his back, how "pompous" he was. Perhaps it was because he had preferred to be addressed as Major, until he took over his father's title, even though he had spent the war in Plymouth, in the Army Pay Corps. He was always jealous of his elder brother Henry, who was handsome and dashing. Henry had been a genuine hero.

Geoffrey had married Sheila Russell, the daughter of Sir Thomas Russell, a career diplomat in the Foreign Service. Sir Thomas had spent most of his life overseas, mainly in India. Sheila had been born in Cairo and had moved to India when she was four. She was sent home to the UK in early 1937 to pursue a writing career. It never materialized because she met Geoffrey through a friend at Cambridge University. He was considered an attractive potential husband by the Russell family. He was good-looking and ambitious. They married in 1938. He was working for his father on the Marsden estate where they made their home. When the war came, he joined the army, but he never saw action.

He decided that he wanted to pursue a career in politics and, using family connections, he was chosen as the Conservative candidate for Plymouth North. In 1946, he was elected to Parliament. He did not impress the hierarchy of the Conservative Party. He became a fairly quiet and unobtrusive backbencher. He felt undervalued. He knew in his heart that his contributions were much greater than he had been given credit for. No doubt someone would offer him a Cabinet post sooner or later. However, in the 1951 election, with the country becoming more socialist, he lost his seat at Plymouth North after running a very poor campaign. Winston Churchill was annoyed. The Conservatives had lost a seat that should have been theirs. Churchill described Geoffrey as "full of wind and puff."

Geoffrey returned to the family estate and took a more active role assisting the estate manager, Carter Evans. The estate consisted of a home farm of about a thousand acres. This included a dairy farm of four hundred acres and sheep on the balance, a game farm that was breeding pheasants for shooting, the villages of Marsden and North Fork, where the estate owned numerous properties and workers' cottages, as well as some other acreage that was rented off to local farmers.

Even though the large estate generated substantial income, it was not enough to meet the enormous cost of maintenance and repairs. Marsden Hall, the seat of the Thornton Family for three centuries, had seventeen bedrooms, two dining rooms –one of which could seat a group of sixty – a ballroom, living room, games room, library, an enormous kitchen, and storage rooms, not to mention the servants' quarters in the attic. The building also had a leaky roof, causing mold problems in three of the bedrooms. In parts of the house, the plumbing didn't work. The wood in the window frames was rotting. No major upgrades and renovations had taken place since the 1930s. In order to cut costs, the number of servants and maintenance crews had been whittled down. By now, Geoffrey and Sheila were looked after only by a very small group. There was John Frampton, an elderly butler, Smythson, the resident cook, and help from the village. In order to meet his financial obligations, pay taxes, and keep the property livable, Geoffrey had sold off certain assets. In 1955, he had been forced to part with a small Rembrandt, and some less valuable pictures, and antique furniture, as well as the Thornton Camping and Caravan Park north of Plymouth and a couple of slightly dilapidated cottages. He had recently opened the house to the public for ninety days in the summer months, in partnership with the National Trust. So far, however, attendance had fallen short of expectations.

These issues had gradually worn Geoffrey down. He felt himself backed into a corner, and now the crunch was coming with his bankers. All of this had driven Sheila to drink. In recent years, things had gotten worse. There were half-empty bottles of vodka hidden behind drapes in the master bedroom or the library, as well as in their little office that served as a TV room where they would often have their meager dinners on trays watching television. Sheila had been a beautiful woman, tall, slim, and dark, with black, wavy hair and piercing blue eyes. Initially, she had loved the country life, but now, after years of neglecting her health, she looked about a decade older than she was. Her black hair had grown grey. It was matted and unkempt. Her clothes, always slightly soiled and old, now hung off her thin frame. Geoffrey wanted to get her help, but he just didn't have the money. The situation at the Marsden estate was precarious.

One of the few joys of their lives, however, was their daughter Amanda, who kept in touch with her parents. She phoned on a regular basis and was always bright and cheery. She worked for a well-established public relations company, Hayden Woodward. When she announced in March that she would be coming down to Plymouth, Geoffrey and Sheila were delighted.

"I'm handling all the public relations for Billy King and the Royals," she said proudly. "Have you heard of them, Daddy?"

"Billy who?"

"They're a successful rock band."

"No, my love," Geoffrey responded. "I can't say that I

have. But I'm not really up-to-date with all this new music. I'm sure they're very successful. Otherwise, Hayden Woodward would not represent them."

"Oh, Daddy, you haven't been concentrating. I'm no longer with Hayden Woodward."

"You're not?"

"No, Daddy. I'm working full-time as the public relations rep for the band."

"Oh. I see." Geoffrey was beginning to feel concerned.

"I'm traveling around the UK because they have a major tour going on right now. That's why they're coming to Plymouth. I've become a personal assistant to Billy King."

"Who?"

"Oh, he's such a great guy."

"Yes, well, Amanda, I didn't realise that you'd left Hayden Woodward. Why didn't you tell me?"

"I *did* tell you, Daddy."

"That was a major decision, Amanda. Hayden Woodward is very well respected. Are you sure you did the right thing? Going from an established business to working for some pop band traveling the country?"

"Oh, yes, I think I've made the right decision, Daddy. I love what I'm doing. The band is very successful. The tour is going well. In fact, we are doing a gig at the Plymouth Argyle football ground in a couple of weeks, and we expect a sellout of nearly 15,000 people."

"That's a lot of people, Amanda," Geoffrey responded, truly impressed. "I had no idea that Plymouth would be such a good location for one of your pop concerts. But leaving the security of a firm like Hayden Woodward to go running around the country? It's not what I would have advised. You should have called me."

"Well, actually, Daddy," said Amanda, "we've had crowds like this all over the country. It's mainly because Billy had a big hit, *Are You The One?* His real name is Ernest Watson, by the way. That song prompted a new album. Perhaps you've heard it, it's been on the radio all the time over the last few months."

"No, I'm afraid I don't know it. But I'm pleased for your sake that it is doing well. That probably keeps you busy."

"Yes, Daddy, absolutely. It's been an endless workload for the past few months, but I love it. It's such fun and Billy is so sweet and nice to me. In fact, so are all the staff that work for him. I'm looking forward to you meeting him when we come to Plymouth."

"Meeting him? I thought we would be able to spend some time together, Amanda. It has been such a long time since you came home," said Geoffrey, now getting a little irritated.

"Don't worry, Daddy, I shall make sure that we have time to have a nice old chat."

"Okay, that's wonderful, Amanda. Your mother and I will be delighted to see you again. It's been fifteen months. Unfortunately, things here on the estate have been quite difficult, so we haven't had much time to socialize with anybody. Would you be able to stay with us?"

"The concerts are on Saturday and Sunday nights, and we'll be at the Metropole Hotel in Plymouth, with the band. But after that, our next gig is in Southampton the following Friday, so I will be able to stay for a couple of nights. I can catch up with the group when they're ready to move on. It would be great to be with you and Mummy for a couple of days."

"That is great news, Amanda. Just let me know as we get nearer the date."

"Okay, Daddy, I certainly will. Love to Mummy."

Amanda was a beautiful young woman, with black hair and bright blue eyes like her mother. She was tall and slim and had a bubbly outgoing personality. She was also academically bright, and well-organized. Excellent credentials for a good PR executive. She had always been a happy little girl who made friends easily and enjoyed the country life on the vast Marsden estate. She treated everyone with respect and was friendly and outgoing. She never took advantage of the family titles. She had gone off to boarding school at the age of thirteen, not unusual among the English aristocracy, and then secured a place at Exeter University where she studied communications. Eventually, this had led to a job in London. She genuinely loved coming back to Marsden Hall and was very much an "outdoors" girl.

Amanda phoned when the band arrived in Plymouth and were rehearsing for the concerts. She arranged to come and visit on Sunday for lunch, together with Billy. And so, on a bright, chilly day, Geoffrey and Sheila were eagerly awaiting their arrival. They had made arrangements for Smythson to come in especially on Sunday and to make a traditional lunch – roast beef and Yorkshire pudding, no less.

Just before noon, Geoffrey heard the roar of an engine coming up the driveway. He went to the front door to greet Amanda. He was surprised, however, to see a man and a woman, both dressed in black leather with large helmets, approaching on a powerful motorcycle.

With one final growl, the motorcycle came to a stop. Amanda and the driver got off. She took off her helmet and shook her hair free. Geoffrey immediately noticed that her black hair had purple streaks in it. The driver also took off his helmet. Geoffrey gathered that this was Billy King. A slim man of medium height, with thick, brown hair, practically to his shoulders! He had long sideburns in the fashion of the times, a sallow complexion, full lips, and grey eyes.

"Hi, Daddy." Amanda gave her father an affectionate hug. "This is Ernest Watson... Billy King. He is my wonderful boss," she said with a little giggle, as she entwined her arm in his.

"Pleased to meet you," said Geoffrey formally. "Do come into the house," he continued, leading the way into the large, marble-floored entrance hall with its suits of armor, magnificent staircase, and the family portraits all looking down, perhaps rather disapprovingly, at the youngest member of the Thornton family dressed in black leather.

"Please follow me into our living room," Geoffrey said, leading the way into the magnificently furnished but rather dowdy and faded living room. There were more family portraits and other pieces of art, sculptures, worn sofas, and upholstered chairs around a large coffee table facing a roaring fire, which had been set earlier in the day.

Sheila was sitting in one of the upholstered chairs, which had seen better days. She stood up to greet her daughter rather unsteadily. "Amanda, sweetheart," she said. "So happy to see you. Why have you got all those purple streaks in your hair?"

"Hello, Mummy. I'm sorry it's been so long," she said with some concern, seeing how her mother had aged since her last visit. Her father, too, looked unwell. He had lost weight. They all took their seats on the dusty furniture. "I dyed my hair for our current UK tour," she said with a laugh. "It's quite a popular thing to do for us bright young things." She immediately lit up the room with her vivaciousness.

"Lord Geoffrey and Lady Marsden. I'm very pleased to meet you," said Ernest with a clear Cockney London accent. "Your daughter is really very special. If I may say so, you should take pride in the great job you have done in bringing her up." Sheila cringed at his accent and demeanor, and she was horrified to see her daughter in a leather motorcycle outfit.

"Well, Ernest or Billy. Which would you prefer?"

"I'm Ernie to my family."

"Ah, so Ernest," responded Geoffrey, ignoring his informal name and not making much effort to hide his superiority over someone of the lower classes. "We are so cut off here, trying to cope with the pressures of managing this vast estate, and

I'm afraid we're a little out of touch with the world. We have not been socializing very much of late, so I was unaware of you, or your band, and the success that you've obviously enjoyed. Congratulations. I'm sure that Amanda is playing her part."

"Absolutely," responded Ernest. "Amanda is amazing. We have never had such good PR. She has had many successes promoting the band. We're always in the papers, and she even got me a spot on the Terry Wogan show on TV." He cast a loving look at Amanda.

"Really, Terry Wogan!" Geoffrey responded. He could see that Ernest was besotted with his daughter. He was beginning to have a queasy feeling that their relationship was more than business.

The lunch proceeded reasonably smoothly. Amanda was nervously laughing over everything, concerned that Ernest would feel uncomfortable. Even though they were sitting in the small dining room, which Geoffrey and Sheila normally used for breakfast, it was still the most lavish and magnificent room that Ernest had ever seen.

"Well, Ernest," said Geoffrey, "tell me a little about yourself. Where did you go to university?"

Ernest laughed. "No chance of that, I'm afraid. I left school at sixteen, after doing my O levels, and went to work for a music publisher in Denmark Street in Soho."

"Is that so?" Geoffrey asked through clenched teeth.

"Yeah, it's the tin pan alley of London's music business. I'd learned how to play the guitar, self-taught when I was twelve. And I messed around with my friends until we got quite good. When I was sixteen, we were doing gigs at the local pubs and community centers. Of course, we all wanted to be stars. We thought all we had to do was show up, play like the Beatles, or the Stones, and make a name for ourselves. But it was not that easy. Of course, my parents were dead against me pursuing a career in music. They thought I should try something where I could have a steady income."

"Well, I can understand that. I agree with your parents. What do they do, incidentally?"

"My dad was a bus driver. He also took an active role in the union. And my mother worked in the kitchens at Guy's Hospital." Sheila's face dropped. Who was this man that her beautiful Amanda found so appealing? "Anyway," said Ernest, "my dad is retired now, and I bought him and my mum a bungalow in Bognor Regis. They love it down there. They're very happy."

"That was a very nice thing to do," said Sheila in a condescending voice, making it clear that she could think of nothing more horrific than a bungalow in Bognor Regis. And then she turned to Amanda, "Why have you got purple hair, sweetheart?" she said for about the fifth time.

The lunch finally came to an end. Ernest had a big appetite, tucked his napkin into his shirt, and asked for "seconds." Awful table manners in Sheila's book.

"Perhaps you would like a walk around the garden before you head back to Plymouth?" said Geoffrey.

Amanda and Ernest both genuinely admired the garden, walking arm-in-arm, occasionally giving each other a little peck or kiss. Half an hour later, they were back on their Harley, in their black leathers and helmets, roaring down the driveway. Geoffrey turned to Sheila as they waved them goodbye. "Oh my God," he said, "what a shock. She is bringing him back tomorrow. Hard to believe she fell for such a man!"

"From the East End," Sheila added, aghast. "No education, no class."

"Perhaps it's just a sign of the times. You don't think she would consider marrying him, do you?"

Sheila brought her hand to her mouth. "It would be a disaster, Geoffrey," said Sheila. "You have got to talk some sense into her. Find out whether this is a truly serious relationship. Make sure she understands that marrying this young man from the lower classes would never work." She paused, unsteadily looking vacantly into space, and then spoke partly almost to herself. "For God's sake, his father was a bus driver."

"Yes, and his mother is a kitchen maid. At a hospital! I just don't understand it, Sheila. What does she see in him?"

"Why did she dye her hair purple?" Somehow Sheila had managed to keep herself engaged and reasonably sober through the whole proceedings. She was having one of her "good days."

"Well, we shall see what happens when they come back tomorrow," said Geoffrey. "I will find an opportunity to give her a good talking to. We are not going to let her throw her life away on some pop star who may be out of work in a year, and relying on our Amanda to support him."

Around midday the following morning, Ernest and Amanda drove up in a rented Audi. It was a beautiful early summer day. Bright blue skies, flowers, trees, and shrubs blossomed everywhere. The sun was warm. Geoffrey was there to meet them. "Hello, hello," he said as the car drew to a halt on the gravel drive. "Frampton will help you with your bags."

The butler moved forward as Ernest got out of the car and opened the boot. Inside were two small suitcases which Frampton took into the house without a word.

"I have put you and Ernest in the Royal suite with its two adjoining bedrooms. I know you love that suite, Amanda," said Geoffrey, looking for clues in response, which were not forthcoming.

"Thank you, Daddy," said Amanda, throwing her arms around her father's neck and giving him a kiss on the cheek. She was, after all, the only warm and affectionate one in the whole family. "The concerts went very well. Totally sold out. A great crowd. We are all over the Plymouth newspapers. I brought some with me."

"I'm very pleased that our tour is going so well, Lord Geoffrey," said Ernest, looking somewhat more appealing now that he wasn't wearing the black leathers. He was dressed in pressed blue jeans and a pale blue Ralph Lauren golf shirt.

"Well. Congratulations to you both. That is very good news. Now, why don't you get settled in? Then you can come down for a light lunch, and then we can take a leisurely walk around some of the property. Tomorrow we can tour the whole estate. How does that sound?"

"That sounds wonderful," Amanda and Ernest said at the same time.

They had a modest lunch, and Ernest noted that Sheila was a little worse for wear today. She had been hitting the vodka bottle all morning, and she had difficulty feeding herself. The only contribution she made in conversation over lunch was to enquire why Amanda had purple streaks in her hair. Amanda looked at her mother with real concern. She had not realised that the drinking problem had got to this stage. She looked at Ernest who held out his hand and gave her a sympathetic smile.

They were waiting for coffee to be served when Amanda, looking very nervous, said, "Daddy, Mummy, I have some wonderful news. Ernest and I are engaged to be married... So exciting!" She gave a nervous laugh. "Look, Mummy," she showed her mother an enormous square-cut diamond engagement ring. "Isn't it beautiful?"

Both Geoffrey and Sheila were dumbfounded. This news was out of the blue. Before they could respond, Ernest intervened. "We are deeply in love and look forward to your blessing."

"Well," said Geoffrey uncertainly. He didn't want to alienate his daughter. But would she really marry so beneath her class? "I have to confess this is a real shock. How long have you known each other?'

"Four months," said Amanda.

"Four months, is that all?" responded Geoffrey, really concerned.

"Of course, we only want Amanda's happiness. She is a very capable young lady who I know makes good choices," he continued.

"You have always guided me, Daddy," said Amanda. Geoffrey recognized, of course, that she was flattering him. Like any good PR person would. "So, I have been able to make good choices in my life up to now."

"Yes. But... Amanda, this is a lifetime decision. You have to consider your long-term relationship. Your interests, your lifestyle. And I have to say, of course, your background and education."

Ernest knew where this was going. The implication was clear. He was from the lower classes. He had been through this many times. How could he even contemplate marrying the daughter of one of the oldest, aristocratic families in Britain? The Thorntons had a 300-year history, and a lifestyle very different from his own.

Geoffrey cleared his throat. "I also have to ask you, Ernest, whether you and your band are going to be able to support yourselves in the future. You know, Amanda went to Cheltenham Ladies' College, and then Exeter University. She has had a first-class education. She was doing very well in public relations in London. In addition, you can see the surroundings, the history, and the tradition in which she grew up. So, I need to ask you a personal question..." Geoffrey paused, choosing his words carefully. "Do you think you will continue to make some sort of steady income once your tour is finished? Can you support my daughter, and perhaps a future family, with all the costs involved?" He wanted to show

Amanda that one could not live on love or infatuation. He hoped she would recognize this choice could be disastrous.

"That's a reasonable question, Lord Geoffrey," responded Billy. "I can see why you would have some concerns, but obviously you don't know much about the music scene, or Billy King and the Royals, and the success we enjoy. To put your mind at rest, I can tell you that last year I earned personally from the band about £880,000, and, in addition to that, royalties from my music and our performances around the world were about one and a half million pounds." Ernest paused.

Geoffrey and Sheila were struck dumb, their mouths open. "Because of the high rate of taxation in this country, my advisers suggested that I move to France. They made a direct agreement with the French government over the maximum level of tax that I and the band would be paying. So, I am now a resident of France. I bought a villa in Mougins, near Cannes. You may have heard of it."

Geoffrey nodded without saying a word. Ernest saw their reaction and was now warming up. He was feeling more confident. "In addition, we are going on a tour in the USA and Canada later this year, which would be our first. I have been guaranteed no less than two million dollars. That tour should generate considerable extra income from royalties, TV appearances, and merchandise sales. So, my Lord Geoffrey, I think you can see that you should not have any worries about my ability to support Amanda." Ernest was happy to spell all this out and to show "class" did not matter in this day and age.

Geoffrey and Sheila were speechless. They looked at each other with the same thought: Could this young man get them out of their financial hole? Eventually Geoffrey was the first to snap out of it. "Well, Ernest, I think you have put our minds at rest. And consequently, as Amanda is over twenty-one, I am sure my wife and I are happy to support her decision. Congratulations to both of you."

"Oh, Daddy and Mummy," said Amanda with tears running down her face, "That is so wonderful. I can assure you that Ernie is fantastic. We are very much in love and we make a very good team."

"That's wonderful, sweetheart. We both hope that your marriage will be very happy."

Amanda butted in excitedly. "Oh, Daddy, you have to come and see us in France. The villa in Mougins is beautiful. There are four bedrooms and a swimming pool, a beautiful garden, incredible views, and Ernie has arranged for help with cooking and gardening. It is just amazing. I love it there."

"I like owning property," said Ernest, realizing he now had the upper hand. As he had learned with the band's success, money talks. "But I have to consider my tax position and try and arrange my affairs before Amanda and I get married, so we don't get caught up in the UK tax net! I suppose you know about these things."

"Well of course," responded Geoffrey. "Highly complicated, and this Labour government is driving away all our talent."

Ernest pushed on, ignoring Geoffrey's comment. "Amanda told me that you have a property for sale, the Dower House, which she says she just adores. Perhaps we could look at it together, if it is still for sale. We drove past it on the Harley when we came for lunch. Most impressive."

Geoffrey's heart missed a beat. Sheila sat upright with a wide-eyed look.

The Dower House had been on the market for over three years and had not received one serious offer. Their estate agent had said no one was willing to undertake the enormous costs of renovating a house in need of serious repair. If Ernest was serious, the sale of the Dower House could solve all of

Geoffrey's financial problems. He was suddenly excited at the proposition. And he saw that Sheila, even in her drunken state, understood what was going on. He answered calmly. "Yes, it is still for sale. The Dower House is about a mile down the road from this property. It was the home traditionally of the widows of previous Lords Marsden when the estate had passed on to the next generation. The last widow to live there was my grandmother, who passed away in 1919. My father, the ninth Lord Marsden, outlived my mother and passed away at the age of 92. It's a six-bedroom Georgian house with a stable block and other outhouses and sheds. It sits on twenty-three acres of gardens and meadows near a large wooded area of the estate. If you have an interest, and the means to modernize the house, it would provide you with a beautiful home." Geoffrey was trying to make a sales pitch now. He no longer spoke with arrogant superiority, but oozing charm to his son-in-law to be.

Amanda spoke up. "You know, I've always loved the Dower House, Daddy, and I hated to see it fall into disrepair over the years since I was a young girl. It really should be somebody's home."

"Well, my love, I would be very happy to show Ernest the Dower House, and indeed the rest of the Marsden estate with all its history and beauty. I'm sure, Ernest, you would enjoy that."

"Yes, Lord Geoffrey, I am sure I would," said Ernest, recognizing that, as a potential buyer, he held all the cards.

They all rose. Sheila did not join them on the walk to the Dower House. Ernest was bowled over by the beauty of the meadows, wildflowers, woods, and the peace and quiet on the estate. He could see himself as the country gentleman living in splendour in the Dower House. They arrived at the entrance in the middle of a long high brick wall. It had once had elaborate iron gates, but these had been contributed to the war effort in 1941 and had never been replaced. The road up to the house, about 100 yards, was overgrown but still beautiful, with two lines of elm trees providing shade. There was a circular driveway outside the magnificent house. It had been built in 1810, in the Georgian style, with large windows, a symmetrical disposition, and aged pale brown bricks. There were four large chimneys at the top, peeking through a sloping roof, and a wide painted wood portico. The front door had a splayed glass semicircle positioned over it.

"Oh, Daddy," said Amanda, "it is still beautiful, but definitely needs some tender loving care to bring it back to life."

"Amanda, you are right. It is a lovely property," said Ernest, "but we better have a good look inside."

"Let me show you the way," said Geoffrey, taking out a large brass key. He inserted it in the front door lock and gently pushed it open.

They entered a large entrance hall with square flagstones, some of which were cracked, and a sweeping wooden staircase going up to the next floor. He showed them around proudly. Every room was in need of some serious renovation. Damp, mold, and water damage were everywhere. All the rooms were very light and airy and, on this magnificent Monday, the sun was streaming in from all angles. Wherever they went, Ernest took note of damp areas on the walls and rotting floorboards caused by a leak in the roof. From the outside, he could see there was considerable tuckpointing required on the corners of the building. All in all, he realised this would be a major construction challenge. Nevertheless, the property was compact, with clean lines, beautifully situated, with a lovely rear terrace with many cracked balusters and flagstones. The potential was there.

"Lord Geoffrey," said Ernest, "this is a beautiful property in a beautiful spot, but it looks like one hell of a problem to bring it back to life." Geoffrey's heart was pounding. Ernest was right. Even on a beautiful day like today, Geoffrey recognized that the property was deteriorating rapidly.

Restoration would be a major headache. "Amanda and I will think about this and perhaps we can talk a little more over supper."

"Of course, Ernest. Please call me Geoffrey, after all, you are joining the family." Geoffrey responded, cringing at the word supper. "I know it's a big decision and a big commitment, but you would be saving one of the most beautiful country manor houses in all of England," he continued with a little bit of over-the-top exaggeration.

They looked at the stable block and a couple of other outbuildings, all in need of considerable work, and then walked back to Marsden Hall. Geoffrey asked Frampton to bring them tea on the terrace. Sheila joined them and just about managed to hold herself together to ask Ernest what he thought of the house. She was as eager as Geoffrey to see something positive happen. They sat at a table with four rickety wicker chairs and enjoyed the sunny afternoon.

After talking about the long history of the estate and the Thornton family, Amanda sought her father's support to have their wedding under a tent in the garden, sometime in the following April. Geoffrey and Sheila readily agreed, convinced Ernest would be paying. Geoffrey then suggested they might like to retire and change for dinner.

Ernest laughed. "Change for dinner, Geoffrey? You must be kidding! I only have one suit. Otherwise it's jeans and T-shirts and my motorcycle leathers all the way. I'm afraid where I come from, we don't change for dinner. In fact, we're happy to get any dinner at all." Ernest was pushing back at his Lordship and their lifestyle. They may have the pedigree, but they needed his money.

"Of course, Ernest. Just an expression you know," Geoffrey said. He felt embarrassed and annoyed that he was being put down by the slick little rock 'n' roll star.

When they went upstairs, Geoffrey and Sheila were able to

talk. "My God," said Sheila. "I wasn't expecting this. So much for you sitting down with Amanda to put her off."

"I know. But he does seem to be extraordinarily successful and caring of her. He is already a tax exile! He obviously has lots of money rolling in and I'm sure he knows that the asking price on the Dower House is £250,000. Amanda has always loved that property. Maybe Ernest would be willing to do that for her. I'm not going to get too excited yet, but who knows? This young man may be the answer to our prayers. Wouldn't that be something, Sheila?"

When they were together in their suite, Ernest and Amanda sat down to discuss the Dower House.

"Mandy, my love, you can see the state of that house. It is lovely, but do you really want to go forward with it? If you do, I will buy it, but I have to have some people look it over to see that we're not buying a money pit."

"Oh, Ernie. I love it. Would you really buy it? I think in the long-term it could be a very good investment. Although I recognize the reconstruction work may be enormous, hopefully, it will prove to be a wonderful family home for us in the future, away from all the hustle and bustle. Like France, but a little bit of England."

"Okay. Let's have a go," said Ernest with a laugh. Amanda let out a squeal and jumped into his arms, kissing him passionately.

"I also think I should try and help your mother, before it is too late," he said holding Amanda's hand. "A few weeks at The Grove might get her sober."

"Oh, Ernie, that would be fantastic. I'm really concerned about my mum. I hardly recognized her. I've known for a long time that she's had a drinking problem. From time to time, she had treatments, but it looks like things have gone down rapidly. She was a striking beauty in her day. To see her like this is really upsetting."

"Listen, Mandy, we've known a whole bunch of people that have gone to The Grove for substance abuse. Sure, many of them have slipped into bad ways, but others have come out on a new path. Maybe your mum could be one of those. But we know from our experience in the music business that if you don't tackle a drinking problem like your mother has, things can only get worse. Do you think I can broach the subject delicately to your father?"

"Let me have a word with him in a quiet corner somewhere. I know he wants to do what's best, but he's got some enormous financial pressures going on at the moment. He just doesn't have the wherewithal to move forward."

"Yeah. That makes sense."

"It would be a bit embarrassing to discuss it over dinner with all of us, but I'm pretty sure he would be over the moon if you could arrange this for him. He will consider it a blessing. He'll probably be indebted to you for life. So, you know what," Amanda said with a little laugh, "between buying the Dower House and doing this for my mother, you certainly will have no in-law problems when we get married." With that, she went over to Ernest, threw her arms around his neck, and gave him another passionate kiss.

Over dinner, there were just the three of them, because Geoffrey said that Sheila had a "headache." They discussed the Dower House.

"Geoffrey, I've discussed this with Amanda. She loves the property, and I love her, so even though I recognize it's going to be an enormous job to restore the house, I think eventually it will become a lovely family home. I'm prepared to pay the asking price, but, instead of the house on twenty-three acres, I want the house with 150 acres, including the woods. If you agree to this, I will make arrangements to introduce you to Roger Miles, our tax accountant and financial adviser, and he will put everything in place to proceed. Is that acceptable?"

Geoffrey could not believe his good luck. He never thought anyone would be willing to buy the Dower House and take on the responsibility of restoring it. He also never thought he would get his asking price and he was quite willing to give up some extra land—the one thing that the estate still had was lots and lots of land. This young man that Amanda was going to marry was turning out to be a real godsend to the family. It would enable him to get the bank off his back and have substantial funds available for the restoration of Marsden Hall.

"Ernest," he said with a smile, "that is a very fair offer. I am very happy to accept. It is also extremely generous of you to buy this property to please my beautiful Amanda. I think you're going to make a wonderful couple. Sheila and I will feel very blessed to have you come and stay and live at the Dower House just up the road from us. I couldn't be happier, Ernest. Thank you very, very much. I think this calls for a major celebration. Let us share a bottle of champagne. I shall ask Frampton to go and get a bottle from the cellar." A couple of minutes later, they were drinking the bubbly, clicking glasses, and smiling and laughing.

"I will have Roger Miles contact you or your estate manager to make arrangements for a visit to look at the property," said Ernest. "I want to bring in contractors, architects, and designers to start work as soon as possible. I think you will like Roger. He is very impressive. Quick, knowledgeable, and pragmatic. He has been invaluable to me and the band. I was introduced to him by Jagger. They met at LSE and have been firm friends ever since. If you are interested, Geoffrey, he might be able to help you with your estate management."

"I would be delighted to meet him. And I would certainly welcome any help he may be able to give to the Marsden estate. I have to confess, it has always been a bit above my pay grade, so to speak. I have left it to others to manage the estate. However, the bottom line is that we have not been doing well. It's been a struggle to cover the costs of maintaining this property. Maybe a fresh set of eyes could prove to be very beneficial."

The rest of the evening passed pleasantly. Amanda had a chance to have a word with her father before she and Ernest went upstairs to bed. Geoffrey was once again extremely grateful. He said he would be very supportive of Ernest if he could arrange for Sheila to go to The Grove for treatment.

The next day, Sheila was up and about. She was delighted and rather tearful for all the good things Amanda and Ernest were doing for the estate and the family. Over the next few weeks, there was a whirlwind of activity. Roger Miles came down to Marsden and brought with him an architect from Bristol and a building contractor, the father of a friend of his in London. Roger called Ernest and told him he thought it was crazy to consider purchasing the property, but he said both the architect and the builder felt that the "bones" of the building were strong. But there was an enormous amount of work to be done. He told Ernest that this was a classic "money pit" and it would be very difficult to assess where the end would be. But he felt he had the right people and he could keep a close watch on the costs and delivery of the services. He also advised Ernest that the ownership of the house and land should be in the name of an offshore trust, in order to not get caught up in the complications of the English tax system. Roger would put the necessary paperwork in place.

Geoffrey really took to Roger, mostly because he found out that Roger had been to Cambridge University, came from a good family, and was very well-spoken. He was clearly extremely able and did not look like he was part of the rock 'n' roll scene. As a result, having explained to Roger over cognac one evening how the Marsden estate and its various businesses were structured, he asked if he would take a little time and look into how his businesses could improve. Carter Evans, the estate manager, was not happy to have Roger Miles on the scene, but couldn't do much about it. Within a couple of weeks, Roger came back to Ernest and said that Carter Evans should be retired and that there was dramatic waste in the operations of the businesses on the estate. He outlined additional sources of revenue that could be generated. These were only preliminary findings, but Geoffrey was both shocked and impressed at the speed at which the businesses had been analyzed. Within a few days, he asked Roger if he could conduct interviews, and find somebody to take over Carter Evans's position.

Ernest had arranged for Sheila to go to The Grove, and, after six weeks of intensive therapy and treatment, she emerged a new person. She put on weight, had her hair colored, was taking an interest in the house, the menus, and what was happening on the estate. She had even started talking to Amanda about planning for the wedding.

The band's UK tour ended in London the last week of June. The tour had been very successful and generated enormous income. Amanda and Ernest went down to Marsden for a few days' rest and relaxation, and to be there on the official announcement of their engagement and exchange of contracts for the purchase of the Dower House. The engagement announcement was placed in the London Times and the Daily Telegraph and both Geoffrey and Sheila were surprised at the amount of interest and excitement that this generated among friends and family. The purchase contract for the Dower House had been signed by the relevant parties, but Roger had insisted that the trust making the purchase on behalf of Ernest could terminate the agreement for whatever reason, prior to the completion of the transaction scheduled for December 15th. He was concerned that the contractor and the architect, as they completed their due diligence and worked out the estimated costs of the restoration, would find some unexpected massive expenditures.

The weather was lovely and the newly engaged couple

enjoyed their few days in the countryside. One afternoon, after a long walk through the village of Marsden, along the cliffs and down to the beach, they returned to the house, tired but exhilarated. Amanda went upstairs to wash her hair. Ernest went to their car because he had left a sweater on the back seat. As he came into the house, passing Geoffrey's study, he heard Sheila on the phone. "I know, what do you think of that? Ha, ha!" Ernest paused. He continued listening.

"Well it was a big surprise to us as well, my dear," Sheila went on. Ernest realised the conversation was about his engagement to Amanda and, although he didn't really want to listen, he was rooted to the spot.

"About six months," Sheila continued. "She works for his band, as their public relations rep, and apparently she has done a wonderful job for them." Sheila paused briefly before continuing. "No, not university, ha, ha, ha. In fact, he's had no education whatsoever. Comes from the East End of London, my dear. Terrible Cockney accent, can hardly speak the Queen's English, no class, and dreadful table manners. And the parents, Daphne, oh my God!"

Ernest had been standing outside of the study door listening to this conversation and getting angrier by the minute. He had dealt with these people most of his life, the so-called upper classes, snooty and superior, and often lazy, arrogant, and stupid. He was beginning to seethe as he listened to this conversation unfolding.

"Well, my dear, he is besotted with Amanda. And of course, she can twist him around her little finger." Sheila chortled with laughter, then she continued. "He owns a villa in Mougins in the South of France". She paused. "Yes, Poppy and Archie Hedley-Young have a place there. Amanda said that Geoffrey and I can go there anytime. Since Ernest and his band are always travelling, we won't have to see much of him or his dreadful family. Instead, we could take long vacations in

France. Perhaps you and Charles could join us. Wouldn't that be a hoot, ha, ha!"

Ernest couldn't believe what he was hearing. He was about ready to blow his top.

"No, the wedding will be held here. Looks like it's going to be an enormous affair under a tent. Of course, we expect Ernest to pay for everything, ha, ha."

That did it for Ernest. He had enough. He marched into the study. As soon as Sheila saw him and his red angry face, she cut off her phone conversation. "Er, Daphne I'll call you back later."

Ernest let loose. "So, Sheila, you think I'm an embarrassment, do you?"

"No, no, no. Ernest you've misheard!"

"I have lived with you people all my life," he said. "You are a prime example. Never done a decent day's work in your life. Totally inept. Geoffrey could screw up a one-car funeral. And I should remind you that, until a few weeks ago, you were a total drunk heading for death row. What gives you the right to insult my parents? They're hard-working people who spent their whole lives doing the right thing, trying to improve workers' rights, and being underpaid and underappreciated."

He was really letting loose now. "You've got a fucking cheek to talk about them, especially since you've never met them." Ernest was shaking with anger. "You sit here, in this decrepit old pile, Lord and Lady Muck, living off your inheritance, and you can't even make that work, even with thousands of acres. You're both pathetic. The truth is I rescued you from the poorhouse. Well, perhaps you're right, perhaps Amanda is marrying beneath her class and perhaps this whole thing is a mistake."

Ernest was bright red and seething. His voice was raised and his Cockney accent was thicker than ever. "So, for starters, you can shove that Dower House up your arse. I don't want to cause you any more embarrassment. I'm leaving. Say goodbye to that twit of a husband."

Sheila now had a complete look of horror on her face. The Dower House! She tried to rescue the situation "Ernest, I'm sorry but you only heard half the conversation. I didn't mean it to be offensive, it was more of a joke and taken out of context. What can I do? This is ridiculous, you can't walk out on Amanda! That would be terrible. She's madly in love with you."

"Goodbye, Sheila, try to stay off the booze."

Ernest turned and marched out of the study at a fast pace straight upstairs to the suite. He burst into the room. Amanda had just washed her hair and was standing in a kimono with a towel wrapped around her head and nothing else. "Come on, Mandy. We're going," he said grabbing his suitcase and throwing clothes in, still red in the face and angry.

"What! What?" said Amanda, not understanding what was going on.

"Apparently, your mother considers me a complete embarrassment, Cockney kid from the East End of London with terrible table manners and awful parents. She's never met them, by the way. So, I'm leaving. I know when I'm not wanted."

Amanda looked on in total disbelief and shock. "What do you mean you're leaving? I'm not even dressed. My hair is all wet," she said in some confusion.

"Well, Mandy, perhaps our whole relationship is a mistake. Perhaps we can't make it work because of our backgrounds. Anyway, I'm going. You can come or you can stay."

"Calm down, Ernie," said Amanda. "I'll talk to Mummy. It's just her way. She can be foolish sometimes. I'm sure she didn't mean anything, Ernie."

"She meant what she said, Mandy. I was there the whole time and heard every word to her friend Daphne."

"Oh, Daphne Walsingham. She's a real airhead. Don't

take any notice of her." Amanda was clearly alarmed. "I shall sort it all out, only calm down."

"Did you tell your mother that she could use the villa whenever she wanted?"

"No, of course not. I would never do that. Is that what she said?"

"That, and a lot of other insulting things, Mandy." Ernest was still hopping mad. "Are you coming?"

"I can't come like this. I will talk to them if you will just stay."

"Screw them. I'm off!" With that, he slammed his suitcase, grabbed his sweater, and marched out of the room.

Within a minute or so, Amanda heard his car revving up and the crunch of stones as he drove down the driveway. She stood there in complete shock. Tears were running down her face. This had only taken a couple of minutes. What the hell had happened? Surely the relationship wasn't over because of something her mother had said to that stupid Daphne. She threw some clothes on and rushed downstairs. Her mother was in the study. Amanda walked in. Sheila was sobbing.

"Mummy, what have you done? What did you say to Daphne Walsingham about Ernie and his family? I think he's called the marriage off!" she said, clearly distraught. "Tell me what you said?"

Sheila was unable to speak. All she could say was: "The Dower House, the Dower House."

Amanda waited a day, in the hope that Ernie would calm down and contact her. She didn't hear anything. She phoned his London flat and left a message and got no reply, and then the villa in Mougins. Maria, the housekeeper, said that Mr. Ernest was not there, but she knew she was lying. She was distraught, unhappy, and totally confused. Did she and Ernie have a future together? She hardly exchanged a word with her mother. Her father was a nervous wreck. Geoffrey had held the bank at bay on the basis of the exchange of contracts for the Dower House. If the wedding and that transaction were not to go forward, he would still be in his big financial mess, although the changes that Roger Miles had made and the appointment of a new estate manager, Simon Morris, were already reaping some benefits.

Out of desperation, Amanda contacted Roger Miles. He knew what had happened. Ernest was still very upset, and wasn't sure about Amanda's love, and whether the marriage would work out for both of them. "Wait a while, Mandy," he said. "I'm sure he will come round."

Amanda moved to London and stayed with her cousin Emma Cowley, in Bayswater. She could not bear to be with her parents, who might have ruined her life. She gave her new London phone number to Roger to pass on to Ernie.

During the second week of August, Billy King and the Royals started their four-month-long US tour. There was still no word. Amanda was lonely and depressed. She began to have doubts about the relationship. Was their love strong enough to overcome obstacles and arguments like this? Ernie had gone off on his tour without a word. She was now angry at him for doing that to her.

At the end of August, just before the Labor Day weekend in the United States, she finally received a phone call from Ernest.

"Mandy, I miss you so much… I have thought this whole thing through, and I don't want to spend my life without you. I am madly in love with you. Your parents are living in the past, but I am not marrying them. I realise that. That's okay. I'm not going to change who I am. I'm not trying to join that club of snooty has-beens, so our relationship will never be warm and fuzzy. But you are not one of them. You understand that this is 1976, and class warfare in Britain is over."

"Oh, Ernie," said Amanda, "I love you with all my heart. I want to spend the rest of our days together. You are my first priority and always will be. My parents will have to continue to live in their world. You've been unbelievably generous and helpful to them. I can't believe how badly they have behaved. I'm not talking to either of them. I just want to see you, hug you, kiss you, and marry you."

"Well, that is going to be sooner than you planned, Mandy. I want you to come down to Mougins. Take a flight to Nice, either late tomorrow or the following day. Let Roger know the details. Maria will meet you at the airport. The band has a five-day break coming up, starting tomorrow night after our final show in Louisville, Kentucky. I have arranged to rent a private jet to take me down to Atlanta where I will get a Delta connection directly to Nice. I am making arrangements for us to have a civil wedding in Mougins with just a few witnesses. That will secure our tax position as well. Don't tell your parents."

"Oh, Ernie, that's wonderful. I am so happy. We will never have a fight like this again. I will always be at your side. I love you so much..." She was so emotional, she could not continue.

"I love you too, Mandy, and always will. See you soon. Can't wait." Amanda was over the moon, and felt her life was back on track. She felt happy for the first time in weeks.

She was sound asleep when a sleepy Emma gently knocked on the door and woke her up. It was 5 a.m.

"There is a phone call for you, Mandy," she said in a croaky voice.

"That's a bit early," Amanda said, thinking maybe Ernest was making a late-night call from the United States. "I'll take it on the telephone at the end of the hallway," she said. "Thank you, Emma."

She padded down the hallway in her nightie. She picked up the telephone. To her surprise it was Roger Miles on the other end. "Amanda, my love." There was a long pause. "There's been an accident," he said with a quiver in his voice.

"What?"

"It's Ernest. His charter plane took off from Louisville. The weather was bad and for some reason, after a couple of minutes, the plane went down." He couldn't continue for a moment. He was crying. "There were no survivors," he said in a quiet, shaky voice. "I'm so sorry, my love, I don't know what to say. I'm going to fly out there tomorrow morning. I will do my best to bring Ernie home to England for burial." He had run out of words.

Amanda, on hearing this news, let out a silent scream and thumped her back against the wall followed by enormous sobs and a flood of tears. She dropped the phone and slowly slid down the wall to the floor.

6 ON THE TRAIN - 1979

It was a beautiful, crisp, sunny autumn day in October when I boarded the train for the short journey from Woldingham to Shaftesbury, where I would change for the direct London train. It was a journey that I made every eight weeks to represent the Regional General Practitioners for the counties of Dorset and Somerset at the General Medical Services Committee meeting, headquartered at the British Medical Association in Euston Square. My role was to negotiate with the government on behalf of rural practitioners in my region. The meetings, requiring an overnight stay, started usually at two p.m. at the BMA offices and continued until about 6 p.m. when the committee broke for drinks and dinner. The following morning the committee would meet from nine a.m. to twelve-thirty p.m., followed by a light lunch. Then, the members went on their way.

The early morning train was quite crowded with commuters. I found a seat in a compartment in the first-class carriage. The occupants were all businessmen, who I knew by sight or personally. They did not greet each other beyond a curt "good morning" and, in true British fashion, were hiding behind their newspapers. I smiled to myself at the sight. For my journey to London, I had put on my good dark-grey, chalk-striped, double-breasted suit, a white shirt, and my red-and-blue RAMC military tie. I also had my faithful, crumpled tweed trilby and a raincoat, just in case.

I had been on the committee for two years and took my responsibilities very seriously. I studied all the papers and made sure that I was well prepared for these meetings.

When I had decided to pursue a career in the medical profession, the last thing I had in mind was becoming a country doctor. However, while doing my residency at Middlesex Hospital in central London, I met and fell in love with my wife-to-be, nurse Claire Burton. Her father had a practice in Woldingham in Dorset but was in failing health. Initially, she persuaded me to come and help out on a temporary basis while her father recovered from prostate cancer surgery. At that time, I had my eyes on becoming a pathologist, but I thought a few months in the country would be a good experience and, of course, I wanted to support my wife and her family through difficult times.

Although Claire's father, Dr. Frank Burton, recovered from his surgery and came back to work, he quickly developed other health problems which forced him to take early retirement. He had been a country doctor all his life and knew all of his patients, their family histories, and backgrounds. They were very personal relationships that he was loath to see disappear.

One afternoon, he sat down with me and asked if I would take over the practice. I was not really surprised, as I could see he did not have the strength to continue working. I discussed this with Claire at length over the next week or so. After all, this was a life-changing decision for both of us. Life in Woldingham was very different from my life in Highgate in London, but it was a healthy, community-oriented family life, and it had started to grow on me. After some intense discussions and some sleepless nights, Claire and I decided we would make our home and my career in Woldingham, and I informed my father-in-law that I would be willing to take over the practice. That brought tears to his eyes. My name, Dr. Peter Darrell, was painted on the surgery door. That was nearly thirty years ago.

After renting a home for three years, during which time two of our children were born, we bought an 18th-century cottage on Forest Lane on the edge of the village. The house was built of pale pink wattle and stucco and had a thatched roof, leaded windows, beams in the living areas, and an inglenook fireplace. It had four bedrooms, two bathrooms and a beautiful garden with a trellis, brick wall covered with wisteria. It was a joy to behold in the spring. It also had eight acres of paddocks and woods. In the spring, the woods were covered with primroses and bluebells. Claire loved to garden and she gradually transformed our little piece of paradise into a beautiful example of the perfect English garden.

Frank Burton enjoyed a fine reputation in Woldingham. He had an outgoing personality, an understanding bedside manner, and he was a pillar of the community. I tried to follow in his footsteps, and, with support from Claire, who worked as my nurse three days per week, we gradually built our own place in the community.

However, I needed Dr. Frank's fine reputation and respect in the community to help me over a very difficult period when I was involved in a murder case where my patient was the victim. Feelings were running high in the village. I came in for a lot of criticism for my handling of the situation and the evidence I gave in court. It's not often, I'm sure, that a young, fairly inexperienced, country doctor is faced with a situation like that.

It took a while, but my father-in-law persuaded the majority of our patients to stay with me, and gradually the practice had prospered and grown, despite the ups and downs of the National Health Service. We had three children, all of whom were now grown, out of University, and pursuing their own careers, but none involved medicine. They had been quite clear that they thought their father's work as a country doctor was far too demanding. But I had developed a love for the life and had become somewhat of a leader in the profession in my region, culminating with my appointment to the General Medical Services Committee. I had taken on a young doctor from Australia, four years ago, to help with the expanded practice. Over these thirty years, I had also lost most of my hair, gained nearly twenty pounds, and was now a rotund, middle-aged man.

I changed trains at Shaftesbury, but stayed on the same platform. The wait for the direct train to London was only six minutes or so. I settled in my first-class compartment to read the newspapers on my way into the capital. Margaret Thatcher had been elected prime minister in May 1979, when her Conservative party took over from James Callaghan's Labour Party after the harsh "winter of discontent." The endless strikes had stopped for the time being, and it had been a pleasant and warm summer, but there were warning signs, as the autumn approached, that the battle with the unions was far from over. Margaret Thatcher was going to dig her heels in on many issues as she attempted to curb inflation. But, on this day, as I headed for my meeting, there were no delays, no disruptions, and no strikes.

As always, I pushed hard in putting forward suggestions for improvements, as they affected my patients. Being a rural practitioner, I specifically raised some issues about two local cottage hospitals. I knew that any feedback would be weeks or months away. The NHS moved slowly. The meeting broke up on time and was followed by drinks and dinner, which was always a good opportunity for renewing acquaintances and friendships and having some professional discussions. After dinner, I headed for my hotel for the night – The Farmers Club on Whitehall Court in Westminster, where I had been a member for more than twenty years. The Farmers Club offered clean, simple accommodations, reliable food, and a comfortable chintzy members' room and bar.

The following morning, I returned for the second half of the meeting, which focused more on the NHS, updates on treatments, payment systems, paperwork, and the allocation of finances to the regions. After the meeting broke up and the members had enjoyed a light lunch, I headed for Waterloo Station and my train home to Woldingham. I had made this journey many times before and timed it perfectly to arrive on my platform a few minutes before the train departed for Shaftesbury, where I would change for the final short journey to Woldingham.

I boarded a first-class carriage and settled down with my newspapers. The mid-afternoon train was not crowded. Just before the train was about to leave, a young man jumped into the compartment carrying a leather hold-all, which he threw up on the luggage rack.

"Phew," I said. "That was cutting it fine. You were lucky to make it."

"Luck had very little to do with it," he responded, looking at me directly with piercing, grey-green eyes. "Timing is everything. It's not always a good thing to have such a regular schedule, as perhaps you have."

I thought that was rather an odd reply but didn't pursue the conversation. The train pulled out of the station and shortly thereafter the ticket inspector came through and clicked both our tickets and said "Change at Shaftesbury for Woldingham." The other occupant asked him: "How long is the wait for the connecting train?"

"You're scheduled to have a seven-minute wait for your connection, but it will be on the same platform, number three," responded the inspector.

I looked across the compartment at my traveling companion. *Going through to Woldingham*, I thought to myself. I *wonder who this young man is?* I looked at him closely. After all, more than half the families in the village of about 700 people were patients of mine, who I treated for numerous ailments, and I had even helped deliver many babies over the years. I prided myself on knowing, even if casually, every family in the village, and I enjoyed playing the recognition game.

The young man sitting opposite appeared to be in his early forties. Dark hair parted on the left, horn-rimmed glasses, nice-looking features, and pale, grey-green eyes that contrasted with his dark complexion. He was dressed in a blue blazer, blue shirt with red-and-blue tie, gold cufflinks, grey trousers, and highly polished brown shoes—a handsome man of medium height and build, prosperous, and smartly, casually dressed. I began to speculate to myself as to who he might be.

London was being left behind and the train was rattling into the countryside. The sun was shining brightly on an autumn landscape, with the trees turning golden, red, and brown, and the fields harvested and now just pale, gold patches interspersed with fields of green vegetables. A beautiful sight of the English countryside at its best. I returned to my newspapers and started to absorb the somewhat depressing economic picture as depicted by the *London Times* and the *Telegraph*. The young man opposite was absorbed in the pink-colored *Financial Times*, avidly reading it page-by-page. I thought, he might be some sort of financial guru, going down to see some of his family or friends for a long weekend. The brown, leather hold-all in the luggage rack had a British Airways hand baggage ticket attached to one of the handles. Maybe he has just landed in London before taking this trip. But he hasn't got much luggage for a stay of more than a day or so. Maybe he already has clothing and other necessities in Woldingham. That could indicate that he was returning 'home' and had whatever he needed for his visit. I thought to myself. But who is he?

I returned to my newspapers, but was only half reading

while I thought about the possibilities. The village had a lot of young men of his age, but most of them were farming, following in the family footsteps. Those that left the beautiful village were few and far between. I started to think of possible candidates. Could it be Neil Braddock, the younger son of Terry and Pam Braddock, chicken and egg farmers on the south edge of the village? Neil had appendicitis when he was about fourteen. I remembered he was now a career officer in the Royal Tank Corps, and spent a lot of time overseas in postings from Germany to the Middle East. I knew that he came back to see his family from time-to-time. I had bumped into Neil once, about ten years ago. But as I remembered, Neil had a very English complexion, fair, with red cheeks. He was also quite tall. Obviously, the man sitting opposite did not fill the bill. Who is he?

I thought of other candidates. How about Anthony Foxton? Anthony was a nice young man, dark-haired and very good-looking. He had grown up on the family dairy farm, a couple of miles from Woldingham. He had always been a sickly boy, suffering from migraine headaches, winter colds, and other ailments. I hadn't seen him for twenty years or more, since he went off to university. However, I had heard on the grapevine that Anthony had been living with a male, artist friend in Manchester. No, I thought this young man opposite is not Anthony.

The train was rattling along towards Shaftesbury, and I was still racking my brains trying to think who this young man might be. He had put away the *Financial Times* and taken out a John Le Carré book, *Smiley's People*. From time to time he looked at me with those piercing, grey-green eyes, but said nothing. I returned to my name game. Other possibilities came to mind but were quickly eliminated. But how about Arthur Seeley? He was definitely dark-haired, the last time I had seen him, which was nearly twenty years ago. He had been a healthy, active, and athletic boy. But Arthur had moved

away from Woldingham, because of a scandal. It was an open
secret in the village that Arthur was not Fred Seeley's son. His
mother, Janet, had been involved with an American airman,
stationed near Shaftesbury during the war. Arthur had been
brought up by Fred as if he was his own, and he wanted him
to learn the family building business, but there was always
gossip, and as soon as Arthur turned eighteen, he had left.
The story was that he had moved to the United States and
was living in San Diego. The man opposite could be a
potential, but he certainly didn't look anything like Janet. But
Arthur's father was an American, I said to myself. Somehow, I
didn't think this young man was Arthur.

I had a new thought. I know who this is, I said to myself,
Jimmy Borthwick! I remembered the young Jimmy vaguely,
having treated him when he had broken his arm falling out of
a tree after stealing apples when he was about twelve. His
father was a landowner in the area, and he also owned one of
only two garages and repair shops in the village. Jimmy was
dark-haired and good-looking, like his Irish mother, Bridget.
He had been a good athlete and student, and he had gone to
Southampton University. I couldn't remember what he was
studying, but then I did remember he had suffered a bad
motorcycle accident which had left deep scars on his face, as
well as a permanent limp after breaking his leg and ankle in
three places. "Damn," I said to myself.

I couldn't see any scars on this young man. I thought of all
the boys I had treated in the village, some from birth until
adulthood. Spotty kids with broken bones, appendicitis,
earaches that would get me out in the middle of the night,
asthma, intestinal problems, or just bloody scrapes and bruises
from boyhood 'accidents.'

I tried to concentrate on my newspapers, but the
intriguing challenge of recognizing the young man
consumed my attention. The sun was streaming into the
compartment, its rays dancing across my lap, and I closed

my eyes to concentrate on other potential candidates. I definitely recognized his face, but I just couldn't pinpoint who he was. Although his identity was on the tip of my tongue.

The train started to slow and then stopped completely in the middle of the countryside. I looked up. The young man opposite suddenly seemed agitated.

"Where are we? Why have we stopped?" he said.

"I don't know," I replied, "but we are still some way from Shaftesbury."

"I don't want to miss the connection, you know," he said looking very nervous. "I have a deadline and a very important mission."

"Well," I said, "I know there's another train to Woldingham an hour later, if we do miss the connection."

"An hour later, an hour later," the man said, now looking rather frantic. "I have a deadline. I set myself a deadline."

I didn't know what he was talking about, but he was getting more agitated by the minute. Just then, the ticket inspector walked down the corridor and passed our compartment. The young man jumped up and shouted, "Why have we stopped? I have a deadline to meet."

The inspector stood at the entrance. "I believe it's a signal problem, sir."

"A signal problem?"

"Yes. Nothing to worry about. I'm sure it will be fixed shortly."

"Shortly? How long is shortly?" he said nervously.

"I'm afraid I don't know, sir, but we will keep you informed." He then continued down the corridor. The young man then lowered the window and looked out, down the side of the train.

"Is anybody boarding the train?" he said to no one in particular.

"I don't think so," I said.

"I hope they're not after me," he said. "They told me I was fine now. I'm fine now."

This young man, I decided, was anything but fine, and was making me a little nervous. He looked out the window again, up and down the track. I then noticed something that made me even more concerned. As he leaned forward, I saw he had a knife inside a scabbard attached to his belt. It looked like it could be a small hunting knife. He pulled his head in from the open window and sat down again looking directly at me. "I'm fine now. I'm fine now, so I have permission to go to the village whenever I like. I've been saving money for a long time, all for this trip." What was he talking about? I didn't know. By now I could see the man was very agitated, and covered in perspiration. I didn't know if he was claustrophobic or had other issues, but there was nothing I could do, sitting in a railway carriage in the middle of nowhere. I would be happy when we got to Shaftesbury.

"I have got some old scores to settle," he said. "Old scores. Yes."

He paused and then continued in a rush. "Against my father and my brothers. I know they did it. They plotted to take away my rights and my inheritance and estate," he said. Having seen the knife I was now concerned as to what this young man was planning.

"Old scores to settle," he said again. "Not only with my family, but with that doctor. It was the doctor who signed the papers. It was the doctor who put me away. Of course, I should not have been in that place. But it was an institution, and they kept me there for more than twenty years. I'm fine now, I'm fine now. They told me I was fine, and I could go to the village, whenever I liked."

Old scores to settle with a doctor. Now I was really nervous. Did I have a patient many years ago who I had to put in an institution? I was racking my brains.

"There's more than one doctor in Woldingham, you know," I said, seeking a bit of comfort in numbers.

"There may be," he said, "but I want Dr. Peter Darrell."

My heart started thumping. Now, I was really afraid. I couldn't move and I couldn't speak. At that moment, the young man stood up again. He came right at me, grabbing my shoulder. I opened my eyes in horror. But the young man looking at me with his grey-green eyes said, "We are pulling into Shaftesbury station." It took me a few moments to calm down and adjust to my surroundings. I then realized that I had fallen asleep, and that I had been dreaming. More like a nightmare really, but I was not going to be murdered, after all!

The young man brought his bag down from the luggage rack, exited the train and waited on the station platform, as many passengers disappeared into the town. I joined him, still rather shaken, waiting for the connection to Woldingham. The local train came a few minutes later. During the quieter travel periods, mid-morning through early evening, the local train from Shaftesbury was only four or five carriages, with half of one of the carriages consisting of four, first-class compartments. This was old railway rolling stock with no corridor. The first-class compartments were opened by turning the door handle on the outside. When exiting the compartment, passengers had to lower the window by moving a leather strap off its little toggle, and then leaned out the window to open the door to the compartment once again from the outside. Once one was in the compartment there could be no additional passengers exiting or boarding other than at scheduled stops. I waited until nearly the last minute not really wanting the young man to join me but he waited also and indeed he did join me in the compartment with a slight acknowledging smile.

"About 25 minutes to Woldingham, I believe, Dr. Darrell," he said. I was taken aback that he knew my name.

"Yes, that's about right," I replied, feeling uneasy.

"You don't remember me, do you Dr. Darrell?"

"Well, actually, I do, but I just can't quite put a name to the face," I responded pleasantly.

"I'm George, Dr. Darrell. George Thornton. I certainly remember you," he said slowly, but emphatically.

Then it came to me in a rush, the whole messy scandal. This young man facing me was the youngest of the three Thornton brothers. The middle son, Philip, always had health and mental issues, and his mother, Penelope, was a fragile creature with many of the same problems. The Thorntons had been farming in the area for hundreds of years, and owned a large estate and Clifton Hall, an 18th-century mansion about a mile south of the village. But the father, Montague Thornton, was very often away from home, being active in Conservative local and county politics for which he had received an OBE from her Majesty the Queen in 1973. Both George and his eldest brother, Sydney, were rather highly strung and unpredictable youngsters.

One winter's night, more than twenty years ago, there had been a big family argument and Philip had fatally stabbed his mother. He pleaded self-defense, and his brother George, a witness, supported him. But he was found guilty of murder. I gave evidence in the case describing the wounds and bruises on Penelope. The judge said he could not accept self-defense, as she had died from seven stab wounds. However, the Judge had called for a mental health assessment. Philip was found to be schizophrenic and sentenced to life in prison at Broadmoor, a psychiatric high-security mental hospital in Berkshire.

The murder scandal had divided the village. Many of the locals, knowing the highly strung, arrogant, and often unpleasant Penelope Thornton, had been sympathetic to Philip. I had come in for some considerable criticism from a number of the villagers for my part in this whole family saga. Many felt I should have been more forthcoming about Penelope and her problems. Shortly after the trial and judgment, the family left my practice for Dr. Archer, the other doctor in the village, and, within a year, George had left the village for Canada. Penelope Thornton had died from Alzheimer's about four years ago.

"Ah yes," I said with a smile, "of course, George. Are you visiting the family?"

"I am, as a matter of fact, Dr. Darrell," George responded. "I shall also be seeing my brother Philip. You remember Philip, Dr. Darrell? He's been in Broadmoor for over twenty years. You played a role in that, didn't you? But now, after years of treatment and good behavior, he is allowed some home visits. I haven't seen him for a very long time, so it will be good to catch up." He paused, perhaps waiting for my reaction, before continuing. I mumbled something about it being so many years ago, but I certainly felt there was something menacing about George. I felt uncomfortable, especially with the knowledge that this was a no corridor compartment. I was stuck with this man until we got to Woldingham.

"I don't think I will tell him that I met you on the train, as it might upset him," he gave a tight smile. I wasn't sure what to make of it.

"I recognized you as soon as I saw you get into the compartment in London."

"You did?"

"Actually, I followed you," he continued. "I wanted to study the man who'd been responsible for putting my brother in an institution for more than 20 years. You certainly jumped when I woke you up as we approached Salisbury station. Guilty conscience?" He paused, and chuckled, but I was rooted to the spot and couldn't come up with a response. Finally, we were approaching Woldingham Station.

"I believe you still live in that pretty pink thatched house on Forest Lane."

"Yes, actually I do…"

"Just you and your wife now."

"Well, yes, my children are all grown up and have left the nest," I responded lightly, trying to hide my uneasiness.

"I know, Dr. Darrell, I am very thorough and like to get my facts straight. As I did during my mother's trial. As I remember, I don't think you were as thorough."

He glared at me. "Perhaps we shall see you in the village over the weekend. Who knows?" He lowered the carriage window and opened the door from the outside.

And, then again with that strange smile, he said, "Have a good day, Doctor." He continued looking at me with those piercing grey-green eyes.

7 TILL DEATH DO US PART – 1980

The Hotel Splendido sits on a steep hill overlooking the beautiful bay of Portofino in Italy. Originally a 16th-century monastery, it was converted into a luxury hotel and opened its doors in 1902. By 1980 it had established itself as one of the finest luxury resort hotels in Europe—small, intimate, with only 64 rooms and suites, an excellent cuisine, swimming pool and tennis court, and a beautiful terrace overlooking the bay.

The hotel had sent a car to pick up Peter Thornton from the airport at Genoa, and he arrived late Thursday afternoon at the end of June. Peter and his wife Mary had been clients of the hotel for over 20 years, always spending the last week of June at the hotel. They enjoyed hiking in the hills behind the hotel that led down to the little town of Santa Margherita – across the bay from Portofino, playing tennis together, swimming in the pool, and walking down the steep hill to the little fishing port of Portofino, with its world-renowned colorful houses, restaurants, cafés, and shops.

The car pulled up to the portico of the hotel and Luigi, the hotel Manager, was waiting. "Welcome back, Signore Thornton. So good to see you again," said Luigi, grasping

Peter's hand and shaking it vigorously. "We're so happy to have you back here at the Splendido." Lowering his voice somewhat, he said in a somber tone, "We also are so sorry to have heard that Signora Thornton passed away. She was always such a pleasant and friendly lady, and certainly beloved by all our hotel staff."

"Thank you," said Peter. "It's been two years now, but life goes on. I wanted to return to the beautiful Splendido where Mary and I spent so many happy times."

"We shall do everything we can to make you as comfortable as possible," Luigi said as he walked Peter into the reception area. "We have a nice large room and balcony for you overlooking the bay, and Paola here will show you to your room and have your luggage delivered," Luigi continued as Peter completed the hotel registration form and handed it to a smiling young lady behind the reception desk.

Within a few minutes, Peter was ensconced in his room, which was indeed large and airy, beautifully decorated, with a little balcony overlooking the bay. He did not remember staying in this particular room on previous visits and was quite grateful for that. He didn't know how this vacation was going to work out without Mary at his side. The last time they had come together was three years earlier when her dementia was beginning to take a grip and her heart condition had slowed her down dramatically. Within a few weeks of returning from Portofino to London, Mary had passed away. For the last couple of years, Peter had no desire to go anywhere on vacation, and, although he spent time with his children and grandchildren, he really didn't want them to keep fussing over him, and this year he had declined an invitation to join them in a rented villa in the South of France. So here he was, all alone except for his books, ready to face a week of luxury, comfort, and good food.

Peter Thornton had been born in 1900 in Somerset where his family owned a large farming estate. He was too young to serve in the First World War and he was not going to inherit the estate because that would pass to his elder brother, Neil.

So, after studying the Classics at Oxford, he went off to India to work for his uncle, George Thornton, who owned a medium-sized tea plantation in the valleys of Bengal south of Darjeeling. Peter was a handsome, dashing, young man from England who enjoyed the social world of the plantations and also working for his uncle. He soon realized, however, that George, a bachelor, was an alcoholic and was doing a poor job of managing the estate. So, Peter had to learn quickly about every aspect of being a tea planter, and, within a couple of years, he was running the business.

As the heat of the summer became unbearable, the planters and their families would retreat to the mountains and the town of Darjeeling, where they enjoyed an active social season, waited on hand and foot by a large number of servants. In many cases the families came with their own entourage, servants, employees, and even furniture and moved en masse to their summer homes.

It was at one of the numerous dances at "The Planters Club" in 1924 that Peter first saw Mary. She was a slim "English Rose" beauty, a brunette with bright green eyes, dressed in the young "flapper" style of the times. Peter Thornton was a suntanned, fair-haired, athletic young man in white jacketed evening dress. Their eyes met across the room and she was soon in his arms, dancing the night away. Peter found out that, not only was she beautiful, but she had a bubbly personality. She was the daughter of Alexander Grant, the manager of a large syndicate-owned plantation estate, and, although she had been educated in England, she had returned to India two years previously.

Their romance quickly blossomed, and, early in 1926, they were married in Darjeeling and settled down at the Thornton Park Plantation, refurbishing a former manager's house. Over the next ten years, they had four children, three boys and a girl. In 1934, George Thornton passed away and left the plantation to Peter. He had already made significant strides in turning the plantation into one of the most efficient and profitable estates in the area. Normally the plantation owners sent their children back to England for their education, but, with a possible war looming, Peter and Mary did not want to do this. So, all their children were educated at the British schools in Darjeeling and the Thorntons stayed in India throughout the Second World War.

After the War, and Indian independence, the plantation continued to flourish, but life was not the same. The four children had all gone off to universities in England and were not going to return to India. So, in 1957, Peter and Mary decided to sell up and move back to England. Peter sold the Thornton Park Plantation to one of the large syndicate groups at a very good price, and they bought a pretty house in the country on the Kent-Sussex border, a flat in London on Sloane Street, and a small apartment in Antibes in the South of France. After spending nearly a year getting themselves established, in what was really a new country for both of them, Peter decided to get back to work. So, he founded Thornton's Tea Blenders, started going to the tea auctions at Mincing Lane, and created his own blends and brands of tea to sell to retailers, caterers, and hotels, which he did with some success. He enjoyed being back in the tea business, and grew his brands over the next fifteen years, until he was seventy-two, when he decided to sell out and retire. He and Mary then spent most of their time in the country, where they still hiked extensively. Peter played golf, they both played tennis, and they loved to work together in the garden. That was until Mary started to exhibit the symptoms of dementia and they found out in one of her annual checkups that she also had a congestive heart condition. Nevertheless, they both felt very blessed, with four great children and ten grandchildren, and they enjoyed a very comfortable lifestyle.

Armed with his John le Carré book, *Tinker Tailor Soldier Spy*, which had recently been turned into a very successful TV series starring Alec Guinness, Peter went down to the Terrace to enjoy a pre-dinner drink, a look around at the hotel guests, and the sun on the bay. After about half an hour, he heard the growl of a car coming up the steep zigzag road to the hotel. A red E- type Jaguar drove into the portico of the hotel and a tall, slightly windswept, tanned young man jumped out, followed by a slim young lady with a scarf wrapped around her head. Luigi came out to greet them. "Hello Luigi, my old mate," said the young man in a well-spoken but very loud British voice.

"So good to see you again," said Luigi.

Peter could not quite hear the name of the guests but he didn't have to wait long. "This lucky young beauty is going to be Mrs. Hugo Farnsworth in a couple of days – ha, ha, ha. May I present Ms. Lisetta di Marco." The group moved into the hotel and Peter Thornton returned to his book.

Mario, the maître d', presented Peter with the dinner menu, from which he chose parma ham and figs, grilled branzino with fried courgette sticks, and a stuffed tomato. The wine waiter came over with the wine list and he selected a glass of Gavi—no point in ordering a bottle or even a half bottle. A few minutes later he was escorted to a table for one, on the edge of the Terrace overlooking the Bay. The sun was going down behind the hills, and the lights in the few villas around the bay and on a large yacht, bobbing on the water, started to twinkle in the dusk.

Suddenly Peter felt very alone. There was no bubbly, chattering Mary at his side, no laughter, and no elegant hand reaching out for his across the pink table cloth. *"This is going to be much harder than I thought,"* he said to himself. Although Mario kept hustling back and forth, inquiring as to whether everything was all right, he passed his time listening to other people's conversations and looking at the elegant guests as they gradually filled up the restaurant on the terrace. There were two small tables on either side of Peter, one occupied by an English couple who hardly said a word to each other, and the other by a German couple very elegantly dressed in cream outfits, with the woman wearing plenty of jewelry, perfectly coiffed, talking animatedly to each other. Behind Peter was an Italian family, a husband, wife, and three children noisily having their dinner, with the table covered with wine bottles, Orangina and San Pellegrino, lots of laughter, and everybody talking at the same time. The children were dressed as elegantly as their parents. The food was delicious as always, but, even though he tried to take his time, he finished his meal in less than an hour. It was all too quick, but there was no reason for him to dither over his wine, so he got up and went into the hotel lounge, intending to get back into his book after ordering a cup of espresso coffee.

Farnsworth and Lisetta were sitting in a corner with a man and woman who it became clear were the banqueting managers for the hotel. "No," said Farnsworth in his loud voice, "we don't want to cut the cake at the beginning of the wedding dinner, but would like to do so just before the dessert and after the speech." Peter couldn't hear the response, but Farnsworth was raising his voice even louder. "I don't care what you think is normal. This is what we want, don't we sweetie?" he said, turning to Lisetta. Again, Peter could not hear her response. A couple of minutes later his voice raised again. "No, we want English Trifle, Zuppa Inglese, as the dessert. This was a favorite of my parents. I don't think it will be too rich, and I'm sure the chef can make it not too creamy."

Peter couldn't hear what the banqueting management was saying to him, but Farnsworth was quite irritated and getting louder. "No, it's really quite simple. The wedding cake can be sliced up and passed around to each table before the dessert is served, and the Veuve Clicquot can be served at the same time."

After a few minutes, the group was joined by two other gentlemen, and Peter quickly gathered that one was the photographer for the wedding and the other was the bandleader. Farnsworth again dominated the conversation with his voice carrying across the lounge. "Well, obviously I would like you to take a family group with the bride and groom; unfortunately, my family is quite depleted, but Lisetta has quite a few members of her family who will be attending the wedding. Luckily not all of them, because they nearly are a tribe on their own – ha, ha, ha. I would also like you to take photos of each table, and Lisetta or I will join some of our guests and you could take casual photos as the evening progresses and the dancing commences. It would also be wonderful to have a background photograph of the bay with the bride and groom and I presume you'll do that early while the light is good." Again there was a response that Peter could not hear.

"I am a keen photographer myself, and love my Leica M5. I've always preferred black-and-white, but these days color seems to be so good that I have been doing more and more. Anyway, I consider myself quite an expert, so I shall be keeping a close watch on you – ha, ha, ha." Peter heard the photographer say that he had done numerous weddings at the Splendido and he was sure that Mr. Farnsworth would be happy with the end result.

Farnsworth then turned his attention to the other gentleman, the leader of the band. "No, I prefer the reliable standards, you know Sinatra, Dean Martin, Tony Bennett, that sort of music. My parents loved that era and I grew up with it, so I love it too. I don't really want too much of that mushy Italian slow-moving dancing stuff. You don't mind sweetie, do you?" he said turning to Lisetta. Peter couldn't hear her response, but Farnsworth plowed on, asking to see a list of suggested song and dance tunes and questioned whether their band singer could speak English well enough.

He then talked about his speech. "Well," he said, "I was blessed by God with the ability of standing on my two feet and speaking without notes, concisely and clearly. Making speeches has never been a problem for me, but, since this is a small wedding, we've only got 65 guests, if they all show up – ha, ha, ha. I intend to keep the speeches down to really one, me. My best man, who is a wonderful chap, Harry Tillson, will propose a toast to the bride and groom and I will then respond. Lisetta doesn't want to say anything, do you sweetie? My speech shall take place when the band has a break and we cut the cake."

The conversation continued for a little while longer and then the group broke up, and Farnsworth and Lisetta headed for the terrace and presumably dinner. Peter's coffee had come and was getting cold because he had been absorbed in this one-sided conversation in the corner of the lounge. How could this lovely girl be marrying this totally obnoxious character? Peter decided that Farnsworth was dreadful and that she was going to make an awful mistake. He had the urge to go over to her and warn her, but of course he couldn't. Gradually the lounge filled up with other diners coming off the terrace. Then Enrico appeared and started playing the piano in the corner, as he had done for the past 25 years, and a gentle buzz settled over the lounge as people enjoyed coffee and after-dinner drinks. Peter ordered his usual Sambuca, and, after that was done, he decided to retire for the evening.

He had a fitful night tossing and turning in the dark bedroom. He woke up convinced that Mary was by his side and even reached out and started talking to her. As the sleep left him, he realised the stark truth, and he felt a blanket of gloom smother him. Later, while not knowing what time it was, he got up and moved over to the French doors to the balcony, which he opened, followed by the shutters, and was immediately blinded by the sunny scene. It was a perfect day, with a cloudless blue sky and the large yacht in the bay below, shimmering in bright sunlight.

He had decided the previous evening that he felt uncomfortable with the "table for one," and resolved to limit that experience as much as possible. So, he decided to order breakfast in his room. It was nearly 9 o'clock when his breakfast arrived, by which time he had shaved and put on shorts and a golf shirt with some canvas shoes. Breakfast was served on his balcony table and he settled down to read yesterday's Daily Mail newspaper and enjoy his breakfast.

After breakfast, he gathered up his John Le Carré, suntan lotion, and his sun hat for a morning on one of the little terraces above the swimming pool, shaded by ancient gnarled trees. He knew from past experience that it would be delightfully tranquil and peaceful. He got into the elevator and there she was, Lisetta, tall and slim, wearing short shorts exposing long tanned legs, and a square-necked silky white T-shirt. Her blonde hair was scooped under a large sun hat. Her face was partially covered by a large pair of round sunglasses. She wore no makeup, and her only jewelry was a twisted, gold bracelet, and a very large, square, diamond engagement ring.

"Good morning," Peter said. "Another beautiful day in paradise!"

She gave a little laugh. "Yes, it really is."

"Congratulations. I couldn't help overhearing your wedding plans."

Again, she laughed. "I'm sure the whole hotel heard about our plans. Hugo's voice can be overpowering sometimes." Peter noticed a slight accent, although her English was perfect. She seemed not only beautiful, but very natural. He wanted to scream at her. *Don't marry that man. It will be a disaster.* But of course, he didn't say that. What he did say surprised him.

"I was happily married for 51 years, until my wife passed away a couple of years ago. We were regular visitors to the

Hotel Splendido for more than 20 years. This is the first time I have come back since she passed away, and it is proving to be quite difficult." *Why did I say that to her?* he thought.

"How wonderful to be married that long! I can understand why it would be difficult to come back here after so many happy visits. I don't think I could even contemplate being married for 51 years," she ended with another laugh. "Well, I hope you have a nice day," she said with a broad smile as the elevator came to a halt and they both stepped out.

Peter saw Luigi in the reception area. "Good morning, Luigi."

"Good morning, Signore Thornton. We have another beautiful day."

"Absolutely delightful. Tell me Luigi, who is this Hugo Farnsworth?"

"Ah, Signore Farnsworth. He is the owner of Farnsworth Industries, which I believe is one of the largest companies in the UK. He inherited the business when his parents unfortunately died in a plane crash in Switzerland three years ago. He and his parents had been coming to the Splendido for some 25 years. They always came in mid-August, so not at the time that you and Signora Thornton visited us. Even as a very young man he was, how you say, boisterous." Peter knew Farnsworth Industries, a very large conglomerate in steel, glass, building supplies, and property.

"I gather he is getting married this weekend."

"Yes, tomorrow in a lavish wedding, even for the Splendido. He is marrying a lovely Italian girl, who I understand he met at a Trade Show in Milano. She will become Mrs. Farnsworth and will live a very comfortable life," Luigi continued with a chuckle. "We have guests and family members arriving all day today and some tomorrow. It is going to be quite an event."

"Well it will be fun to watch the proceedings and the

preparations. I'm sure you're going to have a very busy day, Luigi," Peter said. "I will leave you to it."

Peter went up to his little terrace under the trees and became engrossed in his John Le Carré book. He may have dozed off from time to time, but in any event, he heard, rather than saw, cars arriving and Farnsworth's loud voice greeting guests and family. He decided he did not want to have lunch in the restaurant and chose a seat at the pool bar, where he ordered a salad Nicoise and a glass of white wine. At the end of the restaurant terrace, he saw a lot of activity as the wait staff were setting up a long table, maybe for 20 to 24 guests. Three large candelabras had been put on the table and buckets of water full of flowers were in the shade, ready to be cut and placed on the table at a later hour. There were also a half a dozen free standing lanterns with candles inside to be lit later as well. This was obviously going to be a prenuptial wedding dinner of considerable elegance.

Peter went back to his book for the afternoon and, at about 4:30 p.m., as the pool emptied out, he decided to have his swim. Twenty minutes in the pool was really invigorating, after which he changed into another pair of shorts, went and sat on the bar terrace, and ordered tea. He had only been there for a few minutes before the English couple approached him and the lady said, "We've seen that you are on your own, and wondered whether you would like some company as we are about to order tea as well?"

Peter really didn't want company, he didn't want to make new friends – he was quite happy with his book and the beautiful surroundings – but it would have been rude to say no, so he responded, "Of course, please feel free to join me. I'm Peter Thornton."

The lady, dressed in a rather unattractive sundress covered in a floral design of oranges and green, introduced herself as they sat down. "I am Rosemary Wilson, and this is my husband Charles. We live in London, well, actually Wimbledon. Where are you from?"

"I spend my time between a small flat in Sloane Street and a cottage in the country in Sussex," responded Peter.

The Wilsons ordered their tea as Charles started the conversation, "Are you retired?"

"Yes. I am, but I keep quite busy, and you?"

"Yes. I'm a retired Lloyd's broker. Have you visited the Splendido before?"

"Yes, my late wife and I came here for 20 or so years, until she passed away three years ago."

"Oh, I'm sorry. It must be quite hard to return to familiar surroundings."

"Yes, as a matter of fact it's more difficult than I anticipated, but I am determined to enjoy it. After all, what could be more beautiful than this hotel and this spectacular view?"

"We agree with you, don't we Rosemary?"

"Oh yes. I've never stayed anywhere that is as beautiful as this," said Rosemary. "But there's not a lot to do. Charles and I don't really go hiking or play tennis so I think a few days here is quite enough."

It seemed obvious to Peter that Rosemary was not too happy with the hotel's lack of activities.

Changing the subject, Peter said, "There is going to be quite a luxurious English wedding here tomorrow."

"Yes, we know," replied Rosemary. "Hugo Farnsworth is marrying some Italian girl. He is a very wealthy man about town whose name is always in the papers in England. You obviously know about Farnsworth Industries."

"I know a little, but I don't really remember seeing much about Hugo Farnsworth in the press. Maybe I read the wrong newspapers," Peter responded with a soft laugh. "But apparently it's going to be a very lavish affair so we all have a chance to see the guests, the bride in all her finery, and, even though we are not invited, we will be able to listen to the music and festivities. It should be quite an event."

The conversation continued in this vein and eventually the Wilsons said they were going to retire to their room before getting dressed for dinner. Peter was quite relieved. He'd had enough of chitchat and, contrary to their offer to keep him company, he felt that he was company for them so as they had something to talk about, which clearly from last night's experience, they found difficult.

He took his time over the remnants of his tea before also retiring to his room. He had had quite a lot of sun, a lovely swim, and a pleasant day. He decided to have a nap before dinner because, as he learned from his experience of the previous night, it is far better to be a late diner than one of the early ones, since his meal would be served and consumed very quickly. It was nearly 9 p.m. when he came down for dinner dressed in pale gray trousers, a blue lightweight blazer, a dark blue silk shirt, and a matching tie. The restaurant was full, but he was shown to his table for one promptly, and he exchanged a little nod with the German couple a couple of tables away. The Italian family was hard at it with their table of five, looking like a feast was taking place, with wine, water, soft drinks, and the children bantering amongst themselves and with their parents.

He had a wonderful dinner—Gazpacho, rack of lamb, fresh vegetables, and, for dessert, he treated himself to a coconut gelato with biscotti. He washed it all down with another glass of Gavi.

He decided to have coffee on the bar terrace and a glass of Sambuca. The Farnsworth party had been going strong. There were 20 plus people, including some neat and tidy elderly Italians, who he decided must be Lisetta's parents and family. He took his time over his coffee and was listening to the tinkling of the piano in the lounge when the wedding dinner party started to break up. Suddenly he saw Lisetta coming towards him. She was a little flushed and tipsy. She came right up to him. "51 years," she said, "that must have been true love." Before he could respond, Hugo Farnsworth was at her side, grabbing her by the elbow and quite forcibly moving her back in the direction of the dinner guests walking down the terrace. He didn't say a word to Peter, but, as she started to make her way back under his firm grip, she turned and said, "Sorry, he is in one of his bad moods tonight."

The whole episode only took a minute at the most, but it certainly shot him out of his reverie. Farnsworth's behavior only confirmed Peter's fear that this marriage was going to be a disaster. The man was in a bad mood the night before his wedding! Not a good sign. What a shame, he thought, despite all the material comforts that she would enjoy once they were married, she will be giving up so much more to this loud obnoxious fellow. But, he reasoned, it was her choice.

Peter didn't sleep very well. The incident with Lisetta disturbed him. He was thinking of his long and happy marriage to Mary and all the wonderful experiences they had together and with their children. He didn't see Lisetta's life being anything like that. It made him appreciate how lucky he had been, but also brought on the veil of gloom that he still felt over her loss.

He got up late. It was another brilliantly sunny day. Not a cloud in the sky. What a wonderful day to get married, he thought. By the time he had breakfast on his little balcony, from which he could see the increasing hustle and bustle below as preparations were being made for the wedding, it was midmorning. He went down to the edge of the terrace restaurant and looked down on a grassy lawn area, where preparations were being made for the ceremony. He knew the small ballroom was right under the terrace restaurant, but it was obvious the ceremony was going to be held outside and probably the dancing would be outside later on as well. Large floral arrangements were being delivered and he saw the staff stringing up lanterns for later in the evening.

He turned to see Hugo and Lisetta greeting new guests as they were arriving—three or four car loads within the space of 10 minutes or so. There was a lot of laughing and Hugo's loud voice was overwhelming everything else. Peter made a beeline for his little shaded tree on the terrace above the pool and plowed into his John Le Carré. As always, he was engrossed in the complicated plot, but you have to focus and concentrate on all John Le Carré books to get the full benefit.

When he finally checked his watch, it was nearly 1 p.m. He decided he would not have lunch by the pool, but would instead get changed and take a walk down to the village and have lunch on the quayside in Portofino. Peter Thornton had been blessed with good health his whole life, and, even now at the age of 80, he had no major medical problems and only suffered some mild arthritis in his hands, knees, and feet. He was quite capable of handling the steep descent down the paved path, crossing the zigzag road a couple of times until he reached the back of the village on the plaza of the church, Divo St. Martin. This was a few paces from a small plaza ending in the quayside where the fishing boats were already tied up after their morning work, and the multicolored houses had their windows open with laundry hanging out. The cafés were doing a bustling trade with the tourists. Some large yachts were also moored at the quayside, and as he arrived he saw the ferry leaving the port on its way across the bay.

He found a café to his liking, sat down with the previous day's *Daily Mail*, and ordered a plate of tagliatelle with olive oil and pesto, a small salad and a glass of white wine. He watched the tourists and locals promenading up and down the quayside and took particular note of the fellow diners in the café. A man, probably around his age, with a shock of white hair and a large walrus mustache was sitting a couple of tables away. He had a large belly, but wisely had undone his black waistcoat, which he had over a white shirt and black trousers. He was weather beaten and very tanned, and he wore a black eye patch over one eye. *Corriere della Sera* was lying on his lap as he quietly snoozed in the sunshine. What a wonderful scene, Peter thought. He and Mary would have been so interested in this character and possibly even spoken to him.

After lunch, he wandered around looking at some of the shops and boutiques with their fancy clothes and fancy prices. He would definitely have to find some presents, always expected by his grandchildren, although his own children pleaded with him not to spoil them. However, it gave him much pleasure to find some little knick-knacks and souvenirs which they might like. But he wasn't going to purchase anything today. It was nearly 4 p.m. when he picked up the hotel shuttle bus which came down to the port every 15 minutes for the benefit of the guests who did not want to walk back up the steep hill to the hotel.

He glanced over the restaurant terrace wall and saw that the wedding preparations were well advanced. Sixty or so chairs were laid out on a wood block floor on the grass, facing an elevated stage on which were placed four, large, white columns wrapped in flowers. Paper lanterns and small lights had been strung around the edge of the lawn, which he assumed would be lit once the sun had gone down.

He knew that the ceremony was due to commence at 6:30 p.m., having heard the wedding planning arrangements a couple nights previously. He was sure that he, along with many of the hotel guests standing on the bar terrace, would be watching, so he went back to his room and, after taking a short nap, got himself dressed for the evening. At 6:15 p.m. he went down to the terrace bar and was not really surprised to see a lot of guests already perched on the edge, standing or sitting at bar tables ready to watch the proceedings. The Wilsons were there, as were the German couple and the Italian family. Everybody nodded and said good evening. He was given a little table which had a good view of the area below and ordered scotch and water, no ice.

All the wedding guests were seated and there was a string quartet seated next to the elevated stage playing soft classical music. Just after 6:30, Hugo came down the aisle, followed by his best man. He was smiling and nodding at everybody, and Peter had to admit, he looked really handsome and elegant in a white, evening dress jacket, black trousers, black bow tie, and even a black handkerchief in his breast pocket. Suntanned, with his hair slicked back, he was certainly a handsome picture of the bridegroom to be. He stood on the elevated stage with his best man next to him. About five minutes later, the quartet started playing Mendelssohn's wedding March, and Lisetta appeared on her father's arm and slowly walked down the aisle. She was wearing a white silk dress with a bodice covered in little pearls, pearl earrings on her ears, and a tiara of pearls and diamonds on her swept-up hair, with a chiffon veil covering her face. She had a maid of honor, following closely behind, making sure the train did not get caught on the woodblock flooring. There were flowers everywhere, and a little girl, maybe eight or nine, preceded her and her father, scattering white rose petals from a basket. She was very pretty and very serious. The Catholic Priest was already in place and, within a minute or so, the bride and groom were facing each other. The priest then commenced the wedding ceremony in English, following every sentence in Italian. It was the most beautiful scene with the background of the bay at Portofino. The sun was already going down behind the hills, and the wedding party was sheltered by the hotel and the hills, although the sun was still moving across the bay below. They exchanged their vows, "to have and to hold, in sickness and in health, for richer, for poorer, till death do us part." They then exchanged rings and were pronounced man and wife. Hugo lifted up Lisetta's veil and kissed her on the lips. The quartet started up again and the married couple walked slowly back up the aisle to the small ballroom below, to applause from the audience and even from the hotel guests looking down on the proceedings from the terrace bar.

Peter had been watching the wedding ceremony next to the Wilsons. On the other side of Rosemary Wilson was the German couple.

"What a spectacularly, beautiful event," said Rosemary. "It is not often that we have a ringside seat to a British celebrity wedding," she continued. "I really did not want it to end." She then turned to Peter. "Would you like to join us for dinner while the wedding party is enjoying dinner below us in the ballroom?" Peter hesitated, but then thought, this was one evening that he did not want to have a table for one on the edge of the restaurant terrace.

"Thank you, Rosemary," he said politely. "I would be delighted."

She then turned to the German couple and asked them the same thing. Peter thought they were taken aback a little but, maybe out of politeness, they accepted as well.

"Oh, how lovely. I shall arrange for a table for five with Marco. Just give me a minute or so," and off she scuttled after the Maître d' while Peter, the Germans, and Charles Wilson sat back in their bar chairs on the terrace. Rosemary returned with Marco in pursuit carrying five menus.

"Please take your time," he said to the group. "Tonight, we have lobster thermidor au beurre." In the meantime, the barman had come to see if they would like another drink and they all ordered another round. Wilson insisted on signing for it, which was very nice of him. Rosemary was clearly excited at her social victory and perhaps the thought of company other than her husband for the evening. Fifteen or twenty minutes later the waiter came to take their orders and everyone ordered either the lobster or another fish option from the menu. The Germans, who introduced themselves as Anke and Joseph Merkel, suggested Sancerre as a suitable accompaniment to the fish. After they placed their orders and finished their drinks, Marco escorted them to a table for five in the center of the terrace restaurant.

Rosemary was quite animated and talkative and eager to let her new guests know the details of the Farnsworth wedding. In short order, she found out that Joseph Merkel was a retired chief executive of Becks Brewery in Bremen and his wife was a pediatric doctor at the children's hospital in Bremen. Wilson was very eager to talk about the brewing industry and asked many questions. Merkel responded politely. The group was also very intrigued to hear about Peter's background in the tea industry and his life in India. Rosemary in particular was excited to meet the founder and owner of Thornton's Tea, which she assured everybody was her regular favorite brand.

Rosemary kept coming back to the wedding however. "What an enormous lifestyle-change for this lovely, little Italian lady. I wonder whether she'll be able to cope?"

"I think she's in her early to mid-30s, so she is not a child, and probably is stronger and more sophisticated than we think," said Anke.

"Well the wedding celebration is continuing tomorrow, you know," said Rosemary. "I gather Hugo has hired that enormous yacht in the bay below us and is taking about 50 guests on a champagne lunchtime cruise catered by the Splendido, and going to Santa Margherita, Rapallo, and somewhere else that I've forgotten. Can you imagine what that costs?" Neither Peter nor any of the other dining companions asked Rosemary how she came by that information, but she clearly was a person capable of wheedling out all sorts of details of this wedding celebration.

As they were eating their dinner they could hear soft popular classical music coming from the ballroom directly below them with the sound wafting out onto the wedding terrace. They were finishing their desserts when they heard

Hugo's voice making his speech, and, although nobody could hear clearly what he was saying, it elicited a lot of laughs and ultimately much clapping of approval. Wilson suggested that they "grab a couple of tables" on the bar terrace to watch the dancing. Everyone agreed and they moved to two tables on the edge of the terrace and ordered coffee and liqueurs. Anke Merkel did not seem to take to Rosemary and really had gone quiet as the dinner progressed. However, her husband Joseph continued with the polite conversation and he and Wilson seemed to get on quite well.

As they moved to sit at the little bar tables, they could see the changes made on the terrace below during dinner. All the lanterns around the terrace had been lit and the little stage where the wedding ceremony had taken place was now the bandstand. A six-piece band opened the evening with "*In the Mood.*" Hotel employees had set up roundtables of eight with large bowls of flowers on each table and chocolates and petit fours. The champagne was flowing again, along with other drinks. The guests seemed very merry indeed. The bride and groom then came onto the dance floor and started the dancing to the tune *"You were meant for me."* Farnsworth danced very well and indeed they looked like a celebrity Hollywood couple as they swished around the floor. Peter noticed that the music was exactly as Hugo had requested, namely 1930s and 40s romantic ballads and swing together with some soft jazz and a few songs from The Beatles and Elton John. It was indeed a beautiful spectacle and very pleasant for Peter's dinner group to sit and listen to the music under the stars with a balmy, soft breeze flowing over them.

At about 11 p.m., Joseph and Anke excused themselves and said they were heading for bed, as they were leaving early in the morning. They politely shook hands with the Wilsons and Peter. The waiters had been very discreet and somehow came up with three different bills and the Merkels were presented with their share, which they signed. It was such a lovely evening and Peter was enjoying the music, which incorporated all the favorites that he and Mary had enjoyed over the years. He remembered so many dances, so many galas, so many festive occasions and, of course, family weddings where this music had perfectly fitted the occasion. He wasn't in any hurry to retire. The Wilsons were obviously going to stay until the wedding broke up and Peter decided to do the same.

However, at 11:30 p.m., Hugo stood on the bandstand, thanked everybody for coming,graciously complemented his wife and her family, and said the celebration would end with a bang, and indeed that's what happened. Suddenly there was a whoosh and a rocket soared up from the yacht below in the bay, and, with a bang, sprayed a cascade of white stars. This was then followed by a spectacular 15-minute fireworks display with rockets whooshing and colors splashing reflections all over the bay. When it finally ended, everybody was standing and clapping. The guests started to drift away and Peter decided, as it was nearly midnight, it was time for him to take to his bed. He thanked Rosemary and Charles Wilson and said how much he had enjoyed the evening.

Peter slept late the following morning. It was after 10 a.m. by the time he had breakfast on his little balcony, but he could see and hear Hugo Farnsworth laughing and joking with many of his guests as they boarded two small coaches which Peter presumed were to take them down to the bay where the yacht was bobbing on the sundrenched water. Peter had decided to have a quiet day, it being Sunday. He knew there would be a lot of comings and goings with guests departing during the morning and new guests arriving during the afternoon. That was one of the reasons that over the years he'd always preferred to take his holidays starting and ending in midweek to avoid the crowds, the delays, and the crush.

He went up to his little spot on the terrace above the pool in the shade determined to finish his Le Carré. He had lunch at the pool bar, which was nearly empty due to the fact that it was between the arrivals and departures, and also had the pool nearly to himself for his daily swim. The weather continued to be perfect and he felt really healthy and relaxed after a few days at the Splendido. He was having a cup of tea on the terrace when the two coaches with the grinding of changing gears made their way up the hill to the courtyard of the hotel and deposited Hugo and Lisetta Farnsworth and their guests. He gathered from loud laughing, hugging, and kissing that a number of them would be leaving immediately, which was the case. Lisetta saw him sitting alone and gave him a little wave and a broad smile, which he returned. Hugo put his arm around Lisetta and they were entwined like any young lovers should be. He went up to his room after tea, had a nap, and later came down for dinner, and he was happy to avoid the Wilsons who were deeply in conversation with another English couple who he believed had just arrived. To his relief, they were going to dine together and, although Rosemary gave him a smile and wave, she did not ask him to join them. On this occasion, he decided that a table for one would be manageable.

The Farnsworths appeared in the restaurant, arm-in-arm, smiling and happy, and Peter thought, even more deeply tanned after their day on the yacht. They were joined by eight other friends who were probably the last of the guests staying another night at the hotel. It was a much quieter and subdued group as one would expect after all the excitement of the weekend. He enjoyed another excellent meal: asparagus, followed by Escalope Milanese, fried zucchini, and another glass of the excellent Gavi. After dinner he had his usual coffee and Sambuca on the terrace bar but was pleased to retire early to his bed. He decided that his years were catching up with him after all; he needed his sleep.

The following morning, he had breakfast on his balcony, dressed in shorts and heavy sneakers for a short hike into the hills that he knew well, to where there was a bench with a beautiful panoramic view. It was less than three km up a gentle undulating trail from the hotel. But then he saw Hugo and Lisetta saying goodbye to the last few guests. Hugo's voice, as usual, overpowered everyone. He and Lisetta were dressed for hiking with boots, small backpacks, and Hugo had his Leica around his neck. They both had sun hats and water packs, which were very sensible, as Peter knew they would feel the heat of the day before they returned. He presumed they would be taking the trail over the mountain to Santa Margarita.

He would let the Farnsworths commence their hike ahead of him, as he really did not want to bump into them on the trail. So, he took his time and followed about 20 minutes after they had left.

The magnificent morning was sunny, but with a cool breeze. He took his time, feeling his age, but enjoying the exercise. After about 45 minutes he arrived at the panoramic view and the comfortable bench. He saw nobody else on the trail and sat down to rest and take in the spectacular scenery. After a minute or two, he heard Farnsworth's voice shouting, somewhere up the trail. From his vantage point, the trail began to slowly zigzag up to a steeper level. He was inquisitive to see what was going on. Presumably Farnsworth and Lisetta had taken their time, possibly taking photographs of the scenery. He slowly made his way up the trail and the shouting became louder. He did not hear any response from Lisetta. He came to a turn in the trail behind a promontory of rocks and flowers and suddenly saw them about 40 meters up ahead. Farnsworth was on one knee on the edge of the trail, leaning over rather dangerously, with his Leica camera photographing what Peter knew from experience was a wall of white bougainvillea, a really beautiful sight as the bushes made their way down the steep drop. Peter also knew that, if Farnsworth and Lisetta had gone on another 50 meters or so, they would have been able to look back on the wall of bougainvillea from a higher vantage point—a much less dangerous opportunity to get the photograph that they wanted. Farnsworth stood up and was right in Lisetta's face, shouting again. Peter moved back into the shadows.

"I don't care," he said, "you are now Mrs. Hugo Farnsworth, and you will bloody well do as I want." He was red-faced and angry and it was obvious the argument had been going on for quite some time. Peter could not hear Lisetta's response, but could see she had tears streaming down her cheeks and her body was shaking with sobs. There was nothing Peter could do, but he felt concern for this new young bride. Whatever she said ended the conversation, because she suddenly turned and started to walk away.

"There you go again," shouted Hugo, "another sulking, little girl performance. Sometimes you make me sick. Things will have to change, Lisetta," continued Hugo, still angry as she walked away. "You can no longer behave like an Italian peasant. You're married to me, and you have to learn to behave accordingly. I am not going to put up with this." Lisetta did not respond.

Then Fansworth went down on one knee and was taking shots again with his Leica.

Lisetta was now 20 meters up the trail, but she turned and Peter could see the tears which streaked her cheeks. She was also angry. She stood for a minute, looking at Hugo, not saying a word, and then she suddenly walked purposefully down the trail, right up to him, and, as he started to rise from his one knee, holding his Leica, she lifted her hiking boot and kicked him hard in the shoulder, and, to Peter's horror, he went over the side. There was a thump, but no other sound that Peter could hear as he fell about 10 meters and then presumably bounced out into the steep canyon. Peter was rooted to the spot. He couldn't believe what he had just seen. He was shaking. Lisetta was on her knees sobbing.

After a few moments, he decided there was nothing to be done, so he turned and went down the trail as quickly and quietly as possible. As he did so, out of the corner of his eye, he thought he saw Lisetta look up and see him. He continued shakily to head back to the panoramic view bench and then continued down the trail to the hotel. He went straight up to his bedroom, took off his shoes, and flopped on the bed. His heart was pounding and he was shaking from head to toe. What should he do? He knew that sooner or later the police would be coming and possibly he would be questioned.

He didn't have any lunch and was too shaken up to go down to the terrace. An hour or so later he heard police sirens. An ambulance and police car arrived in the courtyard. He was feeling a bit stronger now and thought it would be more questionable if he did not appear, so he showered and put on a fresh shirt, slacks, and loafers and went down stairs.

"What's going on?" Peter asked Rosemary, who was standing on the edge of the terrace watching the proceedings.

"Oh Peter," she replied clearly upset. "There's been a terrible accident. Apparently, Hugo was taking a photograph on a rocky and dangerous part of the trail, slipped, and fell into the ravine. He could be dead. The ambulance people have gone to find him and poor Lisetta is absolutely overwhelmed." She paused, "Can you imagine? They've only been married for two days."

"Well, this is just awful," Peter said. "I know from experience that there are some dangerous spots on the trail. Let's hope that his fall was not fatal."

Lisetta had been talking to a policewoman, but now the woman, gently holding her arm, took her back into the hotel, presumably to her room to get out of her hiking clothes and freshen up. There was nothing they could do until they found out what had happened to Hugo.

"Peter, do join us for tea?" asked Rosemary. "This is so awful I think we all need to stick together." Peter didn't necessarily understand this logic but he agreed out of politeness. He had decided that Rosemary for all her nosy and busybody personality had genuine concern for fellow human beings and particularly the young lovers whose wedding they had shared just two nights ago. There was lots of noise coming from the ambulance and police cars, with walkie-talkies squawking and fast-talking Italian going on. But within half an hour, two men from the ambulance arrived back in the courtyard, escorted by a policeman holding a Leica, carrying a body on a stretcher. It was completely covered by a sheet.

"Oh no," said Rosemary, with tears welling up. "The worst has happened. How terrible for that poor young woman. How could she ever recover from this experience? Just two days into her marriage with all the beauty and style of the lavish wedding still fresh in her mind." Wilson put his arm around his wife's shoulder, in the first sign of any affection Peter had seen between them, and said, "Now, now love. There is nothing we can do." For some reason they stood up to see the ambulance men load the body into the ambulance at the same time as Lisetta, looking pale and fragile, came back into the courtyard helped by the policewoman. The ambulance doors closed and Lisetta climbed into the back of one of the police cars. The sirens started, and the police car slowly left the courtyard to go down the hill.

Peter had dinner in his room on his little balcony. He was too distraught and nervous to go down to the restaurant. He slept very poorly, tossing and turning, reliving the scene on the trail and worrying about any police enquiries that he may face. What would he do if the police asked him directly if he had seen what happened or if he knew anything about "the accident"?

He was up early next morning. He had just finished his breakfast when there was a knock on the door. It was Luigi. "Good morning, Signore Thornton," he said with a polite smile. "I'm very sorry to disturb you, but the police are still here looking into yesterday's tragedy and they would like to speak to you, as they know you went for a hike on the trail after the Farnsworths had left the hotel. Would you be good enough to come down to the lobby when you're ready, Signore Thornton?"

"Of course, Luigi. I shall be down there shortly." He closed the door.

Peter sat on the bed. He was sweating and shaking. The police would only have to look at him to know his guilt. What was he going to do? Lisetta was well rid of her abusive husband. He knew life with him would have been a nightmare. One of Peter's granddaughters, Laura, was not much younger than Lisetta. What would he do if Laura made a terrible mistake in her choice of husband and took a similar path to extract herself from the marriage? Would he tell the police or give Laura a second chance? He thought about Mary's reaction and even asked for her advice as he often did when he faced troublesome decisions. But should he help Lisetta and risk becoming an accessory to the murder? He tried to pull himself together gathering strength and, after about ten minutes, he went down to the lobby. He had no idea how he would respond.

"Ah Signore Thornton. May I present Inspector Menorini, who would like to ask a few questions about yesterday's tragedy." The Inspector was a tall, slim, stooped man perhaps in his late 50s with thinning, grey hair and a thick moustache, and, as Peter noted, nicotine-stained fingers. He held a little white notepad and was busy scribbling.

"Of course, Inspector," said Peter, surprised that his voice sounded so firm and confident. "How may I help you?"

"Signore Thornton, I understand you were hiking on the trail at the same time as the Farnsworths."

"Well, Inspector, I don't think it was the same time. They left the hotel about 20 minutes before me and I don't move very fast these days," he said with a smile. "They must have been well ahead of me." The Inspector paused and wrote on his notepad.

"How did you know they left about 20 minutes before you?"

"I was having breakfast on my balcony and I saw them." Peter gulped before the Inspector continued.

"Did you see or hear anything of the Farnsworths on the trail?"

"No, Inspector, I walk very slowly and I only went up to the panoramic view where there is a bench, less than three kilometers from the hotel. I rested there for a while and then came back again. I have to confess Inspector," Peter said with a little chuckle, "even that exertion was a bit too much for me and I was exhausted. I went straight to my room and rested for a couple of hours. It was only when I came downstairs to the terrace that I heard about this tragic accident."

"Yes, Signore Thornton," said the Inspector, "indeed, a tragic accident. Did you see anyone else on the trail?"

" No, Inspector. Not a soul. I enjoyed the peace and tranquility," responded Peter.

"Any shouting, or a scream, as Mr. Farnsworth plunged into the ravine?"

Peter gulped again but held himself together. "No, Inspector. Nothing."

The Inspector paused and wrote on his notepad. Peter's heart was pounding.

"Signore Thornton, that bench, which I know well, is only about 60 meters from where Mr. Farnsworth went over the side of the trail into the canyon below. It is where there is a wall of beautiful white bougainvillea. You know the spot, Signore Thornton?"

"I do, Inspector. I did not realize that was where the accident happened. My wife and I came to the hotel for more than 20 years, and we loved to hike the trail all the way over to

Santa Margarita. It is very beautiful, but it was a little too far for me to go to see the bougainvillea as the trail gets quite steep once you pass the bench."

"Can you tell me what time you left the hotel and arrived at the bench, Signore Thornton?"

Peter didn't like the way these questions were going.

"I think I left the hotel about 10:40. I didn't look at my watch when I got to the bench but I did walk slowly, taking my time and enjoying the scenery and the fresh air, so probably it was about 11:30 or 11:45."

"And how long did you stay?"

"Only about 10 minutes, Inspector. The panoramic view is really beautiful, but there was a cool breeze and I started to feel a bit chilled, so I walked back down the hill to the hotel." Peter realised he was putting himself more and more into the quagmire and, even though he felt he was sounding confident and relaxed, his stomach was churning.

"Do you know what time you came back into the hotel?"

"No, Inspector, I am not sure. But probably around 12:30."

The Inspector was scribbling in his notepad. But then he gave Peter a slight smile.

"Thank you so much, Signore Thornton, for your help."

With that he shook hands with Peter and departed. Peter went back to his room and flopped on the bed again as his body and mind gradually calmed down. He hoped that would be the end of it. An hour later there was a knock on the door. He opened the door to find Lisetta standing there. She looked pale, drawn and exhausted. "May I come in, Mr. Thornton?"

"Of course, please do," said Peter.

She then flung her arms around Peter's neck and started sobbing. He held her tightly. Eventually, she calmed down.

"I'm so sorry, Mr. Thornton. I made a terrible mistake. I couldn't take it anymore. Hugo was more abusive than ever. I acted on the spur of the moment. I didn't know what I was doing. But I want to thank you from the bottom of my heart. You are my saviour and I shall never forget you."

Peter held her hand. So she had seen him. He was not really certain whether this had been a spur of the moment decision, as he remembered her purposely walking back to Hugo, lifting her long, suntanned leg and using considerable force, kicking him on the shoulder with her hiking boot.

But he had made his own decision.

"Lisetta, sometimes life gives you a second chance. Not always, but sometimes. It's what you do with those second chances that counts. I hope you have a long and happy life, and find the perfect partner, as I did."

8 MIAMI NICE – 1983

The heat and humidity hit him like a wet towel as he came out of Miami International Airport. He was dragging his luggage and his airline briefcase, full of samples. He hailed a cab and opened the door. He felt a sense of relief as he took his seat. The taxi was air-conditioned. He gave the driver directions.

"Fontainebleau Hotel," he said.

"Never heard of it," came the reply from the balding, middle-aged driver.

"You must have," Keith said, incredulously. "It is a very large resort hotel. They're having a big convention for the Wine and Spirit industry."

At that moment, as they were driving out of the airport, there was a big outdoor advertising board which said, "Welcome to Wine and Spirit Wholesalers of America," and underneath, "Fontainebleau Hotel, Miami Beach."

"There," he said to the driver.

"Oh, you mean the Fountain Blue," said the driver in a drawn-out Southern accent. "Sure, no problem. We will be there in about forty-five minutes."

"Thank you," he said, sinking back into his seat with relief.

Keith Benton had never been to the United States and had no idea what Miami would be like. He knew it would be warm and sunny, but he was not prepared for the high humidity after leaving a chilly London only ten hours earlier. Keith, at the age of twenty-nine, had recently been appointed managing director of E and L Masters Limited, known as Masters of Plymouth, Distillers of Plymouth Gin. He got the job because the long-serving managing director, Fred Thomas, had died of a heart attack three months earlier. Keith had been with the company just over two years, as national and international marketing director. This was a fine-sounding title, but the business was suffering a gradual decline in most of their markets. But Keith redesigned the packaging, which had remained unchanged since 1959, and hired a couple of female salespeople. This caused the Board of Directors to nearly drop dead on the spot, but it had been very successful in resuscitating sales in southwest England, the company's major market.

He also increased the marketing budget for international sales. Soon, they were seeing improvements in France, Italy, Germany, and many countries in Africa and Asia. Masters did no business in the United States. But when he had suggested, four months ago, that the company should participate in the WSWA in Miami, the board was skeptical. The "chairman", Eunice Pettigrew, was nervous about sending Keith to Miami, on what she thought might be an expensive wild goose chase. Her cousin, Charles Pettigrew, was even more critical.

"I don't think the United States is interested in Plymouth Gin," he said at the December board meeting. "I visited that market and tried to interest a number of importers, but found no success."

"When was that, Charles?" said Keith.

"1937," came the reply. Keith bit his lip and did not respond, determined to move forward with his plans.

E and L Masters had been established in 1610, on the

quayside at the old Plymouth dock from where the Mayflower had sailed to America. In 1825, the business had been sold to the Thornton family, descendants of the first Lord Marsden, owner of a very large estate, just north of Plymouth, which had been granted to him by the Duke of Marlborough after the battle of Blenheim. For the past seventy-five years, the ownership of the company had been passed down through the female side of the family. The males in the family had died in various wars, including Afghanistan, South Africa, and The Great War.

Eunice Thornton Pettigrew had taken over the "chairperson" responsibilities in 1945, having been on the board since the 1930s, along with her cousin Charles. The business had prospered on the back of contracts with the British naval shipyards at Plymouth, and had a strong market in the pubs, hotels, and resorts in the west of England. However, increasing competition from the major brands, supermarkets, and gradual declining demand from the shipyards had led to a steady decline of Masters' fortunes.

Keith had grown up in Plymouth. His father worked in the shipyards as a welder, and his mother was a "dinner lady" at a large school in North Plymouth. Neither he nor his sister, Louise, who was two years older, had gone to university. He was a bright boy and had left school with two "A-levels," and got a trainee job at Theakston Brewery in Exeter, in the sales and marketing department. He had taken an evening course in Marketing at Exeter University. Louise, talented and creative, had moved to London at the age of eighteen, and was working in advertising.

Keith was tall, slim, and nice-looking, with brown, curly hair, gray eyes, and a winning smile. He had an outgoing personality and was quite a good athlete, playing soccer every weekend for a local amateur team, Alston Rovers. He had plenty of girlfriends, but none had been the "right one" so far. Two years ago, he moved back to Plymouth and joined E and

L Masters. From that point on, he had been working flat-out trying to turn the business around. He had very little time for romance.

The taxi arrived at the hotel and Keith entered the enormous lobby. It was bustling with columns of people checking in for the convention. He had never been in such a large hotel. He started to feel some trepidation. When he checked in, he was given a WSWA package with his name on it. He did not have a room overlooking the beach, but he did have a beautiful view of the inland waterway. He was amazed at the amount of homes, boats, yachts, and massive cars. And the people! The men were dressed in brightly colored shirts and many were in shorts and sandals. The young women were dressed similarly, in shorts, sandals, and cut-off tops.

As Keith looked through his package, he found a label to be attached to his clothing during the convention. "Keith Benton, Masters of Plymouth, England." Flipping through the brochures, he found the program for the next three days, as well as information about different events. This included an opening night reception due to take place in just under two hours. He unpacked his clothes, as well as the advertising and marketing materials for Masters Plymouth Gin. The convention package also listed all the wholesalers, suppliers and importers, including their suite numbers, as many of them had signed up for "hospitality" suites.

He rested for an hour. Realizing it was already near midnight in the UK, he began to dress for the reception. He put on his gray suit, white shirt, red-and-blue tie, and, of course, his name tag. He went down into the main ballroom and passed through a bustling throng of industry members and their wives. Everyone was dressed up for the evening, greeting each other with slaps on the backs, laughter, handshakes, and hugs. Many were already lined up at three large square dining stations in the middle of the glitzy ballroom, being served everything from sliced roast beef to

Italian ravioli, salads, and cheeses. Some of the guests picked up their food and their choice of spirits or wines and found seats at some of the little tables around the ballroom, busily engaged in conversation and laughter. There were six bars around the gigantic ballroom, all serving the major premium brands of spirits and wines.

After getting a Gordon's Gin and Tonic, Keith started to wander around, noting the names on the tags. He was nodding and smiling and saying "hi" to people that he didn't know. Every now and then, he picked out a tag from one of the English distillers and stopped to talk. Their faces, however, were not very friendly. One person from Haig and Haig even said he was surprised that Masters of Plymouth was still in business. Not very encouraging! He also stopped to talk to a couple of importers that he'd seen on his list. He introduced himself as the marketing director of Masters and asked if he could meet with them to discuss possible representation. On the whole, they were quite friendly, but not altogether forthcoming. A few suggested setting up a meeting. Keith was anxious to grab anything possible, and he was eagerly exchanging business cards.

Gradually, the crowd was thinning out as the reception was nearing its end. It was then that he received a tap on the shoulder. He turned around to face a striking, dark-haired, young woman. "Hi," she said. "I'm Angie Moreno, from Moreno Brothers in New York."

"Hi," Keith said, surprised.

"I saw you walking around, and it looks like you don't know many people. Have you been to a WSWA convention before?" She had an alluring smile. She wore a black dress with a scooped-out square neckline, revealing a suntanned body. Her black hair was pulled back in a ponytail, and she wore gold hoop earrings. She had little makeup, apart from mascara covering her large, brown eyes. Her lips were generously covered with bright red lipstick, matching a belt around her slim waist. She was tall in her high-heeled satin shoes.

For a moment, Keith was overwhelmed by her sudden appearance, in the midst of a generally older and rather staid crowd. However, he quickly found his voice. "Yes, you're right," he responded. "I am Keith Benton, and this is my first WSWA. I don't know anyone. I have been walking around trying to make contacts that might help me get something going for my brands of gin and vodka."

"Oh?" she said.

Keith nodded eagerly. "Yes, I am the managing director and marketing director of Masters of Plymouth."

"I don't think I've heard of it."

"Well, we are a very old distillery from Plymouth, in England. My job here is to try and find an interested importer who will give us a chance to develop our brands in the United States. It is a challenge, but we have to start somewhere," he said with a big smile that seemed to make an impact on Angie.

"Well, we have four houses in New York, Atlanta, Miami, and recently Boston, so we are pretty well established," she said casually. Keith was confused.

"Why do you need four houses?" he said with a puzzled look on his face.

Angie laughed loudly. "Not residences. These are wholesaler houses that we own. Boy, you really do have a lot to learn!"

"Oh, now I understand," said Keith. "So, you're a wholesaler?"

"Yes, I am national marketing director, and we are number four in the US. Maybe if you're very good, I could help you get some business done," she said cheekily.

"That would be fantastic, Angie," responded Keith enthusiastically. "I would really appreciate any help you could give me."

"Okay, Keith. Why don't we meet after the business

session tomorrow morning at our cabana by the pool? I will take you to have lunch at one of our hospitality suites and introduce you to my father. You can give him your samples and anything you have on your company. You can get his advice on possible representation."

"That would be great," said Keith. He was excited at a real prospect. "But excuse my ignorance... what is a cabana?"

Angie laughed again. "A cabana is a private air-conditioned tent around the main swimming pool. Some of the major wholesalers use it as meeting spaces for their own executives, or to meet with suppliers. There are plenty of comfortable seats, and, of course, a large bar. Our cabana number is 115. I'm sure you will find it."

"Thanks, Angie," said Keith again, putting on his winning smile. "I look forward to seeing you in the morning. Now, I have to confess, I am really exhausted. It's been a long day."

Angie looked somewhat disappointed. "Sure," she said. "I understand. Have a great night's sleep and I will see you in the morning."

They were among the last people in the ballroom as members of the staff cleared the food and drink stations. Keith shook Angie's hand firmly and leaned in and gave her a peck on the cheek. They walked out of the ballroom together and went their separate ways. Twenty minutes later, Keith was in bed in a deep sleep.

He woke up early because of the jetlag, and, at 7 a.m. with the sun coming up, he decided to take a jog along the beach. It was a beautiful day, and the sea was calm, the waves lapping quietly on the sands. He got dressed in sneakers, shorts, and a T-shirt and eventually found his way out of the hotel and onto the white Miami Beach. There was plenty of company. Runners, walkers, and guests of the hotel were already spreading out on the large loungers and under the umbrellas. He could not believe how beautiful this early morning scene was. He thought: *If this is America, I'm definitely in love with it.* He had never experienced anything like this before—the hotel, the beach, the size of everything, the prosperity, and the camaraderie of the WSWA convention. So far, he was loving every minute of it. And as a bonus, he had met this stunning girl, who he hoped could help him land some orders. In short, he was in heaven. He jogged and walked for about forty minutes and then made his way back to his hotel room. He put on a pair of tan casual trousers, an open-necked blue shirt, and his identity tag. He had an enormous American breakfast, and, by ten a.m., he was ready for the first business session of the WSWA. He found it all very interesting and took copious notes.

The session came to an end at noon, and the wholesalers disappeared. He quickly found cabana 115. Angie was there, dressed in white pants and a bright red blouse. Her hair was swept up on her head. She had long, white enamel earrings and no other makeup, other than mascara. Keith thought she was very attractive, and he wanted to spend more time with her. He was determined to use his English charm as much as possible, not only on her, but also on her father and the business executives of Moreno Brothers. She approached him with a big smile. "Good morning, Keith. How was the business session? I don't bother going to those anymore. They are pretty boring." Before he could answer she continued, "I would like to introduce you to my father, Anthony Moreno."

She grabbed Keith by the hand and led him over to the back of the spacious and cool cabana. "Pa, this is Keith Benton. Remember I told you about him? He's the managing director of Masters of Plymouth, an old, established English gin company. He is looking for representation in the US market."

Anthony Moreno was a large, good-looking, fleshy man, about six feet tall, overweight, but with a handsome face and a mane of gray-white hair. He had a dark suntan and piercing brown eyes. He was dressed in a white tunic-style silk shirt over beige silk trousers and brown crocodile shoes.

"Pleased to meet you, Keith. Welcome to America."

"I am pleased to meet you, sir," said Keith in his best English. "Thank you so much for giving me some time during your busy day."

"I'd like to introduce you to my brother, Rudy, and my son, Frankie," Anthony continued.

Rudy was a slightly hunched, much slimmer version of his brother Anthony, with black hair, graying at the temples, and was wearing a cream silk suit and a pale blue shirt. He had darting brown eyes. He shook hands with Keith and mumbled something which Keith didn't hear or understand. Frankie was a tall, handsome young man, wearing dark glasses. He had his father's thick mane of hair, except that his was jet black. He was wearing white pants and a black shirt. He had a gold cross around his neck, revealing a hairy and deeply tanned chest.

"Hi, how ya doin'?" he said as he gripped Keith's hand in a firm handshake.

"Pleased to meet you, Frankie," responded Keith. "I'm doing well and enjoying the convention."

"That's great," Anthony chimed in. "Angie tells me you have a nice line of gin and vodka."

"Yes, that is true. Let me show you my samples." Keith opened his airline bag and took out a .75 cl bottle of Masters Plymouth Gin, a bottle of Masters 1610 Gin, and a bottle of Masters Vodka.

"Nice packaging," said Anthony.

"Thank you, sir," said Keith. "We upgraded and redesigned the packaging a couple of years ago, and it seems to be well received."

"Well, I always think packaging is very important," said Anthony. "Do you have a company brochure or anything like that?"

"Yes. Right here," responded Keith, handing Anthony a glossy color brochure. "I also have a dozen miniatures split between the three different products, if that would be of interest to you."

"Yeah" said Anthony thumbing through the brochure. " Also, I would like to see your pricing."

Wow, Keith thought, *this is going well.* Keith took out another sheet of paper from his airline bag. This was the export pricing for all of the products.

"Well, thank you Keith. We'll have some tastings with Rudy, Frankie, and my other people. They're here somewhere at the convention. Perhaps we can get together again after the business session tomorrow morning, and I'll let you know our thoughts. Who knows, maybe we can help you?"

"That would be wonderful, Mr. Moreno. Thank you so much for your consideration," responded Keith. His heart was pounding with excitement.

"Now, Angelina, sweetheart, why don't you take our young friend to lunch on the Seagram's yacht? Just tell them that Keith is a guest of ours. I am sure he'll have no problems."

Turning to Keith, he said, "Seagram's hospitality is outstanding. We'll join you in about half an hour or so."

"Okay, Pa," said Angie. "See you then." With that, she took Keith's arm and guided him out of the cabana. Then they started to make their way through the hotel lobby towards the exit.

"I think my dad liked you," she said. "And he was impressed with your presentation. He might be able to help you. He is not the only one who likes you, by the way," said Angie, smiling and holding Keith's arm more tightly.

"Angie, I can't thank you enough. Without you, I would be like a fish out of water. I wouldn't know really where to start. Incidentally, I also like you Angie. You've been great. Perhaps we could spend the evening together."

"I would like that, and maybe tomorrow as well?"

They walked across the street to a beautiful motor yacht, which Seagram had rented for their hospitality suite. It was about ninety feet long. The upper deck was open to the skies. The rear part of the middle deck was covered with a large canopy and connected to an enormous state room. Keith could see quite a few people mingling, both under the canopy and in the state room. Drinks were being passed around. They crossed the small gangplank and were met by a receptionist at a high desk who checked Angie's convention tag off a list and looked at Keith's. Angie told her that Keith was a guest of the Moreno organization. The receptionist smiled and said, "Welcome to Seagram."

Angie seemed to be well-known among the wholesalers and suppliers, many of whom hugged and kissed her. People smiled at her and asked how she was doing. She laughed and joked. She introduced Keith to them in a whirl of names that didn't really sink in. Everyone was friendly and relaxed. Keith could not believe the beauty and luxury of the yacht. He thought he would have to pinch himself. Here he was, little Keith Benton from the wrong side of the tracks in Plymouth, Devon, now standing on this beautiful yacht in Miami, in the sunshine, with the leaders of the beverage alcohol industry in the United States.

The two bars on the deck under the awning had a wealth of different brands, all Seagram's of course. He thought he would try a Boodles Gin, but he didn't really like the taste, and so he opted for Mumm's Champagne.

Angie was mingling effortlessly with all her peers. "Come on, Keith, let's get something to eat," she said, grabbing him by the hand. Inside the main state room were two large trellis tables with enormous buffets of seafood and salads. There were chefs making omelets and carving beef, hamburgers, hot dogs, and ribs. Keith chose a lobster salad. Angie took a green salad with a hot dog and a couple of ribs and then steered Keith out of the state room and onto the deck, toward a cluster of small tables with pink tablecloths. She found a spot for them both, and they sat down and started to enjoy their lunch.

Fifteen minutes later, Anthony Moreno arrived with his entourage, including Rudy and Frankie. Their arrival created a stir. Clearly they held an important position as one of the largest wholesalers in the United States. Anthony went to the state room. In one corner, Edgar Bronfman was greeting various industry leaders. Keith saw Anthony grip Edgar by the hand and give him a hug at the same time. Surrounded by his brother, son and VPs, they stood in a huddle with Bronfman and some of his senior people. They grabbed some drinks and came out onto the deck, where they saw Angie sitting with Keith.

"Well, son, what do you think? Do you have any yachts on the quayside in Plymouth that can compete?" he said with a laugh.

"No, sir. I've never seen anything like this. It is truly amazing. Thank you for being so hospitable and making it possible."

"You will have to thank Seagram's for the hospitality," Anthony said. "Those guys really know how to put on a party. No expense spared. Of course, we are one of their largest wholesalers."

"Really?"

"We account for a significant volume of Seagram's annual sales, so you can see why they look after us," Anthony said with some pride.

"I'm sure you do a great job for them," said Keith politely.

Anthony turned to Angie. "Well, sweetheart," he said. "This young man certainly knows how to turn on the English charm. You can always be counted on to pick a winner." He was smiling broadly.

"Of course, Pa, I am my father's daughter," she replied, laughing.

"Well, we're going to grab a quick bite to eat and then we're off to meet other suppliers. But you guys enjoy yourselves here and have a good afternoon and evening. Keith, I'll see you at the cabana after tomorrow morning's business session. And then we'll see what we can do for you."

"Thank you so much, sir. I shall be there. I hope you have a nice evening."

With that, Anthony and his entourage began to mill around the industry members for about half an hour, grabbing things off the buffet. Then they disappeared back onto the quayside.

When Angie and Keith had finished lunch, she said, "I'm afraid I've got some work to do this afternoon. But I would love to get together with you for the evening. How about going to a great seafood restaurant on the inner waterway? They also have some music and dancing. I'm sure you'll enjoy it. How does that sound?" she said with a little laugh. "I will make the reservation and we could meet in the lobby at seven-thirty and take a cab."

"That sounds amazing, Angie. I shall be there in the lobby, right on time."

They parted as she made her way back through the hotel to the cabana. Keith decided to spend a couple of hours visiting hospitality suites, large and small. He was tired and still suffering from jet lag, but he was extremely excited about the potential that Anthony Moreno might deliver. He couldn't believe his good luck.

Right on time, Keith was in the lobby of the hotel, dressed in his casual beige slacks and a pale blue polo shirt. Within a minute or two, he saw Angie coming towards him, turning heads as she strode across the lobby floor. She was dressed in tight white pants, high heels, and a tight turquoise sleeveless top, which revealed some of her midriff. Her black hair was framing her face. She had on lots of eye makeup, red lipstick, and long gold drop earrings. A small handbag on a gold chain was slung over her shoulder. He was nervous. He felt everyone in the lobby was looking at them. As she came up to him, she gave him a peck on the cheek.

"Hi, Keith," she said. "You look very handsome."

"Thank you. And you look very beautiful," said Keith.

"Come on," she said, grabbing his arm. "Let's go have some fun. Also, I'm starving."

They got a cab, and, within thirty minutes, they were seated in the Fisherman's Wharf restaurant, over the inland waterway. It had a polished wooden bar and floors, a large stuffed swordfish on the wall, and a deck enclosed in a screen to keep the bugs off. There were large lanterns and small candles everywhere, white tablecloths, comfortable chairs, and a small dance floor.

"So, what do you think of paradise?" said Angie.

"Really great," said Keith enthusiastically. "I love it. If the food is as good as the décor, it should be a wonderful evening."

"I'd hoped you would feel it was a wonderful evening just being with me," said Angie with a pretend pout on her lips.

"Of course," said Keith, taking her hand in his across the table and looking directly into her eyes. "I can't think of anyone in the world that I would rather be with at this moment."

"Ha. You got out of that very neatly, Mr. Benton."

The food was excellent, and they washed it down with a bottle of Chablis. Keith realised that Angie was a really good drinker. She could hold her own. Between them, they polished off the bottle. The trio started playing, and the dance floor quickly filled up. Between courses, Keith asked Angie to dance. Soon, they were dancing cheek to cheek. She looked up at him, pulled his head towards her, and pressed her body close to his. As they moved to the music, he softly kissed her on the lips.

At about ten thirty, Keith was beginning to feel tired. It

was the wine and the jetlag. He suggested they go. She nodded eagerly. Although she offered to pay the bill, he would have none of it. He settled up and they got a cab back to the hotel.

"Thank you for a wonderful evening, Keith," Angie said. "It's such a beautiful night. Have you seen the moonlight on the ocean?"

"No, Angie, my room faces the other way."

"Well, let's go to my room, sit on the balcony and watch the moon on the water for a while. It is breathtaking."

It was beyond beautiful. One part of Keith thought, *I don't know where this is going, but it's all good.* Another part of him was saying, *I don't think I should be mixing business with pleasure. Things could get complicated between us before I've even got an order from these people.* He knew he should resist the temptation, but he would have to be superhuman to do that. The moonlight on the water, the intoxicating smell of her perfume, the balmy night, coupled with the jetlag and half a bottle of Chablis... he was no match for her. She gently pressed her lips to his, and he just melted. He pulled towards her. They kept kissing as she led him back into the bedroom. They were scarcely inside before they were undressing. They stumbled into bed. It was the most sexually charged night of his life. They made love numerous times, until dawn crept into the room around the curtains and onto the walls and bed sheets. He had spent hours exploring her body, smelling her perfume, and admiring her beauty, her deep, brown eyes, dimpled cheeks, and quick smile. They laid in each other's arms for most of the night, and when she finally awoke, she found him staring into her eyes. She gave him a sleepy grin.

"Well, Mr. Benton, that was quite something. I'd love to stay here with you all day, but we both have work to do. However..." she said with an air of mystery around her, "how about the same time, same place tonight?"

"I'd love to see you tonight." Keith responded by giving

her another long, slow kiss. "But now, I have to get back to my room and get ready for the day."

She wrapped the bedsheet around herself and watched him get dressed. As he was ready to leave the bedroom, he gave her one last lingering kiss.

"See you at the cabana."

"I'll be waiting," she said. She slowly let go of his hand.

Keith went back to his room, showered and changed, had breakfast in the lobby café, and was ready for the business session right on time.

The guest speaker was Henry Kissinger. The conference room was packed. Kissinger spoke about multiple threats to world peace, America's role as a reluctant policeman of the world, as he put it – not to mention the importance of NATO – and the ongoing war between Iraq and Iran.

As soon as the session was over, Keith quickly made his way to the cabana.

Anthony and Frankie were talking to three other gentlemen, and Keith waited politely for the conversation to finish. After about five minutes, the group broke up. Anthony came over.

"Good morning, young man. I'm a little disappointed in you," he said with a stern expression. His brown eyes, so similar to Angie's, were boring straight into him. He gripped Keith by the shoulder in a vice-like grip. It was quite painful.

"I think you know that I'm going to do you a very big favor." He paused for effect. "I don't want to hear that you've been running around the convention talking to a lot of chickenshit importers, handing out samples and whatnot. If we're going to do business together, I will make life easy for you, but I expect loyalty. See, someday I may well ask you to do a favor for me." He stopped and once more looked straight into Keith's eyes.

"Yes, Mr. Moreno. I realise you are doing me a big favor, but I thought I would need an importer to clear my shipments, in case you were good enough to agree to take on my brands. So that was why I was talking to various importers."

"If I'm gonna do this favor for you, young man," responded an unsmiling Moreno, "I will make all the arrangements and set you up with an importer who will represent your brands across the whole United States. If the brands take off, you will have an enormous business. We're talking millions of dollars. But you don't know these markets. So, you should listen to my advice. Just do what I tell you, and you will have no problems. Do I make myself clear?"

"Absolutely, Mr. Moreno. That is extremely generous of you. I can't thank you enough."

"Okay. Now that we have an understanding, I can give you the good news. My people like your products. We're going to order three containers from you. I want two of them before the end of June, and the other one by the end of October. I want about eight hundred cases per container. That's probably a normal shipment volume, right?"

"Yes, sir, that is accurate."

"So, the first shipment should be a thousand cases of Masters Plymouth Gin, two hundred cases of the 1610 Premium Gin, and four hundred cases of Masters Vodka."

Keith nearly collapsed from all the excitement. For a minute or so, he was unable to answer Moreno. This order was going to be worth more than $300,000.

Moreno continued. "For these first three containers, we want you to give us $100,000 towards marketing support. Angie will tell you how this should be spent, and what we would have in mind to promote the brands. The money will go to the importer. I've got my eye on a good friend of mine in New Jersey, Jerry Bertoni. He's running a great outfit out of Jersey City, JB Imports. I think he will do a good job for you."

"That is amazing, Mr. Moreno. Your help is truly appreciated. I look forward to working with Mr. Bertoni. And

Angie, of course. I can assure you that Masters of Plymouth will do everything we can to make sure that the brands have every chance of success." Keith could hardly breathe. He wished Angie was there, but she was nowhere to be seen. He needed moral support and a smiling face.

"Okay, Keith. Tomorrow morning is the final business session. We don't usually participate, because things are winding down and we want to pack up and be out of here by noon. But we're always at the closing cocktail reception. So, come to the cabana at ten a.m. I'll introduce you to Jerry Bertoni, and he'll give you the official order. I presume you have all of your BATF approvals and permits?"

"Yes, I have all of those with me, and I can show them to Mr. Bertoni. I also have copies of our company brochures, which I would love to leave with you. You could start getting the word out, so to speak."

"Sure, give me the brochures. But how we're going to inform our customers is up to us, you understand? We certainly won't do that until we have a full marketing package in place." Anthony paused to emphasize his point, and to make sure Keith knew who was calling the shots. "Now, you'll have to excuse me, Keith, but I have other business to attend to."

"Of course, Mr. Moreno. I look forward to seeing you tomorrow morning. And once again, thank you very much for your confidence in me and Masters of Plymouth."

"Yeah. Well, we'll see, but you have to thank Angie. She seems to think you've got what it takes. She's smart. And she knows the market, so you better listen to her. You can learn a lot."

"I certainly will, Mr. Moreno." Keith knew it was time to go. No point in hanging around. He picked up his sample bag and left. He thought about his good fortune. Just forty-eight hours ago, he thought he would be lucky if he got a couple of importers interested, and maybe get a sample shipment set up.

But this was a big chunk of business, by far the largest order that Masters of Plymouth had ever received. He was over the moon. At the same time, he was nervous. He couldn't afford any screw ups. It all had to be spot on in terms of quality, packaging, delivery and everything else.

When he arrived in his room, he noticed a flashing red light on his bedroom telephone. He picked it up and was informed that there were two messages waiting for him. The first was from Angie: "Hi, Keith. Sorry I wasn't with you at the cabana earlier, but it's been a pretty hectic day. Dad told me that things are going well, and that you're going to meet Jerry Bertoni tomorrow morning. In the meantime, I'm really looking forward to seeing you this evening. Seven-thirty in the lobby. I've got another great restaurant for us. Can't wait."

He was excited at the thought of spending another evening and maybe another incredible night with Angie. He checked the second message.

"Hi, Keith. This is Jack Reitman of Red Line Imports in Chicago. We like your Plymouth gin and vodka and would like to discuss the possibility of representing you in the United States. Give me a call, so we can set up a further meeting. I'll be in our hospitality suite, all afternoon, room number 1127."

Keith was surprised and elated. He had met and liked Jack Reitman. He knew that Reitman represented a line of strong regional brands. However, Keith now had a bonanza through Anthony Moreno, and also a forthcoming introduction to JB Imports, and, hopefully, a signed order. The WSWA catalogue listed JB Imports as being established in 1946 in Jersey City, New Jersey. The company represented a long line of imported products, including Scotch whisky, cognac, French brandy, Italian liqueurs, tequila, and Puerto Rico Rum. But no gin or vodka.

He phoned Jack Reitman and was informed that Mr. Reitman was at a meeting and likely to be tied up for the rest of the afternoon, but that he had left a message in case Keith called. Reitman asked if Keith would be kind enough to phone at nine o'clock in the morning at the hospitality suite. Keith thought he was very polite, and he was encouraged by his interest. Still, he would have to tell him that he had made other arrangements. He was confident that no other importer would be willing to place an order for 2,400 cases!

He felt elated. He now had a done deal and decided to take the rest of the afternoon off before getting ready to meet up with Angie. He avoided the hotel swimming pool and the cabanas, and instead headed for the beach. He found a comfortable lounger and spent the next hour or so studying the WSWA catalogue and importers. Then he took a long walk along the beach, enjoying the warm sunshine, and waded out into the ocean for a cooling swim. Keith had always been athletic. He loved to run, swim, and play soccer, and he was an aggressive left half in his local amateur team, Alston Rovers. He trained twice a week and played on Saturdays against other local teams around Plymouth. He also ran twice a week and worked out at the local YMCA. He was in good shape. He swam through the warm waters of the Atlantic Ocean, marveling at the Miami Beach skyline and its miles and miles of white beaches. After a while, he got out, dried off, and sunned himself for half an hour or so. Then he went back to the hotel to get dressed for his evening with Angie.

Right on time she came out of the elevator, dressed in tight, pale turquoise pants and a white, sequined blouse with a deep neckline, revealing plenty of cleavage and a slightly bare midriff. She had on her golden hoop earrings and lots of eye makeup. Her black hair was piled up on top of her head. As previously, she turned many heads as she crossed the lobby. This time, he was ready for the greeting and not at all embarrassed. In fact, he was very proud to be seen with her. She gave him a kiss on the cheek.

"Hi, Keith. That pale English skin is being nicely roasted

here in Miami," she said with a soft laugh "Are you ready to eat? I'm starving, as usual!"

"You look like a film star, Angie. Turning all the heads as usual," he said. "I'm always ready to eat. Let's go."

They grabbed a cab and once again went up to the Bal Harbour area, where she had made a reservation at an Italian restaurant called Leonardo. There was a deck on the inland waterway with an enclosed, screened porch. A pianist was playing near the dance floor. The food was fantastic, as was the bottle of Chianti they had ordered. While they were eating their entrée, Angie took out a pad and pen and gave it to Keith.

"I want to give you some advice about working with Jerry, your U.S. importer," she said and then proceeded to give him a number of tips.

Keith had been writing furiously. "Angie, you are an angel. I don't know much about the U.S. market. I really appreciate your help. Can I contact you if I have problems?"

"Of course. I look forward to working with you. But only because you're one helluva handsome and charming English guy," she said with a laugh.

After a wonderful meal and some intimate dancing, they headed back to the hotel. This time there were no questions asked. They went up to Angie's room, commented briefly on how beautiful the moon was and within five minutes were undressed and lying in each other's arms. The sex was fantastic. The best Keith had ever experienced. Angie's body was perfection. She was strong, and she wanted to pin him to the bed and straddle him. They made love numerous times before dropping off to sleep. Keith awoke when dawn started to creep into the room. He had agreed to meet Angie on the beach at 7:30 a.m. for a jog, and he wanted to be back and have breakfast by 9 o'clock, in order to phone Jack Reitman. It was 6:30 and, because he was still jet lagged, he was wide awake. Angie was stirring slowly. He kissed her on the forehead and murmured in her ear. "See you on the beach in an hour." He got dressed and padded back to his room. He had a shower and changed into shorts and sneakers and a T-shirt. He spent the next half hour rewriting the notes that Angie had given him, getting them in some sort of chronological order. He was on the beach by seven-thirty. Angie was already there, dressed in shorts and a cut-off T-shirt, sneakers, and socks. Her hair was pulled back in a ponytail. She looked gorgeous.

"Okay, Mr. England," she said with a laugh, "let's see what you're made of. Let's run for about 45 minutes and blow away the cobwebs."

"I'm ready, Angie. But I'm a little weak. It's all your fault," he said with a laugh. "But I'll do my best to keep up."

Angie set a hot pace. He didn't think she would be able to maintain it, but she did. He kept up with her, which surprised her. They ran for twenty minutes down an almost deserted white beach as the sun was coming up. Then they turned and headed back to the hotel, arriving sweaty and exhilaratingly exhausted.

"Hey, you did pretty well," said Angie. "There's not many guys who can keep up with me."

"Well, I'm doing my best, day and night," he said with a cheeky grin. They headed back to the hotel and agreed to meet at the cabana at ten, for the meeting with Jerry Bertoni.

Keith went back to his room and had a long slow shower. Then he got dressed, ready for his meeting. At 9 a.m. on the dot, he phoned Jack Reitman.

"Good morning, Mr. Reitman, this is Keith Benton."

"Hi there, Keith," Jack responded. "Thank you for calling back. As I said in my message, we would be interested in discussing Red Line Imports representing your products in the United States, and I'm wondering whether you would like to make an appointment, so we can take this further."

"Well, Mr. Reitman, I really appreciate your interest and

your kind offer, but I have already made arrangements with JB Imports in New Jersey to represent us."

"Oh. So, you're signing up with the Morenos," Reitman said with a chuckle. "You must be Angie's beau of the convention."

"I'm sorry?"

"She is known for finding, uh, new talent at these events, so to speak. She is one hell of a girl—smart, beautiful, and very knowledgeable in the business. But do you know what people call her?"

"No."

"The Black Widow."

"You mean the spider that eats its mates?"

"That's the one. Don't get too friendly." He laughed again. "And you should be aware that working with Moreno means flying near the sun, if you know what I mean. Especially that brother, Rudy. I think he has a rap sheet in at least three states. The police have always got their eyes on him. But anyway, keep us in mind if things don't work out. It was good to meet you. Maybe we'll see each other at future conventions."

"Thank you very much, Mr. Reitman."

Keith was suddenly feeling very nervous. He was certainly more than" friendly" with Angie, and he didn't know where that would lead. Was he just one of her flings? Would it all be all over at the end of the convention? Or was their personal relationship connected to the business relationship? That could be dangerous. And what exactly did Jack Reitman mean about the Morenos? Were these guys connected to the "Mob"? Would they want to suck him in somehow? He couldn't imagine why. After all, he was a small fry by their standards. Perhaps it would be sensible to keep Angie at arm's length from now on, but he didn't know if he would be able to do that. He certainly didn't want to jeopardize the relationship and the major order that they were about to give him. He would need to tread carefully.

At ten o'clock, he presented himself at the cabana and was welcomed by Anthony Moreno.

"Good morning, Keith. I want to introduce you to my good friend, one of our closest import suppliers, Mr. Jerry Bertoni." Bertoni looked like the rest of the Moreno team, dressed in a light cream suit and a black shirt, open at the collar. He had sunglasses and slicked-back black hair. He was deeply suntanned and had a slight but wiry build.

"Pleased to meetcha," Bertoni said, grabbing Keith's hand in a tight vise. "Mr. Moreno is impressed with your gin and vodka. He thinks we should represent you in the U.S. We did some sampling. Good flavor. I like your packaging and your brochure, and I think Mr. Moreno's right. We could really do something worthwhile for you. When it comes to imported gins, particularly from the UK, there is not that much competition."

At that point, Angie entered the cabana. She greeted her father and Jerry with a kiss and a hug. "Good morning," she said with a big smile. "I hope I haven't missed any of the negotiations."

"No, you didn't miss anything. I got the orders right here, Keith. You can check them out. So, let's start with a letter of intent."

"We have a typewriter here in the cabana. I can just draft the LOI based on normal boilerplate agreements and you can fill in any necessary adjustments," said Angie.

"Okay, Keith. Let's get going."

They spent the next hour putting the letter of intent together. At the end, both parties signed it and attached the initial order for 2,400 cases of gin and vodka. Keith was giddy with excitement, but he remained calm and polite to everybody. Angie broke out a bottle of champagne and all the parties toasted the success of the new arrangement.

Then, Anthony apologized to Keith. "We're packing up our cabana. We have to be out of here by noon. After that, we have to pack and check out of the hotel. We're taking an evening flight back to New York. However, we'll be in touch. I hope you'll visit us to see how your brands are doing. We'll do our utmost to make this a success."

"I can't thank you enough, Mr. Moreno. And, of course, Angie. Masters of Plymouth will not let you down. Of course, I hope to see you on a regular basis, maybe in the UK, or when I come to visit Mr. Bertoni."

"We'll see you again soon," said Anthony. He was holding Keith's hand in an iron grip and looking deep into his eyes. "After all, when we have arrangements like this, we like to feel we're becoming part of the same family, if you know what I mean."

"Of course," said Keith, trying not to show his nervousness. "I'm sure this will be a close business relationship."

It was time to go. Angie offered to walk Keith out to the hotel lobby to say goodbye. When they got there, she flung her arms around him, despite all the wholesalers milling about.

"It was wonderful meeting you, Keith. You are a great guy. I enjoyed every minute of being with you," she continued. "We'll keep in touch. It's only a few hours flight. I want us to stay very close."

"Angie," said Keith, "you are the greatest. I'm excited about working with you and your family." Keith was hoping to ease into a business relationship, but he wasn't sure he was getting through.

"You have a good flight home, Keith. I'll be thinking of you," said Angie. She was holding on tight. Tears were welling up in her eyes.

She certainly didn't act like a Black Widow. Maybe Jack Reitman got it wrong. Maybe it was all just industry gossip. But Keith had a nagging feeling that there was some truth to Jack's advice. They parted with a final kiss and hug.

Keith went to his room, armed with a letter of intent and

initial order for 2,400 cases. He felt elated at getting a foothold in the giant U.S. market. The Masters board in Plymouth would drop off their chairs when he told them what he had achieved. He had a five-thirty flight out of Miami to London, and so he packed his bags, checked out, got a cab, and was at the airport with plenty of time for his British Airways flight.

Five weeks after Keith returned from the States, he received a phone call from Angie.

"Hi, Keith. I've got some exciting news. Dad would like you to come to New Jersey to address our annual national sales conference in September, right after Labor Day. You will have an opportunity to present Masters of Plymouth Gin and Vodka as one of our new products of the year and get all the sales teams behind you. This is a great opportunity for you, Keith. We will also be able to present the brand marketing plan through JB Imports. It could give you a boost for a second round of orders. I suggest you try and get a flight directly to Newark, New Jersey. I'll make reservations for you at the hotel where our sales conference will be held. And of course, Keith," she said coyly, "we'll have some quality time together."

Keith was taken aback. He had just seen her five weeks ago. He was hoping to wind back the intensity of the relationship and put it on a business footing. On the other hand, after Keith had absorbed what Angie was saying, it did seem to make sense. He would have to work hard to make an attractive, sensible and informative presentation available. But he had time to do it. He was confident he could come up with something good.

"Wow, Angie, that's great. I think it would be a great opportunity. I will get working on the presentation right now. Please keep in touch, and I will make arrangements for the flight." He realised that this was a bit businesslike, so he changed his tone. "Angie, I know that you're behind this, and that you're pushing everyone to help me. I really appreciate all that you've done. I can't wait to see you again."

Everything about the trip went smoothly. He was impressed with the professionalism of the sales conference, the knowledge of the salesmen, the Q&A sessions that he had to go through, the friendliness of the managers and vice presidents, not to mention the generosity of the Moreno family. Frankie seemed to be the organizer and took the lead, and so Keith spent quite a lot of time with him. They got on well. And then, of course, he had the added advantage of Angie in his corner, pushing the marketing, pushing JB imports, and making encouraging noises to everybody in the room. They all got the message that she and Keith were perhaps an item and that it would be in their interest to keep her happy. As a result, he managed to procure another two orders for 800 cases of Plymouth Gin, one for November, and one more for February. He was over the moon that the business was growing so rapidly. Initial depletions from wholesaler to retailer were encouraging, and JB imports had started to place the brand with other wholesalers down the East Coast. Orders had already begun trickling in.

Keith went back to England, full of the joys of spring. Again, he was able to report good news to the board. Everyone was highly congratulatory, and the initial nervousness that these large orders might be beyond the company's capacity finally abated. He worked hard to make sure that all the orders were executed to perfection, and that there were no hang-ups. He had seen no indication that Angie was a Black Widow. In fact, as far as he was concerned, she was very loving and sweet, except in bed. The other members of the Moreno family had been outgoing and happy throughout the sales meeting. He felt he had no cause to worry.

All that changed in the first week of November. He got a call from Anthony Moreno.

"Hi, Keith. Everything seems to be going well with Masters Gin and Vodka. I'm very pleased with the progress so far. Hopefully, we can keep the good work going. We are making a special effort on these brands, you know?"

"Yes, Mr. Moreno," responded Keith, becoming nervous that this was leading up to something.

"As you know, we are a close family, and Angelina has been working hard for you. She's really your resident sales VP in the U.S." He stopped and chuckled.

"I know, sir, she has been wonderful."

"However, Keith, I need a favor from you. Earlier than I thought. But it's a favor that is very important to our family, particularly my brother Rudy," said Moreno, speaking slowly and deliberately.

Oh God. Here it comes, thought Keith.

"I would like you to get on a plane tomorrow. I made a reservation for you on a British Airways flight out of Heathrow at four p.m. When you arrive at Kennedy Airport, one of my drivers will meet you and bring you to our offices. We'll wait for you in the office. I'll explain it all when you get here." He paused and then continued slowly but emphatically. "This will be an opportunity for you to return the favor to the Moreno family."

Keith's head was rattling with all this information, but he knew he could not deny Moreno's request.

"Of course, Mr. Moreno. I'll be there."

"I knew you would," said Moreno in a mild, but somewhat threatening response. "See you in New York. Tomorrow night."

Keith sat down at his desk. His heart was pounding. His palms were sweaty. He was terrified. When Keith arrived at JFK Airport, he was met by a giant of a man with a sign: "Benton." He approached and introduced himself.

"Good evening, Mr. Benton," the man said. "I'm Carlo. Mr. Moreno sent me to pick you up. Please follow me." He took Keith's overnight bag and briefcase, and they walked out of the airport to the curbside. Keith was greeted by a shock of cold air. It was freezing. He snuggled into his overcoat. Carlo was dressed in a black suit and black shirt, and, for some reason, dark glasses. The man obviously did not feel the cold. Carlo had called into a pager on his jacket, and within a minute or two, a black Mercedes with tinted windows arrived at the curbside. Carlo opened the rear door. Keith got in. The driver did not introduce himself. Carlo joined him in the front passenger seat. A glass screen separated Carlo and the driver from the rear of the car. They drove off. Keith had no idea where they were going. After they left the airport, Keith knocked on the glass screen. He slid it open a crack and asked the driver: "Are we going to Mr. Moreno's office?"

"No, sir. We are going to Jersey City."

Keith had no idea where Jersey City was and felt some pangs of nervousness. He realised that Anthony Moreno was totally in control. He had no idea what this was all about, but he had a gut feeling that it wasn't good. They drove into New York City, a magnificent blaze of light in the cold night, and entered the Holland Tunnel. They came out the other end, and, within twenty minutes or so, they were in a residential area. The streets were small and average-looking, with identical row houses. They eventually pulled up in front of an unremarkable house, just like the others on the street. He could not imagine why Moreno had brought him here.

Carlo bounced out of the car and opened the door for Keith. He got his briefcase from the trunk and led Keith up the steps. Then he knocked three times on the front door. It opened to reveal another tall man in a black suit. "Follow me, sir." He led Keith down the narrow passage to a kitchen. The decor and fittings were all old-fashioned, and there, in the harsh light of an old-fashioned chandelier, sitting around a wooden table, were Anthony Moreno, his brother Rudy, as well as Frank and two other men. On the table was a large bowl of salad and a basket with chunks of bread, together with a bottle of Chianti and two bottles of San Pellegrino.

To Keith's relief, Angie was also there. She was dressed in a thick, grey, roll-neck sweater, blue jeans, and a wide belt. She had no makeup on, and her hair was drawn back in a ponytail. He recognized her gold hoop earrings.

"Good evening, Keith," said Anthony with a slight smile. "Hope you had a good flight. Make yourself comfortable, take off your coat and jacket, if you like. You won't need your briefcase. Angie will serve you some of her delicious ravioli Pomodoro. We just sat down to eat."

Angie came over with a somewhat tight smile on her face. She gave him a peck on the cheek. "Good to see you again, Keith," she said without great enthusiasm.

Keith did as he was told. He took off his overcoat. Anthony Moreno was sitting in his shirtsleeves, with his necktie loosened and his jacket over the back of his chair. His large belly was bursting through his shirt. He was devouring a plate of ravioli.

"Keith, you know my brother Rudy."

Rudy mumbled, "Good to see ya."

Moreno continued, "I would like to introduce you to my lawyer, Vincent Manzoni, and his assistant, Joe Salerno."

Manzoni was a well-dressed, middle-aged man with grey hair and black, horn-rimmed glasses. He gave Keith a tight smile. "Pleased to meetcha," he said, offering a fleshy paw for Keith to shake. His assistant Salerno was a skinny man, with greasy hair and darting black grey eyes. He gave Keith a smile, revealing yellowed teeth. Angie bought over a large steaming plate of ravioli.

"Angie is a great cook, you know," said Anthony. "Enjoy."

Keith started to eat slowly. The ravioli was excellent. He added some salad and accepted half a glass of red wine.

"Well, Keith," said Anthony. "I guess you're wondering why I asked you to come all the way from Plymouth. You know, we have been working hard for your brands, and you have a total commitment from the Moreno organization to make a success for you in the United States. We like to think of you as part of our family. You are young and energetic, and very capable, and Angie is very impressed with you. She's a good judge of character, you know."

"Thank you, sir," said Keith.

"I've asked you here because we need you to help the Moreno family over a little difficulty." He paused. Keith stopped eating. "My brother Rudy had a bad experience with a business associate. He had to teach him a lesson. This business associate had, um, many enemies. And now, perhaps not too surprisingly, his body was found floating in the river, a few weeks ago. Of course, Rudy had nothing to do with his death, but now the police have taken an interest. They want to know where Rudy was at the time of death, you know."

Moreno leaned back in his chair. He wiped his mouth with his napkin and turned his piercing gaze on Keith, who's mouth had gone dry. He had suddenly lost his appetite. He reached for the San Pellegrino. His hand was shaking a little.

"You remember when you came here for our national sales meeting, just after Labor Day? I know that was a very busy couple of days, so you may not remember too well, but on the second day, in the afternoon, from four to seven, you had a meeting in Rudy's hotel suite. It was also attended by Mike Anelli, our Eastern regional sales manager. You discussed your brands and looked at depletions. And you also talked about current market conditions." He paused. "Straight forward stuff, Keith."

Moreno took a large gulp of Chianti and wiped his mouth on his napkin. He turned his piercing stare back to Keith.

"Now, Mr. Manzoni has a deposition document I would like you to sign, confirming the date and time of that meeting. Mr. Salerno here is a notary public and will confirm your signature. Mike has already completed his deposition. After that is done, Keith, Carlo will take you to a hotel, so you can get some sleep. He'll pick you up early in the morning, and take you back to JFK for the flight to London. That will be the end of it, Keith." He paused. Of course, there had been no meeting with Rudy for Keith to remember.

"It is very unlikely you will ever hear anything further on this matter, but if necessary, I know that I can rely on you to confirm what you signed. In court, I mean." He paused again and looked at Keith.

Keith swallowed hard and his mouth had gone totally dry. He felt he would hardly be able to speak.

"You should read the document, Keith, before signing it. But I'm sure you won't have any problem doing us this favor."

Keith was ready to throw up. He felt like a lamb going to the slaughter. He was now sure Rudy was in hiding from the police, in this "safe" house. Vincent Manzoni handed over the deposition for Keith to read. The document described who Keith Benton was, his business occupation, and then went on to confirm what Anthony had told him about the meeting in Rudy's hotel suite. It was a meticulously crafted detailed piece of fiction. Keith realised that if he didn't agree to Anthony's request, the Masters' business in the United States would come to an abrupt halt. It could sink the whole company.

He also wondered if there could be even worse retribution. Maybe he would never make it back to the UK— an "accident" or mysterious disappearance from the hotel? He shuddered at the thought. However, if he did agree to the request, there was a possibility that he might be an accessory to murder.

He looked at Angie for support, but found nothing in her eyes but darkness. She seemed to look right through him. He was in the spider's web. His hand was shaking as Manzoni passed him a pen.

9 NO TURKISH DELIGHT – 1993

He stepped out onto the sidewalk outside their Istanbul hotel on the last day of their honeymoon, clutching both their passports and airline tickets. As usual, the traffic was chaotic, churning up the dust. It was going to be another scorching day. He stood rooted to the spot. *Where was the taxi?* For a moment or two, he did not know what to do.

* * *

Everyone said that the wedding was one of the most beautiful on the North Shore in the summer of 1993. The ceremony had taken place at Christ Church at Tower Road, followed by a magnificent reception at the Nielsen's home, further down Sheridan Road in Winnetka. Maya Britt Nielsen married Peter Alexander Thornton Greenwood. The bride was the granddaughter of Per Nielsen, a dentist who had come from Malmo in Sweden in the late 19th Century and settled in the North Shore of Chicago, where he founded The Dental Equipment Company. Maya's father, Harold, also a practicing dentist, had built the business into a successful international organization with offices and manufacturing facilities around the world.

Peter Greenwood was the great-grandson of a former governor of Georgia, Abraham Thornton, whose family had come from England to the United States in the late 18th Century. His grandfather had been Lieutenant Governor of the state, and his father Arthur had served in the State Senate. The past three generations had all practiced law in the state of Georgia, through numerous partnerships, and still did under the name Tucker, Thornton & Greenwood. There had been various marriages between the Thorntons and the Greenwoods extended families over the past two centuries. It was therefore natural that, after graduating from Duke, Peter went to Northwestern Law School in Chicago where he met Maya, who had passed through Northwestern and was getting an MBA in marketing at Kellogg.

Maya was an outstandingly beautiful bride—tall and slim, with long blonde hair, very blue eyes, and as to be expected, a pearly white smile. She was gracious and charming, with a warm engaging personality. Peter, who had decided to stay in Chicago once he met Maya, was working at Kirkland & Ellis. He was the epitome of tall, dark, and handsome: athletic, and a great tennis player, with an outgoing personality, a slight drawl, and plenty of southern charm. As many people said, including a gushing media, this was a match made in heaven. Two hundred people had crammed into the small church. The reception, afterwards at the Nielsen's mansion on the lake, was held in a very large tent set over the expansive lawn on sections of parquet flooring. There was a large dance area and band stage. The weather could not have been more perfect, and everything worked like a charm. The newlyweds said their goodbyes before the event closed and headed off with loud shouts of appreciation in a rented Rolls-Royce. It drove them to the Ritz Carlton Hotel in Chicago where they had an enormous suite for their first night of marriage.

The following day, they started their three-week honeymoon, flying to London for three days, followed by ten days in Athens and the Greek islands on a small exclusive cruise ship, and then another short cruise from Athens to Istanbul for the last three days of their honeymoon. They were madly in love and oblivious to the fact that they turned heads wherever they went. By the time they got to Istanbul, Maya had developed a light bronze tan, and Peter, who had a darker complexion and more olive skin, had gone deep brown.

They checked into the Hotel Sultan at Sultanahmet, one of Istanbul's oldest established, but still very comfortable, hotels. From here, they ventured out every day for sightseeing, crossing the Bosporus, visiting the Topkapi Museum and the Grand Bazaar. They loved every minute of it. But eventually it was time to go home.

When they checked into the hotel, as was the usual custom, Peter had been asked to deposit their passports with reception, which would be made available upon their departure. As they were checking out, the passports were given back to Peter and he gave his Visa card to settle the account. All their Tumi luggage, a wedding present from one of Peter's doting aunts, was brought down and was waiting on the curbside as Peter and Maya came out and asked the doorman for a taxi to the airport. The doorman blew his whistle. Within a few seconds, a yellow taxi pulled up. They loaded up the small car. Maya got in and Peter was checking to make sure all the pieces of luggage had been stowed carefully in the trunk and on the front seat of the cab. Then he suddenly realized that he had left the passports at the reception desk.

He yelled through the open window to Maya, "I've left the passports at the reception! I'll be back in a minute." He dashed off, dodging hotel guests in the lobby. The two passports were where he had left them. He grabbed them and ran back out of the hotel, but the taxi was nowhere to be seen.

After being rooted to the spot for a few seconds, he grabbed hold of the doorman and said, "Where's the taxi?"

"What taxi?"

"The taxi! With my wife and luggage in it?"

"Oh, yes. I believe, sir, you asked me to tell the driver to go to the airport."

"Well, yes, I did, but I had to dash back into the hotel to get our passports. I can't believe that the taxi would drive off without me. You think they're waiting down the street somewhere or circling because of traffic?"

"I'm sorry, sir, I don't know. I just know that you told me the taxi should go to the airport and presumably that's where he has gone."

"But that's crazy. My wife can't go anywhere because I have got her passport," said Peter, a certain amount of panic rising in his stomach.

"Then perhaps she will be waiting for you at the airport. Would you like a taxi to take you there?"

"I don't know, I don't know," said Peter, nervous about making a decision to leave the hotel in case the taxi and his wife should turn up. Perhaps Maya had asked the driver to circle a couple of blocks while she waited for him to pick up the passports.

Highly, unlikely, he thought, *but should I leave the hotel or not?* He made a decision. Perhaps they had gone to the airport, and the driver could not understand Maya's protests.

"Okay, get me a taxi and I will go to the airport." He had the passports, and he also had the tickets for the BA flight to London for the connection to Chicago. Presumably, the taxi driver did not understand what she was saying. He must have just gone to the airport. No doubt Peter would find her there.

With the early morning traffic, it took an agonizing hour to get to the airport. Peter paid the driver and rushed into the terminal, scanning the large crowd of passengers lining up at the check-in desks for various airlines. He ran to the BA desk, but Maya wasn't there, nor was their luggage. *Where else could she be?* He was getting worried now. There seemed no sensible explanation. If she had come to the airport, surely she would have had a porter deliver the luggage to the BA desk and wait for him to arrive. Maybe she was somewhere else in the airport.

He dashed over to a large information desk in the middle of the terminal, found an English-speaking assistant, and asked if she would put out a call for Mrs. Peter Greenwood to come to the information desk as soon as possible. He waited for fifteen minutes. There was no response. He then asked the young lady to put out the same message again. Still no response, and still no sign of Maya. He dashed back and forth to the British Airways desk to see if she was there. He asked the BA check-in personnel if she had made herself known. No one of her description had spoken to them. Panic was starting to grip him like a fever. It didn't make sense to stay at the airport. Obviously, she wasn't here. *What should he do next?* He gave all necessary information to the BA desk, showed them Maya's passport photo, and asked them to phone the hotel if she showed up or they had any news.

He decided to go back to the hotel and see if she had returned. Maybe the taxi had a mechanical breakdown. Or perhaps there had been an accident. He would have to seek help from the hotel management. They had to find her. *This is crazy,* he said to himself. *She can't just disappear like this.*

After another agonizing one-hour drive through the traffic back into the city, he arrived at the hotel and ran to the reception desk. "Excuse me," he said to the receptionist. "Has my wife been looking for me? Mrs. Peter Greenwood?"

"No, sir, I believe you checked out earlier this morning, but I'll ask the concierge." She went over to the concierge desk with Peter following at a fast pace.

"I'm sorry, Mr. Greenwood, I haven't seen Mrs. Greenwood today."

Peter then explained what had happened and how Maya had just disappeared into thin air.

"Would you like to talk to the manager?" asked the concierge.

"Yes, I think that would be helpful."

The concierge disappeared into the back office and a couple of minutes later the hotel manager came out to greet Peter. "Good morning, Mr. Greenwood. I am Walter Orban, the hotel manager. How may I help you?"

Peter explained the situation at length, and Mr. Orban took on a worried expression.

"I'm very sorry, Mr. Greenwood. This is most distressing. If you wait here a few moments, I shall go and speak to the doormen, our security staff, and lobby personnel, including our receptionists, to see if they can cast some light on the situation. Why don't I have a pot of coffee delivered to you while you sit here in the lobby? I will be no more than a few minutes."

The manager escorted Peter to one of the deep leather chairs in the highly decorated Ottoman lobby. Within a minute or two, a tray of Turkish coffee and a couple of biscuits were placed before him. His thoughts were jangling like mad. He was in a cold sweat and everything was shaking.

About ten minutes later, Mr. Orban came back and sat down next to Peter. "Mr. Greenwood, I have checked with all our staff and they all confirmed that they saw you and Mrs. Greenwood leave the hotel with your luggage. The doorman confirms that he called a taxi for you and you told him to tell the driver to go to the airport. You, then, left Mrs. Greenwood in the taxi while you ran back into the hotel, presumably, as you told me earlier, to pick up your passports. And when you came back, the taxi had left. The doorman doesn't know the driver of the taxi, cannot remember the license number, and only confirmed, as you did, that it was a yellow taxi, one of the thousands in the city." He paused pensively. "Technically,

Mr. Greenwood, you have checked out, paid your bill, and left the hotel, and therefore we have no further responsibility to you as a guest, but in these strange circumstances we would like to help you in any way we can. Accordingly, with your permission, I would like to call the police and have you explain the situation to them."

"The Police! I really don't want to bring the police into the situation," said Peter. But then he thought; there was probably no other option. "Yes, maybe you're right. I'm very worried and I think that is a sensible suggestion."

"I will make a phone call on your behalf and I'm sure we will have an officer here within thirty minutes. So please relax, enjoy your coffee, as I'm sure we will find an explanation," Mr. Orban said with a gracious smile.

It was less than half an hour when Mr. Orban, accompanied by a tall, dark-haired man with a luxurious black moustache, followed by a smaller man in a light raincoat, approached Peter, who had been anxiously checking his watch every few minutes.

"Mr. Greenwood," said Mr. Orban, "this is Detective Inspector Mustafi from Istanbul Central Police and his assistant, Detective Kamal. With your permission, I would like to talk to him in Turkish, so that he will quickly understand the situation." Peter shook hands with the inspector while the hotel manager launched into a long explanation of what had happened. Peter could only understand, from time to time, his name and his wife's name. The inspector was nodding as his assistant was taking notes on a little white pad. Peter, again, felt the panic rising. *Oh my god*, he thought to himself, *maybe Maya has been kidnapped.*

When the Inspector turned to Peter, he spoke in accented English. "Mr. Greenwood, could I see both your passports?" Peter handed them over and he looked at the passports, particularly at Maya's passport photo. "You have other photos of your wife?"

"Well, I do, but they are all in my camera, which is in my luggage with my wife. Other than that, I only have one small photo which I carry around in my wallet." With shaking hands, he withdrew a photo of a beautiful, smiling Maya.

"Mr. Greenwood, I don't want to ask you to have the indignity of coming to our police station, so I would like to sit here and have you explain exactly what Mr. Orban told me, but in English. Please speak slowly and deliberately." Peter described every minute of the past four hours or so. Detective Mustafi turned to his assistant and said something. The assistant produced some paperwork from his briefcase.

"Mr. Greenwood," said the detective, talking slowly and deliberately. "I would like you to take a few minutes to complete this missing-persons form that we need as a standard procedure in order to conduct a search for your wife."

Peter noticed that the questionnaire was in Turkish, Greek, and English. He put the forms on the coffee table in front of him and, with a shaking hand and pounding heart, he started to complete a detailed description of his wife and the events surrounding her disappearance. Within a few minutes, he had completed the forms. During this time, Mustafi had been talking to his assistant in rapid Turkish. They seemed to be arguing. But, at the end, they were nodding in agreement.

"Detective, I have to ask. Do you have any idea what may have happened to my wife?" Peter said, with a crack in his voice.

"Well, Mr. Greenwood, there could be many simple explanations. The taxi driver may have driven off to the airport because that was what he was told to do. Many of our taxi drivers do not have any English and so, even if your wife had been asking him to stop or to turn around, he might not have understood. I know you've been to the airport and you couldn't find her, but I have already put out a call to the airport to check if there is any sign of her or your luggage. We are also checking two other small municipal airports."

"Oh? You have other airports?" said Peter, now clutching at straws.

"Another explanation," continued the detective, "might be that the taxi had a breakdown and maybe he had to wait two or three hours for a tow truck to come and take them to an auto service shop."

"Yes. That could be," said Peter.

"Although it is surprising we haven't heard from them yet, this may happen at any minute. Alternatively, they may have been in an accident. We are checking the hospitals right now to see if there is anyone of your wife's description."

"An Accident?"

"I think we will know very shortly if this is the case. There could be many other explanations. After all, it is not easy to communicate, unless one can get to a telephone, and our phone services are somewhat antiquated. Maybe your wife has been trying to call the hotel or the airport. Nevertheless, we are going to start the procedures as though this is a missing person's case. Hopefully within a few hours this will resolve itself."

"Oh, I hope so, but I just have to ask you one other question," said Peter. "I saw you nodding very seriously with Mr. Orban as you were talking about my wife's disappearance. Do you think there may have been some criminal involvement? Maybe a kidnapping?"

"Well, as a worst-case scenario, that is one of the possibilities," responded the detective, still talking slowly and quietly. "In the meantime, while I am awaiting responses from various sources, I suggest you might like to check into the hotel, say, for another four or five days, while we do our best to resolve the case."

Peter nodded. He was in a daze. He had no clothes, and, at the moment, nowhere to stay. "I will. Thank you."

"Because all your luggage has disappeared, I think you might want a little time to go and buy yourself some extra clothes and toiletries. I'll return to the police station, but can meet you back here, say, at eight p.m. I can give you an update of what we have discovered."

"Eight p.m. Yes, of course."

"However, in the meantime, if your wife and your luggage return to the hotel, please let me know. Here is a card with my phone number and fax number on it. Our receptionist speaks English and, if you need any help, I'm sure Mr. Orban would be glad to provide any assistance possible. I can assure you, Mr. Greenwood, we shall be doing our best to resolve this situation and have a happy ending."

"Thank you very much, Detective Mustafi." Peter liked the solid look of this man. He believed him.

Mr. Orban gave him a quiet corner room overlooking the hotel gardens. Peter went shopping and bought a cheap holdall bag, into which he stuffed a pair of jeans, sneakers, some casual slacks, two shirts, two T-shirts, some underwear, and toiletries. He was back in the hotel by late afternoon. Although he did not want to panic his family or Maya's family, he felt he had to make a call to the US to explain the situation. After all, the newlyweds were expected back in the States the following day.

With some difficulty and with help from Mr. Orban, he was able to put through a call to his father in Atlanta. "Hi Dad," he said. "I have a problem and I'm still in Istanbul."

"Good to hear from you, Peter. Are you guys having a great time? Aren't you due back tomorrow in the US?" responded David Greenwood.

"No, Dad. I think I need some help." With that, he explained the situation to his father in detail.

"That is unbelievable. People just don't disappear into thin air. There's got to be some reasonable explanation. I remember going to Istanbul with your mother, and those taxis were awful, always overcharging, wanting to take you in a different direction, and driving like lunatics. Maybe there's been an accident."

"The taxis aren't any better, Dad. The police are checking."

"Okay, son," responded David Greenwood somberly. "I will reach out to the State Department and call you back at your hotel later today. I'll also tell your mother and the family, although at this stage, I don't want them to worry too much. Give me the name of your hotel and the telephone number." Peter provided the information and confirmed that he would contact Maya's family as well.

When he got through to Maya's mother, she started crying and handed the phone to Maya's father. Peter explained the full details of Maya's disappearance. Harold Neilson was very upset and angry. "You've only been married to my daughter for three weeks! You have a responsibility to protect and look after your wife's well-being. How could you leave your passports at the reception and then not at least tell the doorman or taxi driver you were going back into the hotel? Peter, you are not a schoolboy, but that was so irresponsible!"

Peter told him about the police help and said he had spoken to his father who was going to contact the State Department to provide Peter with assistance in Istanbul.

"I am going to call Paul Simon, our senator for Illinois. He's a friend of mine. He is very knowledgeable and experienced." Harold then said that, if Peter didn't find Maya in the next day or so, he would jump on a plane to Istanbul. He also offered the help of one of his corporate subsidiaries based in Athens.

"Thank you," responded Peter. "I really appreciate your support, but there is nothing you can do at the moment," said Peter, not wanting Harold to make a bad situation worse.

Peter promised to keep Harold fully informed of what was going on and was somewhat relieved when he was able to put the phone down.

His father telephoned back within three hours. "Peter," he said, firmly and businesslike. "I've contacted the State Department, and they sent a message to the US Ambassador in Istanbul. His name is Bobby Daniels. He went to Georgetown. He's a year or two older than I am, but I do remember him. I think we may have met from time-to-time in Washington. He is a good man. I explained what has happened and they say they will do everything to help get this resolved, and quickly."

"The Ambassador? Thank you."

"Yes, he will be expecting your call. Please let me know what your inspector says when you see him."

"I will, Dad."

"You can call me at any time, morning or night. I'll also be making enquiries to find out how these situations are resolved in a country like Turkey. If I have any important information, I will let you know." He paused for a moment. "Peter, I know this must be terrible for you. And no doubt for Maya's family, too. Stay strong. We are totally behind you. We are praying that there will be a quick resolution."

"Thank you, Dad. I'll contact the ambassador after my meeting with the police. It will probably be tomorrow morning, Istanbul time, but I'll keep you posted."

At 8 p.m., Peter was anxiously pacing the lobby checking his watch, awaiting the arrival of detective Mustafi. He showed up a few minutes late with his assistant, armed with his notebook in tow, just like before.

"Have you found her?" said Peter, pouncing on the detective.

"Good evening, Mr. Greenwood," said the detective calmly. "I want to give you an update. Let's sit down over here." He pointed to three small chairs. "We have checked all the hospitals in the area and there is no record of any accident involving any person of your wife's description. In addition, we have checked every police report for any vehicle accidents that might have involved a taxi. Nothing. We've also increased surveillance at our airports, land borders, and ferry services and shipping in the Bosporus. We have issued a missing persons alert to all police stations in every city and town in the country. We have taken your photograph, enhanced and improved it, and attached it to all the notices that we have sent around the country. Finally, we are checking all our street and border surveillance cameras for any indication of a woman of your wife's appearance. This includes our survey of yellow taxi services in Istanbul. So far, however, Mr. Greenwood, I regret to say that we have no leads on this case."

Peter's shoulders sagged. "Surely, detective, someone should know what has happened to her. She can't just disappear into thin air. You have millions of tourists a year coming through Istanbul. This disappearance seems unthinkable in such a big city. Is there any way you could identify the taxi that picked up my wife?" said Peter, pushing back and agitated.

"Unfortunately, Mr. Greenwood, that is very difficult. Unless we had a license number of the cab, or some other indication that could differentiate that particular taxi from the thousands of others in Istanbul. We have nearly 15,000 yellow taxis in Istanbul. Although each one has a licensed driver, the drivers often 'sublet' their licenses to other drivers when they don't want to work or to give them a rest period. This makes it even more difficult to identify a taxi and its driver. What I am saying, Mr. Greenwood, is that it may not happen. I think, however, that there is a chance that we will have some news for you over the next couple of days from all the other actions that were taken. And, of course, I will contact you as soon as anything comes to my knowledge."

"You can imagine how concerned I and our families are about the situation, so I would really appreciate you keeping me up-to-date at all times."

"Of course, but I have to tell you, Mr. Greenwood, that it

is our experience in these sorts of cases that, if we don't find the missing person within 48 hours, the case becomes extremely difficult to solve. I feel it is only right that you should know this."

Peter was shocked that the detective was saying this. *Forty-eight hours is no time*, he thought. He would not want to think that the police were giving up so quickly. He had a sinking feeling in his stomach.

"You can't give up after 48 hours!! I have been thinking, Detective, that if this is a kidnapping case, I don't understand why my wife would not have jumped out of the car or banged on the windows at the first opportunity."

"I am not saying that this is a kidnapping case, as we have not received a ransom note, but most of our yellow taxis have no air-conditioning, so the windows are tinted to keep out the sun, which also makes it difficult to look into the vehicle. In addition, we have seen kidnapping and robbery cases in taxis where the driver sprayed a nerve gas into the rear passenger seats and closed the glass partition between the driver and the passenger. The passenger is immediately immobilized and unable to move." The detective paused. "But, Mr. Greenwood, none of this may apply to your wife. It is too soon to draw any conclusions as we have no evidence. We shall just keep following our process."

Peter couldn't believe what he was hearing. Kidnapping in broad daylight outside a leading hotel in Istanbul? Could this be possible? He responded to the detective quietly and politely. "I appreciate your honesty, Detective. Could I ask you to let me have a few enlarged photographs of my wife? I'm sure you won't mind my doing everything possible to try and see if I can turn up some leads," Peter said, somewhat implying that Turkish police probably were going to be too slow and incompetent to get the job done. He was going to do the grunt work and try and find someone out there who might know what had happened.

"Of course. I fully understand you don't want to be sitting here doing nothing," the detective responded, but with a condescending tone, experienced in the knowledge that Americans always thought they could get immediate resolution of any problems and were far more able than the local police. But he smiled and kept his mouth shut. He turned to his assistant who pulled out three, 8-by-10 photos from the pocket photo that Peter had in his wallet and handed them to Peter.

As soon as the detectives left, Peter headed out to the taxi rank and then the grand bazaar and started showing Maya's photographs to the stall owners. He did this for nearly three hours, only stopping to have a snack and a coffee half-way through his endeavors. He had no luck. Although the stall owners were cordial and polite, none of them had seen Maya. He went back to the hotel, emotionally drained and physically tired. However, he could not sleep, racked by guilt and frustration. In the early hours, he got up, got dressed, and walked out through the empty lobby of the hotel into the deserted streets, wandering around until early dawn, when he went back to the hotel and crashed out, fully dressed, sleeping fitfully for a couple of hours.

He had a light breakfast and anxiously watched the clock until he thought it was a respectable time to contact the US Ambassador. He made his phone call and was put through to the Ambassador's assistant.

"This is Elisabeth Dixon, Ambassador Daniels's assistant." Peter introduced himself. "Ah, yes. The Ambassador has been expecting your call, Mr. Greenwood," Ms. Dixon said. "I'll put you right through."

The ambassador picked up the phone. "Mr. Greenwood. Your father has been in touch with me through the State Department and explained the traumatic disappearance of your wife. I know that you have been dealing with Istanbul police on this matter. Do you have any news?"

Peter explained the outcome of the meeting that he had the previous evening with Detective Mustafi.

"Peter, if I may call you that, I am so sorry. I can only imagine what you and your families are going through at this terrible time. The US Embassy and all of my staff will do everything we can to help. I would like to meet with you later today. Perhaps you could come to the embassy at four-thirty. We can discuss what additional efforts can be made. Does that work for you, Peter?"

"Yes, Ambassador. Thank you very much."

After meeting with the ambassador, and bringing him up-to-date, Peter left the embassy feeling a little better in the knowledge that the US Government was now involved in Maya's disappearance. Surely bringing all this muscle into the search should bring some news quickly.

Promptly at 8 p.m. Peter received a call from the detective. "Good evening, Mr. Greenwood. I promised to give you a call, but I regret I don't have any major news at this time. We believe we can eliminate the car accident, crossing the Bosporus, and leaving the country through one of our airports. We have a team of detectives making inquiries throughout the city and will continue to do this until we get some answers. We are also reviewing surveillance footage from cameras at the borders. Getting that footage is more laborious than the surveillance that we have at the country's airports and will probably take another day or two. Rest assured, Mr. Greenwood, we are doing everything that we can."

The next couple of days brought no real news. Detective Mustafi gave Peter an update every day, but they were no nearer to solving Maya's disappearance. Peter was depressed, not sleeping, not eating, and beginning to look gaunt and ill. He called the ambassador a couple of times, although there was not much to tell. He spent his days pounding the pavement, showing Maya's photos to shop owners, taxi drivers, restaurants, and even went to the railroad station, all to no avail. He now believed that it was quite possible that Maya had been kidnapped and murdered for her jewelry and the contents of their luggage. Detective Mustafi would not comment on Peter's concerns, only saying that there were still many possibilities to be pursued.

Early on the fourth day of her disappearance, Peter got a call from Mustafi saying that they had recovered some Tumi luggage and he wanted Peter to examine it. With a sinking feeling in his stomach, Peter grabbed a taxi and, within 15 minutes, was at the Central Police Station, an old, dusty, grubby relic from the early 1920s. He was ushered into a conference room near the reception and entrance. The detective and his assistant were waiting for him with three pieces of luggage. "As you can see," said the detective, "we have recovered three pieces of empty luggage. We believe they match your description, Mr. Greenwood. We would like you to examine the luggage and confirm whether it is yours."

Peter examined the large suitcase and the two smaller ones, which certainly matched ones that they owned. The holdall was not with the suitcases. The little leather-strapped pocket attachments for the owner's address or business card were empty, but, when he opened the cases, he could smell Maya's perfume and quickly opened one of the inside storage pockets and felt down in the corners and came out holding a bright copper penny which he flourished in front of the detective. "This is definitely our luggage, detective," Peter said, his voice cracking. "Maya put this penny into one of the pockets in the suitcases for luck. Where did you find it?"

"One of our officers found the luggage in the Grand Bazaar. The stall owner purchased it about 48 hours ago from a Kurd, probably from southeast Turkey according to his accent. He was unable to give us a detailed description or any further information. Frankly, it would be no use bringing him to the station to cross examine him at this stage. However, what I am now able to do is focus our efforts in continuing to review our surveillance cameras at our borders with Syria. The Kurds and many other people go back and forth across the border on a daily basis."

"Syria! I suppose this is progress of some sort, Detective," said Peter, feeling sick.

"Yes, it is progress, Mr. Greenwood. Our hope is that our enquiries through the Kurdish communities might give us some leads. I definitely think this should be the area that receives our maximum attention. We should be able to complete our analysis of all our survey cameras within the next 48 hours and will let you know if we have any further news."

Peter was making regular telephone calls to his father in Atlanta and his in-laws in Chicago. He had persuaded Harold not to come to Istanbul. Then he called the embassy with this news. The Ambassador's assistant, Miss Dixon, said that the Ambassador would like to see him and asked him to come to the embassy at four that afternoon. Later in the day, he phoned both his father and Harold with the latest news.

When Peter presented himself at the embassy, he was quickly ushered into the Ambassador's large, comfortable office. "Good afternoon, Peter. I'm pleased that the police have made some progress. I checked out Detective Mustafi and he is considered one of the best in the Istanbul Police Force. Now that they have recovered the lost luggage, it would appear your wife is no longer connected to her luggage, which was probably forcibly taken from her."

"Yes, Mr. Ambassador, I'm not sure whether this is progress or whether this indicates that this case may not be resolved any time soon."

"Now, Peter," the Ambassador said in a fatherly manner, "you must remain hopeful, but I wanted to lay out for you one of the worst-case scenarios that might regretfully apply to your wife, Maya." The Ambassador came around from his desk and sat on the edge facing Peter, who was seated in a large comfortable leather chair. "Even now, at the end of the 20th Century, human trafficking and hostage taking is alive and well. It can take many forms, including kidnapping of young women smuggled into mainly Middle Eastern and North African countries. With all the continuing turmoil in the Middle East, an American woman hostage can be useful currency for these people to try to extract concessions or prisoner swaps. These problems are also prevalent in the United States. During the past few years, an average of twenty young women per year disappeared in California alone. None of these young women have been rescued or have escaped their captors."

Peter was horrified. "That sounds unbelievable in this day and age. Surely the American government doesn't allow that sort of thing to happen?"

The Ambassador paused, gathering his thoughts. "These cases can be extremely difficult to solve, Peter. More often than not we don't get cooperation from the governments of the relevant countries where terrorist organizations, warlords, or just rich sheiks operate often with an anti-American bias. I sincerely hope that Maya has not fallen victim to one of these crimes, but I felt it was only right to advise you that, regrettably, this could be an explanation of Maya's disappearance."

Peter felt sick to his stomach. He had considered Maya might be dead, murdered, if not for ransom, but had not given any thought to the fact that she might have been whisked out of the country and sold as a hostage to some warlord. "Mr. Ambassador, I don't know how to process this information. I'm living in hope that Detective Mustafi and his team will find Maya and rescue her from wherever she is being held captive."

"I know how difficult this is, Peter. We are using all our diplomatic sources, contacts, and intelligence connections, but, like your detective, we have uncovered no leads so far.

However, I do believe that sooner or later we will get some answers. In the meantime, stay close to your hotel, keep in touch with the police, and please update me on any further progress."

Peter left the embassy feeling more despondent than ever. He felt powerless, and it seemed the US government was as well. The ambassador's revelation about human trafficking was a horrific thought. He really didn't want to think about it, but, as the days went by, the chances of finding Maya alive and returning to his arms was fading minute by minute, hour by hour.

Two days later, early in the morning, Peter received a phone call from Detective Mustafi. "Mr. Greenwood, this is Detective Mustafi, we have some surveillance footage that I would like you to view. Could you come down to our police station?"

"Of course, Detective. I'll be with you within the hour." Peter got off the phone with his heart pounding. *Was the surveillance footage of Maya? Was she alive? Were the police in a position to rescue her?* He was conflicted. *It could be good news, it could be bad news.* He had suffered through a couple more sleepless nights thinking about the ambassador's concerns and warning. He took a taxi to the Central Police Station where the public and the police officers were milling around, rushing up and down long corridors.

He checked in at the reception area, as instructed by Mustafi, and was escorted to an office at the end of one of the long, cream-colored corridors. They stopped at a half glass wooden door, with a painted sign in Turkish and in English: "Detective Mustafi." He entered a dingy, stuffy office. The detective was in his shirt sleeves, sitting behind a large cluttered desk. Piles of papers were everywhere. There was a fan whirring on the ceiling that just seemed to move the hot air around. It was stifling. The window overlooked a narrow courtyard, so there was limited natural light coming in.

"Good morning, Mr. Greenwood. Please follow me."

"Where are we going?"

"To a secure office where we can review the footage together," the detective said.

Peter followed him down some stairs to a basement area. They went down another long corridor and stopped at a black door. The detective pushed it open, ushering Peter into a room with a row of outdated computers. The detective's assistant was waiting. He turned on his computer. "Here is some footage from the Mursitpinar border crossing into Syria. It was taken on the day after your wife disappeared. I'd like you to look very closely at these images. They are, of course, never very clear, but we think that one of these may be your wife." The assistant brought up a rather blurred gray image of two men and three women descending from a Toyota pick-up truck. One of the men went into a border post while the other man stood with the women. All three women were dressed in black niqab head-to-toe coverings, with only their eyes showing. The men were wearing traditional kaftans and Kurdish headgear.

One of the women was tall and slim; she towered over the other two. Her niqab did not come all the way to the ground, and a part of one foot was exposed. One could also see part of her left hand in the sleeve of the niqab. The assistant magnified the image.

"Mr. Greenwood," said the detective, "do you think the image of the tall lady could be your wife? We are able to see that her toenails are painted, even though we do not have these images in color. We also believe that the man standing with them in Kurdish clothing is concealing a weapon under his Kaftan. I would like to show you the rest of the images." The assistant restarted the surveillance. The other man who had been accompanying the women came out of the border post and they all climbed back into the Toyota truck. Then the vehicle drove away.

"Well, Mr. Greenwood?"

"Could you run the images again, Detective?" Peter looked closely at the grey images. "I don't know. The images are blurred. It is possible that the tall lady is Maya. She painted her toenails. In fact, she put on a coral color varnish the day before we were due to leave Istanbul. It's impossible to see anything clearly under those garments, but it looks like part of her left hand is showing in her sleeve. I am not sure, but there appears to be a white band where her engagement and wedding ring should be." Peter paused, eager to see the surveillance images, but shaking with fear. "If it is her, Detective, are you able to launch a rescue attempt? I'm sure you have the number plate of the Toyota truck."

"We shall treat that as a positive identification. I believe your wife is still alive which, of course, is wonderful news. However, she has left Turkey, and we have no jurisdiction across the border that would allow us to pursue this case any further. What we will now do is contact the Syrian authorities and try to get their support to pursue the evidence that we have. Perhaps your contacts through the American Embassy may be able to help. We've checked the Toyota number plates and found that this vehicle was stolen a day before your wife was abducted. Chances are, however, that within an hour of crossing the border into Syria someone would have changed the number plates."

"Oh, Detective, you can't give up now," said Peter in anguish. "There must be a way to pursue the truck and identify the men with her. We are getting near, we must find a way to rescue my wife." Peter was almost pleading.

"We will do everything we can, Mr. Greenwood, but I have to be honest. This seems to be a case of human trafficking or hostage-taking. These women will be sold to sheiks or local warlords, maybe in Syria or in other countries. They'll become part of their harem, from which it is virtually impossible to escape. A young American woman such as your wife would be an extremely valuable hostage. She could be traded many times and looked on as a security asset to be used in any possible future negotiations with the Americans on military or other matters. Unfortunately, we have seen other cases involving Western women over the past few years. I know this is not what you want to hear, but I feel pretty certain that this is what happened."

Peter felt ill. His hands were sweaty and clammy.

"We will continue to pursue this case with interrogation at the Turkish border post and try to obtain positive identification from other sources. We shall do this for a few days, but then the case will have to be handled outside of Turkey."

"That's crazy! Can't you at least work together with your counterparts in Syria to pursue the case and not just hand it over for the whole thing to be rehashed while precious days pass?" Peter responded with his voice rising and his frustrating showing.

"Mr. Greenwood, our diplomatic relations with Syria, particularly in the Kurdish region, are not good. It is difficult to obtain cooperation on almost any matter. It would be better to get the American government to pressure the authorities on the other side of the border. As I say, we will do everything we can over the next few days using our contacts and security apparatus. But having said that, Mr. Greenwood, I don't think there is anything more that you can do. You might like to consider making arrangements to return home to the United States and to work with the US authorities."

Peter felt relief and depression at the same time. He was confident now that Maya was alive and had been abducted. The thought was excruciatingly painful. The detective was right, however, that he probably could not do any more in Istanbul.

"Detective, I would like to ask a couple of questions. How could that group pass from Turkey into Syria without passports? And why do you think my wife did not make an attempt to escape at any point, including at the border post?"

"Unfortunately, Mr. Greenwood, it is not difficult to pass through our border posts without the necessary papers or passports. We will, of course, investigate and probably arrest the officers in that post. With regard to your wife's attempt to escape, I think we have identified the fact that at least one of the two men had a weapon under his Kaftan, and we could see the outline of something protruding through the folds of his garment. The women would have been threatened with death."

Peter could see the detective was sticking to the facts.

"Yeah, I was expecting that answer, Detective. I think I will stay on in Istanbul for a few days, to see if you can make any further progress. Would it be possible to have three copies of this surveillance tape? I would like to give one to the US Ambassador and keep the others, just in case they may prove to be useful in the search."

"Of course. I will organize that straightaway and have them sent over to your hotel later today. I'm truly sorry we were unable to rescue your wife from her captors while she was in Turkey, but I sincerely hope you will be united again soon." Peter was moved by the genuine concern of Detective Mustafi. When he got back to the hotel, he phoned his father even though it was 4 o'clock in the morning in Atlanta. "Sorry to wake you, Dad, but I wanted to tell you the latest news."

"Don't worry, son. What is happening?" Peter described his visit to the police station and the review of the surveillance cameras at the borders.

"You must contact the American embassy, Peter, as soon as possible, and give them a copy of the surveillance tape, so they can use their Syrian connections to try and trace Maya's captors."

"The police here are sending three copies of the surveillance tape to my hotel. I just wanted to update you. I have to balance the relief that I know Maya is alive, with the wrenching knowledge that she has been abducted for sale to some sheik or warlord. It just doesn't seem possible that this would happen in this day and age, but apparently it is more prevalent than I realized." For a moment or two, he was unable to continue. "Unless some other news breaks here, I will probably fly back to the States in a few days, and, if so, would like to come to you in Atlanta, rather than returning to Chicago, if that's okay with you?"

"Of course, just let me know your plans."

Peter then had the rather gruesome task of phoning Maya's parents and telling them the news. This time he got through to Maya's father, but, as the conversation progressed, he could hear her mother crying in the background. Harold was relieved that Maya was alive, while sounding shell-shocked and distraught, but was more understanding.

Harold continued, "I met with Paul Simon and he made some enquiries. If it was a Kurd who sold your luggage to one of the vendors in the bazaar, he may have been connected to the PKK."

"The PKK?"

"It's an insurgency group based in Turkey and Syria, fighting the Turkish government forces in a low-level war of independence. It's been going on since 1978. Apparently, there are numerous PKK militias, many of them led by pretty ruthless characters, and they are hiding in the mountains, in small villages, and even caves and are extremely difficult to dislodge and defeat. I tell you this, Peter, as you might like to question the US Ambassador about these people and see if the US intelligence people have contacts with any of the militias."

"Thank you, Harold. I'll let you know what the ambassador has to say." Peter then phoned the US Ambassador and was told to come to the Embassy at 6 p.m. that evening.

Copies of the surveillance tapes arrived early in the afternoon. He busied himself by making notes and questions for the ambassador and the State Department. *Did they have a list of sheiks, warlords, and militias who participated in human trafficking? Was there a department within the State Department that dealt with these cases? Did the State Department, FBI, or CIA have spies or contacts who would be able to identify Maya's possible or probable captors? Because of her height and appearance, would it be easier for the authorities to identify her when she was travelling around? In a case like this, would she be kept under guard all the time? Would she be in some sort of prison cell?* All these questions and others rattled around Peter's head. He was physically and emotionally exhausted, but was eager to go and talk to the US Ambassador.

After giving details of the meeting at the police station, Peter asked the Ambassador how the State Department or other US agencies could help in the search for Maya now that she was out of Turkey and into Syria.

"Of course, Peter, the US State Department will do everything possible to help in this terrible situation. The US Government and key departments treat kidnapping of its citizens extremely seriously and they do everything possible to pursue leads and resolve these cases," said the Ambassador in his diplomatic speak.

"I wanted to ask a few questions, Mr. Ambassador," said Peter, reading off his notes. But, as he got to the end, his voice was cracking and he had difficulty continuing. "Is she... is she..." he could hardly get the words out, "going to be a sex slave to some sheik or warlord?"

"Peter, I know how painful this must be, but I'm afraid she may be sold many times over as time goes on. She will have no freedom, but, as long as she does not try to escape or put up a fight, she will not be tortured or treated badly, although this is not necessarily always the case. It will be virtually impossible for her to escape as she will be confined to her captors' compound. She will be under guard, along with other young women, at all times. She will, however, have female company and will probably be well fed and allowed to have reasonable hygiene facilities. Escape is very rare. Extraction is a better possibility if we can get a good lead, and that is what we will do right now. I wish I didn't have to describe such a bleak picture, but I want to give you a realistic appraisal of the situation based on my knowledge of similar cases over the past twenty years."

"Thank you," responded Peter with his voice cracking and tears welling up. He couldn't continue. When he thought his voice was strong enough, Peter said, "I don't think there's much more I can do in Istanbul. I thought I would stay a couple more days to see if Detective Mustafi comes up with any additional information. Then I think I will go back to the States and try with the help of the US State Department to pursue Maya's captors from there."

"I think that is very sensible, Peter. I will let you know if we have any information over the next few days that could be helpful. Otherwise, we will continue to communicate with you when you are back in the States. If anything else transpires from the Turkish police, please let me know. However, I know you recognize that the matter is now out of their jurisdiction."

Peter left the embassy exhausted and shattered. He was living through a nightmare and could not believe how within a few days his honeymoon had turned into hell.

Two days later, Detective Mustafi phoned Peter to inform him that they had arrested the officers operating the border post. Under interrogation, they had confirmed that they had been bribed to let Maya and the rest of the party through the border into Syria. They also confirmed that the captors were Kurds, but could not say if they came into Turkey on a regular basis, couldn't identify the Toyota pickup truck, and did not have a record of the number plate. Basically, the detective was saying this lead was going nowhere.

Peter left Istanbul the next day, flying Turkish Airlines

direct to New York, where he changed flights to Atlanta and was met by his father and elder brother, Ted, at the airport. Then he was taken to his father's beautiful home in Buckhead. He was wiped out and jetlagged. His mother burst into tears when she saw him, pale and gaunt and ill-looking. He had lost ten pounds. Back in his old bedroom, he crashed into an exhausted sleep with the help of a sleeping pill, which knocked him out for eleven hours.

The following morning, he staggered downstairs, wearing some of the clothes he had bought in Istanbul. He had missed breakfast, but his father, mother, and brother were waiting for him and lunch had been set up in the conservatory. "Hope you feel rested, son," said Arthur, all business. "I've made arrangements for us to visit with State Department officials in Washington, and also representatives of the FBI who have had experience with human trafficking. They have already initiated a number of moves in Syria, using their intelligence contacts with Kurdish leaders to help in the search for Maya."

"Thanks Dad. Let's hope to God they will come up with something."

"In the meantime, I think you need a couple of days rest to build up your strength."

Arthur and Peter went to Washington and met with officials from the State Department. Regrettably, they painted a bleak picture, similar to the US Ambassador in Istanbul. They assured Peter and his father they would do everything possible and promised to give a regular review and update of the findings within the next couple of weeks.

Peter returned to Chicago and met with Maya's parents. They were, of course, totally distraught and overcome by the updated news. Harold was more supportive and softer in his approach to Peter, probably recognizing how much he was suffering. Maya's mother was tearful throughout the discussion.

"I know you're doing everything you can, Peter, and your

father is using all his contacts within the US government to help, but I have one more thought, Peter, that you may like to consider. Although the State Department and other agencies will be as helpful as possible, we must recognize that they are the large, slow-moving, and overpowering US Government. I think it would be a good idea to hire a detective agency to help us in this case. Pinkertons, as you probably know, have been around for more than a hundred years and are still in business in this high-tech age and have offices and contacts around the world. I think they could do the ground work for us and be focused just on this one case. What do you think, Peter? I have contacts at the highest level who would be happy to represent the family."

"I think that's a good idea, Harold. I am in favor of anything that could possibly lead to Maya being rescued."

A visit to the Pinkerton agency a few days later also confirmed the difficulty of finding and rescuing abducted young women in the human trafficking chain. However, Charles Turnbull, an old friend of Harold's, agreed to take on the case and pass all the available information updates and surveillance tape to their Middle Eastern agencies and 'foot soldiers.' They added one other point which had not been made clear previously. Maya may not be in Syria at all but may have been sold on to other Arab countries such as Iraq, Yemen, Libya, Morocco, and, maybe, Sudan. He also said that if Maya was "purchased" in Syria, she may well be in the Kurdish mountain areas. It was an extremely dangerous place with many competing tribes. None of this information boded well for Maya and added to the depression that engulfed Peter. But he was resolved to use all his energy to continue to chase every possible connection and devote his life to rescuing his wife.

Peter and Maya had bought a two-bedroom apartment on East Pearson Street and had only purchased a few pieces of furniture, including a large double bed. The apartment was full of wedding presents, many of which had not been opened. Peter could not face going back to the apartment and resolved he would not return unless it was with Maya. He arranged for all the bills, assessments, and other charges to be sent to him in Atlanta.

Over the next weeks and months, the State Department came up with nothing. The Pinkerton agency came up with a couple of possible leads and sightings, but nothing came of it. A sighting on the Iraq-Syrian border of a tall young woman of Western features with some blonde hair peeking out from her niqab appeared to be a good possibility. The agency quickly followed up, but the lead went nowhere.

Peter remained totally consumed by the search. Although he stayed in Atlanta and joined his father's law firm, he did not function very well. He still had trouble sleeping and made numerous visits to various doctors to try and help him with both depression and lack of sleep and appetite. Many of his old friends rallied around and tried to include him in their plans. He appreciated their kindness, but did not want to be part of any social group or activity.

After four months in Atlanta, he told his father and Maya's parents that he had decided to go back to Istanbul and then to Syria, or wherever there had been any sightings that could lead to Maya's rescue. Both Arthur and Harold told him he was looking for a needle in a haystack. However, he was determined to go. He couldn't bear being so far away from Maya. He was convinced she was alive. If she wasn't, in his mind, he would feel it. He flew directly to Istanbul and met with the US Ambassador, who was embarrassed that the State Department and all of the various government agencies had been unable to produce any concrete leads on Maya's disappearance. Then he met with the Pinkerton's local agent. They both crossed over into Syria, with renewed promises of rewards for information leading to Maya's rescue. However, Arthur and Harold had been right; it was like looking for a needle in a haystack. The Pinkerton agent was very smart and had many connections with the Kurds and Arabs, and, although Peter sat in for at least a dozen interviews with people who thought they could help, he realized that all they were interested in was a possible financial payout. He moved from Syria to Erbil, the capital city of Iraqi Kurdistan, and met with some government officials, accompanied by a US consular representative. He got to understand that the quest for independence and the creation of Kurdistan as a sovereign country was a driving force for all Kurds around the world. People in Erbil were well-educated, cordial, and helpful. Peter realized very quickly that, even though there were groups of militias fighting various forces from Turkey, those in power in Erbil did not have any control over the groups and their warlords.

After four months, Peter returned to the US, no nearer to solving the mystery of Maya's disappearance. He suffered from severe depression and a personality change and had become addicted to some of his medications. He had considered suicide a couple of times, but still felt deep down that Maya was alive. His family and friends were worried about his health. They tried everything to rouse him from his despair, to no avail. He continued to push the State Department, keep in touch with the US Ambassador in Istanbul, and have regular communications with Pinkerton's management and their agents. He would not give up the search, nor would he give up hope. Even though he knew that his family and Maya's family now believed that she was dead.

At the beginning of 1997, he got a call from Pinkertons. One of their agents had information relating to a possible lead in Yemen. Simmering North-South tensions erupted with President Saleh sending armed forces to crush a southern independence civil war. One of the northern militias of Shia, led by Anwar Mansoor al-Hadi, also known as the "Lion of the North" had been seen in Sana, with his harem of women, one of whom was very tall and rumored to be an American or Australian. When Peter got this news, his heart jumped, and within a few hours he was on a plane to Yemen, landing in Aden after a grueling nineteen-hour journey. He was met at the dilapidated airport by a Pinkerton agent. Peter sensed there was some bad news coming. He was right. After the agent, Ababa introduced himself, he told Peter he had something to tell him.

"Mr. Greenwood, my informants have told me that Anwar Mansoor has disposed of four of his harem by cutting their throats. He considered them troublemakers. He disposed of the bodies, but one of my contacts photographed all four of them without their niqab coverings. I will take you to my office so you can look at these photographs, which, I should warn you, are very disturbing."

Peter's heart sank and he started to shake. He could hardly respond and was praying that one of the photographs was not of Maya. However, it did not sound good because he knew that Maya would never submit or give in. She must have been passed on by quite a few different sheiks or warlords since her abduction in Istanbul and landed up in this godforsaken country of seething religious conflict.

The office, fifteen minutes from the airport, was a shoddy, off-white building. The elevator was not working, so they hiked up three flights of concrete steps to get to his office, a stifling room with a glass door and a rattling air conditioning unit in the window that seemed to be doing nothing for the clammy heat or the flies. "Take a seat, Mr. Greenwood. I should warn you again that these photos are really gruesome." Ababa pointed to one of the wooden chairs facing the cluttered desk. Without saying anything further, he produced a buff envelope which he opened and slid out four photographs. He spread them across his desk.

Peter quickly focused on the one photograph of a tall, slim, fair-haired young woman whose throat had been cut, and one of her eyes gouged out of her skull. Her face was battered and bloody, as was her body. Two fingers on one hand had been cut off and were still oozing blood, and she appeared to have many broken bones from her feet upwards. Peter knew straightaway that this was not Maya. The other women were similarly horribly disfigured. Peter felt sick to his stomach.

"I'm sorry, Mr. Greenwood, that I have bought you on a wild goose chase, but I didn't get this additional information until late last night. I'm relieved that one of these poor women is not the young lady that you are seeking."

"This was a genuine lead. Obviously, I am relieved at the outcome, but I'm appalled by the brutal killing of these young women. I suggest that you inform the authorities so that they can pass this information around to various embassies."

Peter returned to the US totally exhausted and more depressed than before. He had to believe that Maya was still alive, but, after he had seen such brutality from one of these militia leaders, he was not so sure. His heart still ached for Maya.

In 2003, ten years after Maya's disappearance, both Peter's family and Maya's came to him and suggested it was time to plan a memorial service for Maya and for Peter to get on with his life. Peter argued against this. Despite the efforts of various family and friends to introduce him to available women or include him in social gatherings, he could not abandon Maya. And, although there was no closure at this stage, he would never give up, and he would never remarry. He would continue to search for her for the rest of his life, or until there was proof without a doubt that she had died. Peter had gone prematurely grey. He was no longer the boisterous, young, handsome man he once was. His hair was thinning, and he had a sallow complexion. There was nothing anybody could do to bring him out of his despair. He remained close to a few of his old friends and he pursued a healthy regimen of working out and playing tennis, one thing that seemed to relieve the stress. He worked hard at the family law firm, but he did so unenthusiastically. He followed every twist and turn of the various upheavals, wars, and insurgencies throughout the Middle East, always looking for that hopeful lead. But it never came.

The years went by. There were sightings from time-to-time in various Arab countries, but nothing that could lead to a positive identification and rescue. Eventually the family terminated their arrangements with Pinkerton.

The Arab spring in 2011 was a turning point for millions of people hoping for democratic government and less corruption, leading to prosperity, peace, and healthy economies. Unfortunately, this was not to be. Revolutions quickly turned into crackdowns by military dictatorships and increasingly brutal civil wars. The US and its NATO allies were eager to support the revolution in Libya and gradually got sucked into the efforts to overthrow Colonel Gaddafi, the Libyan dictator. Eventually he was caught and killed by what was considered legitimate opposition, but the oil-rich country divided into tribes and clans and quickly descended into civil war. Battles raged along the coast of Libya between Tripoli, Tobruk, and Benghazi. NATO supplied aerial cover, which gradually turned into bombing raids on rebel and terrorist organizations fighting the efforts to establish a democratic government. Adding to the turmoil and suffering of the people were thousands of refugees streaming from one battle zone to the other. The US opened and closed its embassy in Tripoli and its outlying consulate offices in Tobruk and Benghazi on a regular basis depending on the level of fighting. In April 2012, fighting intensified in Benghazi as different rebel factions and terrorist organizations supported by a Salafist group, Ansar al-Sharia, battled with "government troops."

The military commander of Ansar al-Sharia, Muhammad

el-Yousef, was living in a beautiful white villa on the outskirts of the city. It had been commandeered from an oil executive who had fled the country. It was set in three acres of lush gardens surrounded by an eight-foot whitewashed wall, in which there were large, ornate entrance wooden doors protected by a guardhouse. Within the grounds was a sixty-foot swimming pool and a lavish pool house consisting of two small bedrooms, a small living area, a kitchenette, and a bathroom. This building, with iron grills on its windows, housed four women from his harem. The exit doors were locked and there was a guard located outside the entrance door morning and night.

On the night of April 7th, the fighting and explosions intensified, and the villa was attacked by three rocket-carrying NATO helicopters just after midnight. The target was the main villa, which suffered direct hits from two or more rockets. It was set on fire. The guardhouse was destroyed with one strike, which also shattered part of the surrounding compound wall. The pool house also suffered a direct hit. The four women were asleep when the strike hit. Part of the pool house was totally destroyed and was on fire. One rocket hit the pool itself, sending up a gush of water. Much of the building was reduced to a pile of rubble, but one of the women survived, and staggered out into the grounds. The guard lay dead and she could see at least two other bodies of her former friends under the rubble.

She was deafened, because of the rocket blast. There was smoke, fire, and dust everywhere. She felt a severe pain in her shoulder and realised she was bleeding.The compound was under attack from the ground as well. Artillery shells landing in the lush grounds and small arms fire raking the villa.She was in a panic. There were bodies everywhere, armed militia, some women and even a couple of children.She staggered around ,not knowing what to do or where to go .She felt she was watching a silent movie,with all the characters rapidly moving in different directions.But then, through the smoke, she saw that the guardhouse had been destroyed and that, in the chaos, she might be able to leave the property through the demolished wall. Guards and others were running towards the villa. She staggered out into the road. There was nobody else there.

She had been living in the villa for the past fifteen months, having been transferred from her previous location in Yemen via a cargo plane, bound from head to foot, and blindfolded. Over the years, she had been moved from place to place in northern Syria, Iraq, Iran, Sudan, and, most recently, Yemen. A couple of weeks after she arrived at the villa, her captors dragged her out of bed, early one morning, and told her to dress in an orange jumpsuit. They blindfolded her and frogmarched her to a location against the wall of the villa. Even though she could not speak Arabic fluently, she could certainly understand the language. She realised that she was being prepared for a video of her own death. The guards who had come to collect her put on masks. They were all dressed in black, with only their eyes showing. They were carrying Kalashnikov rifles and ornate knives. She was shaking. She felt that death was near. However, much to her surprise, nothing happened and she was marched back to the pool house, and that particular exercise was never repeated.

She had seen American helicopters many times, passing over the compound and heading to what she knew was the American consulate about two miles away. She started staggering along the road, covered in dust and blood. The battle was raging behind her. There were no shoes on her feet. The US consulate was on the Fourth Ring Road on the edge of town and was extremely well fortified with a watch tower, roadblocks, barbed wire, and a contingent of Marines. Before the recent increase in fighting, things had been reasonably quiet, but the bombing raid was heavy. Parts of the town were on fire. There was sporadic fighting between rebel units and government forces.

It was just after dawn that a woman in a full-length torn kaftan, with mud caked feet and holding a bloodstained roll of material at her right shoulder, staggered towards one of the American roadblocks. She was weak and traumatised. An armed soldier in the watchtower turned on a spotlight and shouted for her to halt immediately and kneel. She was still deaf and could not hear him.

Two guards came out of the guard post as she approached. One raised his rifle. She staggered towards him. He fired one shot. She stumbled to the ground on one knee. She was a gaunt-faced, blonde woman. Her hair had grey streaks, and her mud-caked face showed a scar, long healed, from her right eye to her mouth. Her hands were bloodstained and dirty. She keeled over. The two soldiers approached her warily. "I am an American, Maya Greenwood," she said in a shaky voice. Tears were running down her face "I escaped, Peter, I escaped," were her last words.

10 BOOKENDS – 2003

I stood in front of the mirror in the familiar room at the Bay View Inn, a B&B in Camden, Maine, tying my black-tie. This went with my dark-grey suit, white shirt, and black shoes. My wife, Laura, was slipping into a black dress befitting of the funeral that we were about to attend. Neither of us had slept well. I knew that she had been quietly crying again in the bathroom. Her eyes were red rimmed. Nobody likes to go to a funeral, and this was our second in Maine within the last few months.

While she was getting ready, I went out on the veranda and sat down in one of the wicker chairs looking out over the sea, which was shimmering in early spring sunshine. It was a chilly and slightly windswept day. My thoughts turned to how the years had passed so quickly and how our visits to Camden had been such an important part of our life experiences. I remember every detail, particularly of our first visit.

If you think about it, we often make decisions that can have a profound effect on our lives, just by chance, or maybe even by the flip of a coin. That's how it happened for Laura and I. Twenty years ago, we flipped a coin to decide where to go on our first "empty nest" vacation after the kids were off to college, and that coin flip was to have a profound effect on two decades of our lives. Laura had chosen Vermont, heads, and I had chosen Maine, tails. Tails it was... We were looking forward to some well-earned rest. Our daughter, Patricia, had been accepted at the University of Wisconsin in Madison, and we had just dropped her off and helped to get her settled. Laura had been tearful and concerned, even though we had previously sent our two boys off to college, which she had handled much more calmly. After a few days of check-up phone calls, Laura realised that Patricia was happily settling into college life. When I look back at those moments, and at that fateful coin flip, I still find it unbelievable that twenty years have passed. Now, Patricia has three children of her own, and they are starting to talk about college themselves. So much has happened.

But our first vacation on our own for many years was settled. I had done my research and had chosen an attractive looking B&B in Camden, Maine. The weekend after Labor Day, we flew to Portland, picked up a rental car, and arrived at the Bay View Inn, at the top of Bay View Road, overlooking Camden Harbor. The B&B was a large, Victorian house painted creamy-yellow and white. We approached through a sweeping drive up a slight hill, flanked by a large lawn and flowerbeds with an outstanding view of the bay. The Inn had eight guest rooms and was owned and managed by Roy and Mary Beth Thornton. Roy was English, from the Plymouth area, where he had met Mary Beth towards the end of the war. Roy had been in the Merchant Navy and, after their marriage in 1946, secured a job as assistant harbormaster for the Port of Portland. He took over as harbormaster in 1964 and held that job until his retirement in 1978. That's when he and Mary Beth purchased the Bay View Inn.

On registering with the friendly owners, we soon realised there was a definite British influence. All the guest bedrooms were named after British naval heroes – Drake, Nelson, Howe,

Anson, etc. ‒ and, because the season was winding down, we were given the largest bedroom at the front of the house, Drake. The B&B had an English chintzy feel to it with nautical accents. Our large, airy bedroom had dark, hardwood floors, a four-poster bed with yellow and blue furnishings, and a small veranda with two rocking chairs and a wicker table, facing south with a perfect view out to sea. On the walls were several attractive nautical prints. There was a large print of a British 18th-century man-of-war over the wood-burning fireplace. Fresh flowers, a pile of books and magazines, and a small bathroom completed the accommodations. Laura had a big smile on her face, so I knew straight away that she was happy with the room. It seemed like a good start to our vacation.

Another English touch was the daily tea service. Tea was served between 4 and 5 p.m. Since it was four-thirty when we had unpacked, we were able to participate in a true English tea with two other couples. There was a large urn of English breakfast tea on a refectory table, together with milk, lemon, and sugar and two plates of small finger sandwiches, cut up in triangles, two plates of chocolate cake, and a plate of English biscuits—Walkers shortbread and McVitie's digestives. Laura and I helped ourselves and took our plates out onto a large sweeping veranda. It covered the whole south and east side of the house. We sat on some wicker chairs arranged around a table, munched our sandwiches, drank our English tea, and took in the idyllic view. "My God," said Laura. "This is perfection." We sat there in the warm sunshine, looking at the sparkling blue sea. I agreed wholeheartedly.

After finishing our tea and obtaining a map of Camden from the front desk, we decided to walk down to the town, take in the sites, and maybe have an early dinner. We took a slow walk down Bay View Road, with the warm sun on our backs, admiring the view of the harbor and passing some historic landmarks, such as the Camden Harbor Inn and the Camden yacht club.

We turned right and headed onto the dock and found ourselves at MacGregor Boatyard. There, out of the water, was a 27-foot Pearson sailboat for rent, exactly the same as my own, which I kept in Wilmette harbor, a few minutes from where we lived. I turned to Laura and suggested we could rent the boat and sail around the bay.

Although Laura had crewed for me many times, she is not an enthusiastic sailor. Her main complaint is that sailing on Lake Michigan is not too exciting, there are no islands and hardly any harbors, or even lighthouses, in the Chicagoland area. Sailing from Wilmette to some of the downtown Chicago harbors, I have to confess, can be boring. But, as I pointed out, Camden has a lot to offer. A large bay named Penobscot sheltered a rocky shoreline, hidden mansions, some small islands, lighthouses, and, of course, lots of lobster boats, seals, and even the occasional bald eagle. I persuaded Laura it would be quite fun, and she agreed with a knowing smile.

I went into the small office and met Mr. McGregor. He said that because it was the end of season I could take the boat out whenever I liked and he would charge me a reduced hourly rate. We agreed on the terms and I said I would come back in a couple of days. I didn't think it was fair to Laura to take her sailing on the first full day of our vacation. I walked out of the office feeling pleased. If the weather stayed fine, we could enjoy some wonderful sailing.

We walked back to Main Street, casually looking at restaurants and little shops and boutiques, and then we came across the JAGO Gallery. Outside was a big sign that said "Grand Opening." Inside, we saw quite a crowd drinking wine, laughing, and having their photographs taken.

"Come on in," said a willowy, blonde lady at the door. "I'm Janet Chatsworth. My husband Gordon and I own this gallery. It's the opening night. Have a glass of wine and look

around. I'd be happy to answer any questions you may have."
We joined the crowd and were soon offered a glass of wine
and some canapés. We took in the contemporary art, colorful
glass, and bronze sculptures.

Laura and I love art. She is interested in sculptures,
whereas I prefer paintings, but our home has an eclectic
collection of various styles. It didn't take long before I found
something that I really liked. Of course, it had a nautical
connection. The painting was of a couple of men at the end
of a little pier, fishing over a very placid sea early in the
morning. I was struck by the tranquility of the picture, but
also the coloring. It had an almost Turneresque quality, and I
thought the artist captured the early morning light perfectly. I
saw the name, David Hawkes, oil on board, priced at $1750.
It was a good-sized painting, maybe 36 x 24. Laura and I
discussed the possible purchase. She liked it just as much as I
did. We approached Janet and asked some questions about the
artist. He was a local, but quite well known, with exhibitions
in museums in Portland and other towns. We agreed to
purchase the painting.

"Wonderful," said a bubbly Janet. "You are our first
customer. Congratulations, and we hope you get many years
of enjoyment from this painting. I must tell Gordon and
introduce you." She scuttled through the crowds and came
back with her husband, a man of medium size and build, with
a shock of whitish, gray hair, reddish complexion, glasses, and
a silver mustache.

"Hi, I'm Gordon Chatsworth, and you are our first
customers. I'm so pleased to meet you. Where are you from?
Are you on vacation?"

"We're from Chicago. Yes. It's our first time in Camden,
and we only arrived this afternoon. It looks beautiful, and we
are looking forward to a lovely week." We chatted for a little
while, then Gordon went off to talk to other customers.

We continued to view the gallery's art, which we both

agreed was beautifully presented. But, after drinking another glass of wine and having some more canapés, we decided it was time to leave. We went over to say goodbyes to Janet and Gordon and make arrangements to pay for the painting.

"Why don't we get it all wrapped up for you to be collected tomorrow?" said Janet. "As you can see, we have quite a crowd here at the moment, and things are a bit hectic. Would that work for you?"

"Of course," I responded. "What time would you like us to come over?"

"How about five p.m., just about the end of the day."

"Would you like me to pay for the painting now or tomorrow?"

"Tomorrow will be fine."

We sort of waved goodbye to Gordon, who was surrounded by four people, looking at a large landscape painting. Then we made our way back to the dock area. Although it was getting dark, it was still warm, and we found a nice fish restaurant where, of course, we both ordered Maine lobster, after some clam chowder, and a lovely crisp salad, washed down with an excellent Sauvignon Blanc. After dinner, we slowly walked back to our B&B and sat on the veranda for a while, admiring a beautiful moonlit scene across the water. "The end of a perfect day," said Laura.

The next evening, Sunday, we went down to the gallery to pick up our painting, as arranged. Janet was just closing up shop and gave us a welcoming smile. She presented us with our well-packaged purchase and an invoice, which I paid.

"If you're not doing anything," she said, "perhaps you'd like to join Gordon and I for dinner at our local French bistro. It's really authentic, and you won't find any tourists."

I looked at Laura. We had no plans.

"We'd love to."

"Well, let's put this package in your trunk and you can follow us up to our house outside of town. We can have a drink together and then move on to dinner later. Does that sound good?"

"Absolutely. That's very nice of you."

With our new painting safely in the trunk, we followed Gordon's grey BMW up the main street. After a mile or so, as Camden retreated, we turned right onto Sunset Lane and wound our way up the hill until we entered the driveway of a whitewashed, Victorian villa. It had pale, grey shutters and a bright red front door. However, when we entered, we found a light, airy, modern house with spectacular views of the harbor.

As to be expected, the walls were covered with paintings of various types, styles, and colors, and there was a liberal smattering of beautiful glass pieces and bronze sculptures in the living room and in the attached conservatory. We were ushered out of these rooms and onto a wide stone terrace overlooking an expansive lawn with rose bushes on the edge. The lawn fell away to a gray stonewall. Behind the wall appeared to be another lane, and then rocks leading down to the water's edge.

"Make yourself comfortable," said Gordon, gesturing to a number of wicker chairs on the terrace. "What would you like to drink? Scotch, gin, vodka, wine, or beer? We've got the lot." He said, laughing.

"I would love a scotch whisky, with a lot of water and a couple of rocks," I replied. Laura said she would like a white wine and chose a Chardonnay. Gordon disappeared into the house just as Janet came out with a tray of cheese and crackers.

"You have a beautiful home," said Laura. "How long have you lived here?"

"We have owned the house for about four years now, but only moved in about two years ago," said Janet. "It was a bit of a wreck when we bought it. We probably spent too much money bringing it up-to-date and trying to make it a little more cheerful. Of course, the plumbing, electrics, and nearly everything else cost twice as much as we thought, but we're happy with the result. We're comfortable here now."

"Well," said Laura, "It looks like your perseverance paid off. It's really bright and cheerful."

Gordon returned with the drinks and we chatted for the next half an hour or so. I found out that Gordon Chatsworth was a retired stockbroker, having worked for Merrill Lynch for twenty-five years.

"I just got fed up with the whole thing," he said. "I realised that, despite all the efforts we made in managing our clients' wealth, all the meetings and the endless newsletters and market commentaries did not do much better than the S&P 500. In fact, in some years we fell behind. In other years, we might have been slightly ahead. If you consider the fees, many of our clients were really no better off than if they had just put their money in the S&P 500."

I thought that was a refreshing response from a former stockbroker. Gordon went on to say that he'd always loved art and artists. He and Janet had visited Maine as vacationers for years. They finally decided to buy a home and set up the JAGO Gallery. It was a labor of love, but he was confident that he would enjoy it immensely. Janet, who came from the Midwest and had studied art history at the University of Wisconsin, was an eager participant and contributor to these plans. Even though they were quite young to be retired, it was clear that they were going to enjoy their new career.

They were both interesting and fun, and it was only when we realised the sun was disappearing rapidly that Gordon said, "We'd better make a move to Chez Pierre." Again, we arranged to follow him down into town so that we could drive on to our B&B after dinner.

They told us that Chez Pierre was owned by Pierre Giroud and his wife, an elderly couple who opened the tiny restaurant and patio a few streets back from Camden Harbor on Friday through Sunday. They had a limited menu, which they put up on a chalkboard. Customers were told to bring their own wine, or, as in Gordon's case, leave bottles of their personal wine selections at the restaurant for future visits.

The restaurant was quite crowded when we arrived. I could see that the capacity was only about thirty covers, with maybe another sixteen outside on the patio. For that Sunday evening, the chalkboard menu was French onion soup, or Soup de Poisson, or crudités, and then entrées, carré d'agneau lamb chops, or lobster thermidor, and finally apple tartin or raspberry tart.

Janet and Gordon seemed to know everyone there. They were greeted warmly by Pierre and his wife Marian. It was noisy and smokey, so we chose a table out on the patio. In due course, a young girl came and placed a half bottle of Sancerre and a full bottle of Châteauneuf-du-Pape on our table and took our orders.

The food was excellent. It had the taste of a real French bistro. Everything was cooked to perfection. It was amazing that this little place in the middle of a backstreet in Camden could provide such a wonderful experience.

At the end of the evening, Gordon and Janet guided us back towards our B&B. Gordon and I arranged to play golf at his club, Seaview, on Wednesday afternoon.

The weather remained calm and beautiful, and Laura and I enjoyed some sailing on Monday. On Tuesday, we drove up to Acadia National Park and spent the day hiking through the woods and hills. On a spectacular Wednesday afternoon, Gordon and I had a great round of golf, which I lost on the last hole. The course was challenging, but it was beautiful. Most holes had lovely views of the sea.

Gordon was a heavy smoker—one cigarette per hole. He said it was too difficult for him to quit. It was one of the pleasures of his life.

The ladies joined us at the clubhouse for dinner, and it was so mild that we were able to sit on the terrace and watch the moon rise over the silvery sea. Laura and I already felt like Janet and Gordon were old friends. We didn't know it at that time, but it was the beginning of a long and close friendship.

We were sorry to leave Camden at the end of the week. So much had happened. We vowed to return, which we did every year for the next twenty years. We kept in touch with the Chatsworths. Over the years, we spent time with them, not only in Camden, but also in New York, visiting the museums and taking in some Broadway shows. We visited Door County, Wisconsin, on more than one occasion and invited them to our home in Wilmette and proudly showed what Chicago had to offer. We even went on a river cruise together in Europe. These vacations were not always smooth sailing. Janet and Gordon would often bicker, and some arguments left them in silence and us embarrassed. Laura and I talked about this and put it down to artistic temperament.

Their children got married and had their own children, as did ours. We shared happy celebrations of weddings and births and the joys of grandchildren together. The JAGO Gallery flourished and expanded into the next two stores, while developing a list of artists of some repute and a loyal following. Janet and Gordon loved the business, but as the business grew, their artistic differences caused more arguments. On one occasion, Janet left Gordon for a few weeks, and went to Europe on her own. But she came back and all was well again.

I retired, but I kept busy with a number of board appointments and my sailing and golf, while Laura pursued her passion for theatre. We visited Camden every year, around September, staying at our lovely B&B for the first few years. As our friendship developed, we began spending our week at the Chatsworth home. But, after one particular visit was ruined by loud and extended arguments, we decided to return to our B&B. Of course, we got to know some of the locals ourselves over the years. Eventually Pierre and Marian retired, and the bistro closed, which was a great loss. I became quite friendly with McGregor, and he always made sure I had a good sailboat at a great price. Laura and I got to know other store and restaurant owners and we always received a warm welcome. Of course, going to restaurants with Janet and Gordon, who knew everybody, made a difference. We continued our hikes, but cut down the distances as I got older and my knees started to give out. Still, we always looked forward to our Camden visits and felt we were home away from home.

But then, as is often the case, life got in the way of our idyllic relationship. One day in July, I got a call from Janet. I immediately knew from her voice that she was distraught.

"Gordon has been diagnosed with lung cancer, stage IV," she said in a trembling voice.

"What," I replied, totally stunned. "When did that happen? I just spoke to you both, what was it, four, six weeks ago? You were both fine."

"I know, but Gordon has had some stomach issues for the past couple of months. We thought it was just indigestion, initially, and then maybe some infection, but the pain got worse and more regular. Our doctor was concerned, and so, through one of Gordon's old New York contacts, we went to see a doctor at Sloan Kettering. He had some tests, and, unfortunately, this is the result. They're putting him on a course of chemo straightaway. They are making optimistic noises. But, at the same time, they're telling me to prepare for the worst. I just can't believe it," Janet's voice was cracking. "It's all so sudden."

"My God, Janet, I am so sorry, what can I do to help?" I felt my response was rather lame. I supposed it was the shock.

"Nothing, at this time," Janet responded, "But I appreciate your offer."

"We are going to rent an apartment in New York for the next few months, while Gordon goes through this treatment, so we can be near to his doctor. He's a good guy with a great reputation. If anything can be done, he is probably the best man available." She paused and sniffled. "You know, John lives in Manhattan. He and my daughter-in-law, Rita, will be with us. That will be very good for Gordon as we get through this. We can only pray."

"If there is anything we can do, we will come to New York to be with you," I said.

"Thanks, but I think this is the best choice we have at the moment. I'll let you know our New York address in the next week or two after I have made all the arrangements. You are the only people I have told so far. Nobody in Camden knows, or anywhere else, for that matter."

"I understand, Janet. You've got to be optimistic. Please tell Gordon that we will be thinking of him. We will certainly keep in touch. If you need anything, and I really mean anything, please just call and let us know and we'll be there."

"Thank you so much," a tearful Janet said. Her voice was cracking.

I was in total shock. How quickly lives can turn around. Gordon had sounded fine when we had spoken recently on the phone. Laura was out at one of her theatre board meetings. I told her when she came home. She sat down and started sobbing.

Within a couple of weeks, Gordon and Janet moved into a rented apartment on East 61st Street and Gordon started his treatment. Laura sent a giant orchid to their temporary new home and kept in touch by telephone. Gordon felt awful after the first batch of chemo, but gradually he got stronger as his body got used to the regular onslaughts of the treatment. He told me that he was worried about Janet. For a couple of years now, her breathing had become labored from time-to-time. She had coughing bouts and even struggled with climbing a few stairs. I was concerned to hear this, as we knew how secondhand smoke could impact one's health.

After four months, Gordon had further tests and scans and the doctors said that his tumors had shrunk and they were encouraged. This was great news, especially when they said he could go home to Maine. He had to come back to New York for checkups every four weeks.

We arranged to pay them a visit. And so, we arrived in Camden on a blustery, cold day in early December. The little town with the beautiful harbor looked so different in the dead of winter. Many of the stores and restaurants were closed, but our B&B stayed open throughout the whole year, since the Thorton's son and daughter-in-law, who had taken over the inn, lived on the premises, and so we were able to get our usual room. They were pleased to see us, and we were pleased to see them. By this time, most of Camden knew about Gordon, and they understood why we were visiting.

We drove up the hill to their house through driving rain and wind. Janet ushered us into their living room. There was a roaring fire. Gordon was sitting in a chair near the fireplace, with a blanket around his lower legs. He gave us a big, welcoming smile. He had lost weight and looked pale, but he seemed better than I had expected. His shock of grey hair had turned white, but, before his diagnosis, he had not changed much over the past 20 years. Perhaps put on a few pounds around the middle, as we all had. Janet, on the other hand, did not look good at all. She had also lost weight, and her skin had taken on a gray pallor, which I knew was sometimes connected to people with heart conditions. None of us were spring chickens, and we were visiting in the middle of winter, when nobody had a healthy summer tan.

Gordon was tearful as he greeted us. "I'm so pleased to see you guys," he said, his voice breaking. "So nice of you to come all this way." Laura was also tearful as she replied and hugged him.

"We're so happy you're back in Maine. Hopefully the

good news from your tests will continue." I gave Gordon a hug as well and livened up the proceedings.

"You are looking good, Gordon. I hope Janet is looking after you. How is her cooking?"

"Pretty awful, actually," responded Gordon with a laugh. "We are having most meals sent in from all our friendly restaurants. Our daughter-in-law came to stay for a few days and she's really a good cook. I think my appetite is improving now that I'm home. I'm also getting out and about a bit. I'm taking walks down to the harbor, when the weather permits. Of course, not on a day like this, but last week was sunny and crisp and everything looked beautiful."

"Fresh Camden air, after three months being cooped up in a small apartment in the middle of New York," interjected Janet. "This break is really welcome."

"When you go back to New York for your checkups, how long do you have to stay?" I asked.

"I'm still receiving treatment, but they can usually get it done in a full day, so we just stay a couple of nights."

They wanted us to stay for dinner, which they were going to order from one of the fish restaurants in town, but we declined. I could see that Gordon was beginning to flag and Janet looked exhausted as well. We said we would leave them alone for the evening and that we'd be back the next day. It was a shock to see them both. Janet was pushing hard to be her usual bubbly self, but just couldn't keep going. Gordon was laboring to breathe and was not leading the conversations like he had done in the past.

We went back the next morning and brought them lunch, which we all shared around the fireplace. The weather was still cold, but at least it had stopped raining and the wind was not so biting. The sun was breaking through the clouds, from time to time, and when that happened the view of the harbor was transformed and everything looked happier. We spent most of the day with them, talking about old times, catching up on the children and grandchildren, and this certainly gave them a boost. They seemed more energized and bright-eyed by the time we said our goodbyes.

Janet saw us out and, as I kissed her goodbye, she said, "Sometimes, I feel this is a payback. I don't want him to suffer, but at last I can make my own choices." I was taken aback by this comment. I didn't know what she was talking about. Laura and I discussed it later. Perhaps she was just feeling the extreme stress of the ongoing medical treatments.

The following morning we flew back to Chicago. We kept in touch. A few weeks later, Gordon phoned to say that the latest test had shown the cancer was still there and spreading. They had increased the treatments, although he was still allowed to come home to Maine for breaks in between.

We spoke on the phone to Janet, who seemed to have come to terms with the inevitable. A couple of weeks later, on a Sunday evening, I phoned and asked how they were doing. Janet said they were both sitting in bed reading books, as they so often did. She said she was okay, but Gordon was having difficulty breathing. She was pushing him to go to the hospital, which he was resisting. I got on the phone. I could hear him laboring to breathe. I added my weight to push him to check into the local hospital and see what was going on.

"Call me in the morning, Janet, and let me know how Gordon is doing," I said. Laura was very upset to hear the news. Neither of us were able to sleep. In the morning, I didn't hear from Janet. I was about to call her when I got a call from their son, John, in New York.

"I'm afraid Dad passed away last night," he said, his voice breaking.

I called Janet, but she was too distraught to talk to me. I left a message to say we were coming out to Maine immediately. As soon as I got off the phone, I made reservations to fly out that day. Laura was crying and red-eyed. By the time we arrived, Janet had her three children and their spouses and grandkids around her.

The funeral was a few days later, and it appeared that half the town showed up. The eulogy described Gordon as a kind and generous gentleman, a pillar of the community who had set-up home in Camden and brought beauty and culture to the town.

We decided to stay on for a few days to help as best we could. Laura busied herself in the kitchen every day. Janet received friends and neighbors and had her children and grandchildren around her for most of the time.

A couple of days after the funeral, Laura and I went up to the house. Janet was sitting on the terrace in a garden chair, all alone, dressed warmly, with a blanket around her legs. It was a windless, chilly day, with weak sunshine shimmering on the bay.

None of the children were there. I pulled up a couple of chairs and gave her a kiss on the cheek.

"How are you doing, Janet?"

She looked at me strangely. "How am I doing? It may be too late for me to do anything," she said with a wry smile. "And I have waited years for this." She looked at Laura and then me intently, as though she didn't know us.

"You waited years? For him to…?" Laura said, but stopped herself from continuing.

"It was all a lie, you know," said Janet.

"What? I'm sorry," I said, confused.

Janet made a vague gesture with her hand. "All of it. Gordon and me. The happy couple, our wonderful life together. It was all a lie."

"What are you talking about?" said Laura, turning slightly pale.

Janet chuckled mirthlessly. "He didn't take early retirement from Merrill, you know," she said, her face hardening.

"He didn't?" I said. "But I thought..."

Janet brushed my words aside. "He was sacked. He was lucky not to go to jail."

"Gordon?" said Laura with a hollow laughing sound. "I don't understand."

Janet looked at her, then at me. "He swindled a whole bunch of his clients. And not just once, but over a period of nearly fifteen years. He cost them millions of dollars while he made a fortune."

Laura put her hand over her mouth as she looked at Janet in wild-eyed horror.

Janet continued, "In addition to our Central Park apartment in Manhattan, we had a place in the Hamptons and a yacht. We were living the good life. I just thought I had a brilliant husband, but it eventually caught up with us." She paused, gathering her thoughts.

"I can't believe this," Laura said in a hushed whisper.

"Merrill wanted to avoid a major scandal. They paid off his clients for all their losses. Of course, we had to be part of the settlement. So, the apartment went, as did the house in the Hamptons and the boat, and Gordon's substantial stock portfolios. We left New York with our tails between our legs. We had less than a million and a half left, which was in my name, luckily. We hid in Camden, where nobody would know us." She paused, laughing mirthlessly. "Of course, Gordon always had the charm. He was a smart guy, although the devil to live with. It was his way or the highway. We put on a good show for you guys, but I threatened to leave him many times. Well, he has gone now and I am free."

Laura and I exchanged a glance. Then I looked at Janet. "Why are you telling us this?" I said quietly.

She shrugged. "I want you to know. Before it's too late."

"Too late?" Laura said.

Janet inhaled nervously and ran her hand over her blanket, as if to pick lint off it. "I'm not well, you know. I think my golden years won't last very long." She gave us a wry smile. "We did a good job hiding the truth, didn't we?"

I stared at Janet in disbelief. We had been friends for twenty years, and, although we didn't see that much of each other, I really thought we knew each other well. I was shocked. Laura, too, was speechless.

After a moment or two, I responded. "Janet, I had absolutely no idea.Gordon was always so bright, smart, generous and charming. I really thought he took early retirement, because he just 'had enough' of the system."

Janet chortled sarcastically. "It was the line we used with everybody."

"You said you're not well?" Laura interjected.

"Yes,"said Janet, pausing while she gathered her thoughts.

"You have been through enormous stress these past few months and you need to look after your own health now and decide what the future holds for you. Even at our age, we have a lot of life to live." I said, still totally shocked over the news about Gordon.

Janet sighed and leaned back in her chair. "Thank you," she said. "God, I needed to get that off my chest. I wanted to tell you about Gordon for many years. I feel better, now that you know. Even my children don't know the full story. Let's keep it that way."

"Yes, obviously, we won't repeat this to anyone," I agreed.

"Someone once said that the true measure of a man is how he treats you when others are not looking," Janet said, sounding wistful. "Unfortunately, Gordon was a much bigger man to the world than he was to me."

"Janet," Laura said, quiet and seriously. "Are you ill? Are you feeling alright?"

Janet nodded. "I'll go see a doctor and probably have some tests. But I've had a heartache for years."

"A heartache," I repeated. My throat felt dry.

"We had many good times," Janet said. "And I stayed with

him, despite all our ups and downs. I suppose you could say we loved each other." She looked out into the distance, and her voice was breaking. "But he lied to me and dragged me into his fantasy world of a retired Merrill broker." She paused. "He destroyed my trust. And now I am alone." She stopped talking and looked exhausted. It was obviously time for us to leave.

I told her to call me after her doctor's visit. I also told her that we would always love her and Gordon. Janet nodded emotionally, and Laura hugged her. A few tears were rolling down her cheek as we said goodbye. We left the house in a daze.

"My God," Laura said," I certainly didn't expect that. It's unbelievable!"

"Well, they kept that from us for 20 years, but, as they say, you never know what goes on behind closed doors."

My mind was racing. Had our long relationship with Janet and Gordon been a charade all these years? Had we been taken advantage of? I couldn't think how. We had enjoyed each other's company, travelled together, and shared the ups-and-downs of life. We very rarely discussed the stock market or investing.

A few weeks later, Janet called to say that she had a serious congestive heart condition. She would have to be very careful and follow instructions with regard to her diet and lifestyle. She was not happy about this. "The golden years don't look so golden now," she said.

Laura and I telephoned at least once per week. Janet told me she didn't want her home to be like a hospital room. The regimen of injections and pills made her feel even more fatigued and depressed. So, I wasn't too surprised when, a few weeks later, she called to say she was not continuing her treatment.

She said she didn't think there was much point now that Gordon had gone. I didn't know what to say, but I respected her decision. We phoned her every day, and, although she tried to be cheerful, especially when talking to Laura, we could tell she was getting weaker.

A couple of nights ago she passed away, and now we are back in Camden for another funeral and another eulogy.

Spring is on its way in Camden. Its harbor and the Chatsworth home and garden are beginning to emerge from the winter with a new lease on life. But I could not help but reflect on how two lives, their families and close friends, had been changed over a matter of weeks. Of course, the one certainty in life is death.

Laura and I know how lucky we have been, and we treat every day as a blessing.

As we left Camden, I held onto Laura very tightly. We both knew without saying a word that Janet's death had bookended an era and we would never return.

ABOUT THE AUTHOR

Ellis M. Goodman CBE is a successful businessman with a background in Public Accounting, the Beverage Alcohol Industry and Commercial Real Estate. In the late 1970's Mr. Goodman was also an investor/manager in the Music Industry (GTO Records) and Film Production (The Greek Tycoon) and Distribution (Picnic at Hanging Rock).

More recently, he was an Associate Producer and Executive Producer of the award-winning documentary feature films, "Louder Than A Bomb," and "Mulberry Child," (recently seen on PBS – national coverage). He is also the Executive Producer of the recently released documentary "Art Paul of Playboy: The man behind the Bunny," and was one of the Executive Producers on the movie "Judy," starring the Oscar-winning Renee Zellweger.

In addition, Ellis Goodman was a Producer of the Broadway show, "End of the Rainbow," and was one of the Investors/Producers of "An American in Paris."

Mr. Goodman has served on the Board of American National Bank, The Kellogg School of Management at Northwestern University, The Chicago Sister Cities International Program, Steppenwolf Theatre, The Chicago International Film Festival, and Chicago Botanic Garden.

Mr. Goodman was invested as Commander of the British Empire by Her Majesty Queen Elizabeth in 1996.

ALSO BY ELLIS M. GOODMAN

Non Fiction:

Corona: The Inside Story of America's #1 Imported Beer

Espionage Fiction:

Bear Any Burden

The Keller Papers

CPSIA information can be obtained
at www.ICGtesting.com
Printed in the USA
LVHW091138040821
694441LV00003B/13